Praise for Rhiannon Leith's
Edge of Heaven

"...not only does this book sizzle with unbelievable lust, it will also tug at your heartstrings"

~ *Blackraven's Reviews*

"Micah's and Sam's chemistry alone and along with Lily will keep you panting and wondering what will happen next for this trio."

~ *IReadRomance.com*

"Not only is the storyline well-constructed and entertaining, Ms. Leith did a wonderful job of creating sizzling chemistry between the two men and Lily. It was very interesting to witness the power struggle – good and evil, light versus dark – that plays out through most of the story between Micah and Sammael."

~ *Two Lips Reviews*

Look for these titles by
Rhiannon Leith

Now Available:

The Guild Chronicles
With a Touch

Edge of Heaven

Rhiannon Leith

Samhain Publishing, Ltd.
577 Mulberry Street, Suite 1520
Macon, GA 31201
www.samhainpublishing.com

Edge of Heaven
Copyright © 2011 by Rhiannon Leith
Print ISBN: 978-1-60928-090-1
Digital ISBN: 978-1-60928-059-8

First Samhain Publishing, Ltd. electronic publication: June 2010
First Samhain Publishing, Ltd. print publication: May 2011

Dedication

For "himself".

    With thanks to the usual suspects, Crystal, Elaina, Rowan and Mima. And super-editor, Deb.

Chapter One

Sammael kept his eyes trained on the uneven stone floor and tried not to listen to the pleas coming from the woman currently entertaining their master. It didn't do to interrupt him, no matter what the circumstances. Eons had been spent in torment for lesser transgressions, and Sammael had no wish to join those who had earned the displeasure of the Nameless.

Her begging faded away to inarticulate cries, part pain, and part pleasure, each one degrading. Sammael closed his eyes but it didn't help. He felt himself harden at the thought of her. Lara, that was her name. She had been beautiful when she entered, afraid, desperate, but very beautiful. The scent of her fear still lingered, tantalisingly sharp. She had walked right by him and he could still smell it, hovering on the air like a trail of smoke. Who knew how she would emerge, if she was released at all?

Abruptly the sounds stopped. Still Sammael waited until his name was called. Only then, his head still carefully bowed, did he approach the dais on which sat the throne of Hell.

The Nameless lounged back, his immortal gaze distant and cold. At his booted feet, the woman lay very still. Rumour had it that when she lived, she had been a light, one of those rare and evolved souls who could make a difference to the lives of others. Until her guardian angel spoke of the forbidden and upset the balance. The demon Asmodeus had stepped right in to secure her fall. Sammael would have felt pity for her, but she had brought it on herself. She had made her own choices. They all had.

"Sammael," said the Nameless, his voice a whip-crack that snapped Sammael's attention back to him and him alone. A thin and knowing smile graced his luscious mouth with a curve. They had all been angels once. But only he had been the Morningstar.

His eyes were hazel. Always unexpected, that. Sammael had never become accustomed to seeing the eyes of the Nameless, the face that spawned all evil. Part of him wondered where the Nameless had picked them up. But somehow they belonged in that face. That was the hardest part of all, to see such human eyes in the face of the inhuman, to face that, and bow his head.

"You seemed to enjoy Lara's little display." The smile broadened as his gaze trailed down Sammael's front to the erection visible through the tight fabric of his pants.

"Master?" Sometimes it was best to be vague and subservient.

"Do you want her? She's yours."

Lara lifted her head, her mouth slack with fear, her beauty all but drained away by whatever he had put her through.

"You're generous, Master," said Sammael carefully, "but I don't think she wants me."

The Nameless laughed, throwing back his head. "What she wants is irrelevant. Just take her. I'll have someone hold her for you if you cannot manage it yourself."

Rape had never appealed to Sammael. It was crude, lacking in skill and finesse. He didn't need to force himself upon anyone. Besides, why would he take someone against their will, when the delight was in seeing them succumb, to hear them beg for more? The Nameless knew this, of course. It was Sammael's special talent, and the reason Hell kept him as a pet.

Sammael was about to try another excuse, but Lara got in before him. "Please, Master, don't cast me aside. Not yet. There is more I can do for you. I swear I will please you. I swear." She crawled to her knees before him, nestling between his thighs, fawning like a bitch. Her hands trailed up towards the God Knife, the blade whose forging caused the Fall, but she skirted around its edge. They all knew never to touch it. Even a god would die from that knife's kiss. That had been its express purpose when it was made, to kill the Creator and put the being now known as the Nameless in His place.

The Nameless reached down and tangled his fingers in the lengths of Lara's golden hair. He jerked her head back so he could look in her face, and whatever he saw there made him relax his grip just enough so she could lower her head. Her shoulders shook, and though no noise came, Sammael felt certain she was weeping.

One damned soul was the least of his worries. The attention of the Nameless had returned to him, and under that kind of scrutiny he didn't dare blink.

"There's a new light that needs putting out, Sammael. I think you're just the man to do it. Here."

The Nameless stretched out his free hand and the necessary information slammed right into Sammael's head like a full-blown migraine. The force with which the Nameless delivered it nearly sent Sammael sprawling onto the slick stone floor. He kept his footing, barely, but staggered back a step or two. The soles of his boots skidded before they found purchase. Blood on the floor again. There was always blood here. There was always death.

And there too, it seemed, in the mind of the woman he saw now, his intended victim. His prey. The light in her was dwindling, her hope going out. Fear as strong as Lara's, and just as intoxicating to a demon. It surrounded her. And with it went despair.

11

He tried to see her face but couldn't. It didn't matter. Not really. He would seduce her, and he would lead her down the paths so she would damn herself, but he preferred it when they were beautiful. No matter though. Vulnerable was almost as good.

"You know what to do," the Nameless said, his gaze straying from Sammael, back down to Lara. The woman began to shudder, her skin shivering. "You may depart as soon as you are ready."

He pulled Lara's head to his crotch and Sammael heard a choking sound as she took his cock fully down her throat. The Nameless tightened his grip on her hair again, moving her head as if she was nothing but a tool. Which she was. She just didn't know it yet. As Sammael turned to go, he heard the Nameless speak again, calling forth Asmodeus, and despite the best of Lara's efforts, his voice was perfectly calm. Soon enough he would cast her aside once more and let whichever of his legions had pleased him for that moment have her. Each and every one of them. Then he'd take her back and do it all again. She couldn't escape it. No one could.

It was worse when the voices came unexpectedly, out of a quiet afternoon, when Lily was doing nothing more than reading or listening to music. When she wasn't expecting it, relaxed and at peace, completely unaware that such harmony was about to be snatched away from her.

"Do you know where I am?"

It was a young voice, a man, hardly more than a boy. He sounded so scared, so alone.

"Can you hear me? I know you can hear me! Help me, please help me."

A woman, older, but not by much. Lost, terribly afraid and bewildered.

"*Where am I? What's going on? There was a crash, and it hurt and then... Oh God, am I dead?*"

The third voice chilled her, carrying the weight of years and dreadful deeds.

Lily's shaking hands folded into fists, her nails digging into her palms, a prickling of sweat standing out on her cold skin. Why couldn't they just come one at a time anymore? She forced a steadying breath into her aching lungs.

"*It's all right,*" Micah said, his voice clear as a bell, cutting through the confused babble. "*I'm here. Just take it one at a time.*"

The smell of cinnamon swirled around her and for a moment she thought she felt a hand close on her shoulder, like a dream, or a memory. So vivid, but not real. She was remarkably good at discerning real from unreal. Or at least she had been.

But having him with her was the comfort it always had been. All her life.

One at a time. Right. One by one.

One.

"*Where am I? C'mon, this isn't happening! Help me. I know you can help me.*"

"Listen to me. You need to step into the light."

"*A light? What the hell are you—*"

The voice—young, male, brassy—paused and Lily heard the relief flooding the next words.

"*Oh God, I see it. Oh God.*"

And he was gone. One down, and the knot of tension inside her loosened just a little. Next.

The sound of sobbing filled her mind. Despair stretched its clammy fingers into her brain.

"It's okay," she said. "Really, just find the light. Go into the light." Moments ticked by and the voice stilled to silence. Lily waited, rocking forward and backwards.

"I see my family."

There was no hesitation. The spirit rushed on its course.

One remained. She reached for him, only to find a shadow, a slick of tar in spirit form. Her mind and soul recoiled, repulsed by what she found.

"You have to help him," Micah insisted.

"But he's..." She couldn't say evil, but it was true. This was a stained and miserable soul. He'd done dreadful things. He was terrified, not of death, but of what came afterwards.

"Am I dead? Talk to me, you bitch."

She shrank back, wrapping her arms around her body, curling in on herself as his presence assaulted her mind.

The floor shook and the lights in the living room flared, bulbs popping in unison. The room plunged into darkness and from the next apartment the alarm started up, an insistent whine as painful as the spirit battering against her.

"Micah, I can't do this. I can't."

"You can, my bright one. Just keep calm and bid him depart. If he will not pass to the light, send him—"

With an almighty crash, the coffee table before her was tossed aside like a child's toy. Lily screamed and her heart jerked up in alarm. Bile burned the back of her throat.

"Get out," she yelled, her voice thin and sharp with terror. "Get away from me. If you won't go to the light then you can go to Hell and be damned. Those are your only choices now. You have no place here. Not anymore. You're dead, you hear me? Dead!"

Abruptly, the assault on her stopped and the room around her fell silent.

Her strength drained from her, leaving her like a wrung-out dishcloth. She slumped onto the sofa again, still clinging to herself.

"*That's it, my bright one,*" came Micah's soothing voice. "*There, there, rest now.*"

If she closed her eyes she could feel his fingertips smooth back her sweat-drenched hair from her forehead. But closing her eyes meant succumbing to sleep and, exhausted though she was, her dreams brought only nightmares.

"It's not fair, Micah." She stared at the ceiling. It blurred in and out of focus, and lights danced before her. "Are you here?"

His hand stroked her neck, strong and gentle fingers.

"If only you were real."

"*I am real,*" he assured her. "*And I'm here for you. Always.*"

"I wish you could show yourself to me. I wish..."

His sigh broke over her like a wave, regret and pain combined, more weight than she had ever heard from him before.

"*So do I. But it's impossible. Rest now, my bright one.*"

"I don't feel bright, Micah. I feel—"

"*Sleep, Lily. Sleep and let your body and mind replenish themselves.*"

She tried to obey. Her heavy eyelids slid closed and her breathing relaxed. It only took a moment. His touch lingered, stirring the sensitive hairs at the back of her neck, almost as if he were lying by her side, breathing with her. The hand strayed lower, insubstantial and yet perfectly real, a sensual touch that was at the same time comforting. Her spirit guide, her beloved companion, her friend.

If only he existed in more than her addled mind. Twenty years of his voice, keeping her back from the brink, calming her and soothing her fears, she needed him as surely as she needed air. Ever since she was a teenager, Micah had been with her.

"I wish you were real," she repeated, exhaustion muffling the words.

"*I am.*" His breath played on the skin of her ear. If she

15

turned, her lips would meet his, if he were real. If he weren't a figment of her fevered imagination.

She moved, rolling on the sofa, her mouth opening to greet his lips. He drew in a breath—an illusion, she assured herself. He didn't breathe. He wasn't alive. Not anymore. If ever. His hand closed around her shoulder, tightened, and she held her breath, waiting, praying that his lips would brush against hers.

Half dazed, she tried to lift herself but the dream washed over her. This was a dream, wasn't it? Or a vision. She knew them, knew the difference. But right now she didn't care. She wanted it to be the future she was seeing and not some fantasy. Right now she wanted—

A fist thundered against the door of her apartment and Lily started, tumbling off the sofa and landing heavily on the floor.

"Lily?" The building superintendent yelled from the other side of the door. "Lily, are you okay?"

She scrambled to her feet, picking her way through the jumble of books and papers, piled up and abandoned newspaper clippings, printouts and journals. Her shin glanced off one pile, sending it skittering across the carpet in an avalanche. She stumbled, but caught herself.

"I'm okay," she called, tripping forward and catching herself just as she fell against the door. She fumbled with the chain and jerked the door open. Cassini's reddened face peered in at her, more concerned than angry, but both emotions were there. She smiled, but when he didn't return the expression, her face fell. "Again?"

Cassini nodded slowly. "Every fuse in the building, *bella*."

"I'm sorry."

"I know. You're okay though?"

"Yes. Fine."

He turned slightly and behind him she could see Mr. Hopkins, her only neighbour on this floor. Middle aged and grey, of hair, clothes and manner, he wrung his hands in front of him, gazing at her with concern.

"See, Mr. Hopkins. She's fine," said Cassini, a little too heartily. "Not a thing to worry about here."

"Well," Hopkins muttered, shuffling from one foot to the other as if reluctant to withdraw. "If you're sure, Lily. I'm right next door, you know?"

She tried to smile. He meant well, she knew that, and he'd been here longer than anyone could remember, even Cassini. He took care of things in a proprietary manner, and sometimes that included the tenants.

Cassini waved at him cheerfully until his door shut, then rolled his eyes before giving Lily a conspiratorial wink.

"Listen, can you try to keep it down tomorrow? I'm showing the next-door apartment. I don't need no weird while I'm with prospective tenants."

Damn, she was lucky to live here. Lucky in so many ways. "I know. I'll-I'll do everything I can."

"Can't ask no more than that." He patted the door. "You take care now, honey. Get some rest. Say hello to my mama, will you? Tell her we still miss her."

"When I see her, I will. Thanks."

Lily closed the door as he walked away, twirling his screwdriver between his fingers. She pressed her forehead against the wood and tried to breathe calmly.

This couldn't go on. This simply couldn't go on.

Micah hated it when Lily left her little apartment. The city streets were not her friend—too many dead voices, too many lost souls. It was worse when she was between contracts, like now, and had nothing to distract her. Sometimes the need to just get out of the apartment would strike her forcibly and she had no choice but to obey. He understood that. Fear, that was the problem. She was afraid of staying inside all the time, afraid of losing her mind if she did, afraid of being locked away, alone.

She was never alone.

Sometimes he wondered if he should stop pretending to be just another spirit guide and reveal himself as her guardian. At first, when she had been just a teen—confused, terrified, lost—she had desperately needed a spirit guide. The rules had been put in place for a very good reason. The balance between Heaven and Hell was precarious at best. To tell her would influence her free will, her ability to choose light or dark. The last guardian to do so had lost his charge to Hell, removed from her side just when she needed him most.

He longed to tell Lily the truth. But he couldn't risk it.

Still, he wondered how she would take such a revelation.

Her light was so bright. It drew him to her effortlessly and the struggle to maintain his distance grew worse with every passing day. She was worth it, though. Micah knew that with all his heart. He had to be there whenever she needed him.

And she needed him. No doubt about that. His bright one, brightest of the bright even with the flicker that had entered her light recently, Lily attracted the supernatural like a lodestone, both the good and the ill. More darkness these days as well, he thought mournfully as he walked behind her through the grime of the city. He shielded her from the worst of it. That was his duty. But still, she was weakening. Her task of ushering the souls of the departed onwards was taking its toll as more of them seemed to be the twisted and damned.

He reached out and brushed his fingertips against the tight pleat of her copper-coloured hair. Electricity sparked between them and her step faltered. When she glanced back Micah was relieved to see a ghost of a smile grace her lips.

"You're here." Her voice was so low that no mortal could hear it. To hear her voice pitched so, just for him, made his body throb with a need forbidden to him.

"*Always, bright one,*" he assured her. Her smile spread a little, but it didn't reach her eyes. Her smiles never did anymore.

He was losing her. Even as he tried to hold her to him, to keep her in the light, in the world, she was slipping away, her presence a little more insubstantial every day. She lived with ghosts, she lived like a ghost. No wonder she seemed more distant all the time.

She bought groceries—barely enough to keep a grown woman alive—and spent an hour in a bookshop. As they crossed the park she watched the children playing, listening to their squeals of joy, and Micah felt the bonds of love in the place, the strands that tied parent to child, husband to wife, lover to lover. They glowed like dewy spider webs in sunlight, linking all those lives together.

Lily had no such ties. She was alone.

Spirits normally kept their distance in the daylight, for which he was grateful. For now she was safe, so he allowed himself to relax and enjoy the pleasures of being abroad in the world. The touch of the sun on his face, the feeling of the breeze and the way it brushed his skin. Standing there with Lily, Micah could imagine nothing more perfect, nothing more like Heaven.

He felt the change at the same moment she did.

"Time to go," she whispered.

Micah's head jerked up. A group of shadows hung amid the trees on the far side of the grassy expanse where the children played. They weren't doing anything, not yet, but they were as aware of Lily as she was of them. And Micah knew he was the only thing keeping them back right now.

"*Very well,*" he conceded. "*Go calmly. Do not run. Don't let them smell fear from you.*"

"I know the drill." She gritted her teeth as she obeyed.

Micah shook off her annoyance. Of course she knew what to do. They had been doing it for years. He waited until she had walked behind him and then spread his invisible arms wide. Sunlight poured into him, invigorating and dazzling. He smiled and the brightness grew. Then he turned it on the shadows.

They shied back, retreating hurriedly.

"Look, Mummy," one of the children shouted. "Look there."

Micah glanced at the child, a boy, no more than five years of age. He was pointing towards them, his eyes dazzled. His mother knelt at his side.

"What is it?" she asked.

Micah smiled and turned away to follow Lily. She trudged ahead of him, head bowed so strands of her red-gold hair fell in a curtain on each side of her face. She shoved her balled fists into her jeans pockets and her shoulders formed a hard line of tension. He reached for her again, but just as he did, the child's reply caught his ears.

"An angel. In the sunlight."

Micah turned back, startled. Only the most sensitive could ever hope to catch a glimpse of him or any of his kind. And even then, only in the most stressful of situations. Not unless he chose to reveal himself.

He walked back towards the boy, who looked past him. No, if he had seen Micah for that instant, he didn't see him now. Reaching out, past the mother's amused face, Micah laid his hand on the boy's head in blessing. There was no spark, no jolt such as he felt with Lily.

"There's no angel there, honey," said the mother, smoothing her hand across her child's hair, just as Micah had done.

"Yes, there is. There was. She's gone now. The lady with the light in her hair."

The lady. Micah spun around, but there was no sign of Lily.

She'd walked on ahead of him. He could sense her at the gates of the park now, turning left, walking home. Taking the short cut.

There were two men in the alley. Waiting.

Fear burst upon Micah, fear for her as she walked right into danger without him. He drew his consciousness in, ready to evanesce to her side. Nothing happened. The pull of the world out here was too great, too strong. It anchored him, holding him away from her and refusing to let him go.

Micah sprinted across the open grass, his legs pounding beneath him. He needed to be there, to shield her again. Weaving through the traffic as he crossed the road, he wished he truly had the powers that his kind were reputed to have, to be anywhere in the blink of an eye, to fly to her side. To protect her.

He felt the spike of her terror.

"*Lily!*"

Micah flung himself around the corner. Her groceries spilled across the alley. The light caught the flash of a knife. Lily screamed.

Too late. He was too late.

Something black barrelled into her attackers from the shadows. A snarl ripped through the air as this new defender hurled a punch at the nearest, heedless of the weapon he held. Blood glistened as it flew through the air and, while one mugger went down in a heap, the other turned and fled.

Micah rushed to Lily's side, but the dark man was there first.

"Are you all right? They aren't going to harm you now."

She nodded, swallowing hard as if trying to find words.

Micah slipped in beside her. "*I'm here.*"

"Where were you?" she asked.

Her rescuer answered, a chuckle in his voice. "I came down

the other way. Didn't see you there until you cried out." He offered his hand and Lily took it gingerly.

A wave of foreboding swept through Micah. He knew that voice, or something like it. His senses shivered and he gazed into a face almost as old as his. But not the same. Nothing like the same.

Handsome, chiselled features, an expressive mouth with just the right mix of gentleness and a promise to seduce even the most flawless souls. His eyes, rather than being black and endless, were the deepest brown and had seen a thousand tragedies, had understood them all. His eyes were compassion.

"I'm Sam," the demon said. "Are you sure you're okay? Here, let me help you."

Micah froze as Lily allowed Sammael to draw her away from the wall, as he called the police and stayed with her, comforting her. Micah watched, closed out and terrified, as Sammael, the Angel of Death, the Seducer of Souls, moved into Lily's life without so much as a misstep.

Chapter Two

Lily didn't quite know what to say, but Sam seemed comfortable enough talking for both of them. The police took her statement, most of which was filled in by Sam, and her attacker was taken away. There was no trace of the other one, the one who had run.

"I wouldn't worry," said Sam, his warm voice as reassuring as the gentle hand with which he cupped her elbow. "He's probably high-tailing it for the hills." He grinned at her.

To her surprise Lily found herself returning the smile. His good nature was infectious. "How can you be so blasé about it?"

"We're both okay. That's all that matters. Can I at least buy you dinner? I don't think you'll be making much from these."

The salad and fruit she had bought were squashed to slime on the alley. The eggs had shattered and milk pooled with blood.

She looked up at Sam and saw the drip coming off his fingers.

"You're hurt." Without a thought, she grabbed his arm. The knife had cut through his jacket and the cashmere sweater beneath it, right into the skin. "Oh my God, Sam. Why didn't you say anything?"

He frowned, turning his arm this way and that, examining the wound. "It's just a scratch."

"Just a— Look at it!" She pulled his hand towards her so

she could peel back the material. Up close, she had to admit, it didn't appear as bad as when seen through the shredded material. "Look, I'm not far from home. At least let me dig out a bandage or—"

"*Stop it, Lily. Listen to yourself. You just invited a complete stranger into your home. Get away from him. He's dangerous.*" The tone in Micah's voice left her stunned for a moment. He had never spoken to her that way. Never!

Her face must have frozen. People told her she sometimes got that fazed-out look when she heard the voices. When people spoke to her at all. And here was a person, a man, who had saved her life, a knight in shining armour—well, expensively casual clothes anyway. And she had never seen a man so handsome. No, beautiful. He was beautiful. His face captivated her, and her breath caught in her throat when she gazed into his eyes. A deep, rich brown, like polished walnut, framed by long, thick lashes, they made her feel like she was falling. She held his hand against her chest, his long fingers only a fraction away from the curl of her breast. His own chest rose and fell, and his mouth, sensuously expressive, rose in the tenderest smile of confusion she had ever seen.

And something else.

Desire.

For her?

Awkwardness washed back through her system, like being drenched in a bucket of water. She dropped his hand, but it didn't fall.

Sam towered over her, broad-shouldered and slim-hipped. Now free, his hand closed against the curve of her waist and slid down until he reached the flare of her hip. He leaned in and his lips began to part.

Oh God, he was going to kiss her. She knew it and knew there was nothing she could do to stop him. She didn't want to stop him. She barely knew this man and here she was standing outside an alley where half an hour ago she might have been murdered, ready to kiss him. Almost begging to kiss him.

"Lily! Listen to me. Please. Don't do this. You don't understand." Micah's voice in her mind was sharp and acidic, afraid. Why was Micah afraid?

"No," she told him softly, but Sam was close enough to hear her murmured response to her spirit guide.

He stiffened for a moment, and disappointment registered in those endless eyes. Then he drew back. "Of course, I apologise." He bowed his head, oddly formal. "At least allow me to repeat that dinner invitation."

Lily's breath escaped in a rush. A mix of disappointment and anger made her head swim. Damn it, Micah had no right to interfere.

"I'm here to protect you."

She had to fight to keep her face from dropping into a scowl. And more, because she wanted to tell him that this was not an area of her life in which he had any jurisdiction. But she couldn't say anything, not with Sam there.

"Of course," she said, feeling a surge of glee as Micah's dismayed gasp rang around her head. "I'd love to. But only if you'll let me see to that cut." She smiled. "It's my fault you got it, after all."

He laughed. "How can I refuse that?"

She fell into step so easily beside him, as if she had always belonged there.

When they reached her apartment building and Lily ran inside to get a bandage, she stopped in the living room, breathing hard. It was a mess. She thanked God she had asked him to wait in the foyer.

"You weren't thinking of bringing him up here?"

"And why not, Micah?"

"He's dangerous, that's why. He's not human."

"Micah!" she exclaimed. "That's an awful thing to say. Anyone would think you're jealous."

"Lily, I know about these things. And he's..."

"He's what?"

Micah paused, almost as if he was trying to formulate an excuse, or force out a word he couldn't quite say.

Instead, he sighed. *"He's not human. I can't tell you anymore."*

"And why not? What are you hiding from me, Micah?" He'd never been like this before, so threatened, so demanding. Lily knew Micah hid things from her. She'd be a fool to entirely believe everything a voice in her head told her. And while she didn't want to be accused of insanity or schizophrenia, she had made some subtle enquiries which had turned up nothing physically or mentally wrong with her.

Well, apart from the visits from ghosts, the visions, the paranormal activity and the voices she heard. Especially the one who watched over her.

"If you're going psychic stalker on me, Micah, I swear to God... And you are not to come with me on this date, do you hear?"

"Then be careful, if you won't listen. And remember that I will always be here for you. Should you need me. I will never be far."

"Promise." She had to hold firm.

A pause followed, like someone grinding their teeth to get out of answering. Lily waited.

"I promise."

"Everything okay?" Sam's voice made her jump like a startled cat. He stood in the doorway, leaning on the frame, his jacket draped over his uninjured arm. He had rolled up the sleeve of the other. The cut looked quite small now. It didn't need a bandage. It barely warranted a band-aid.

"I'm fine. How did you get up here?"

"The stairs. Your super said to go right up. I think he wants to show me an apartment."

"You're looking for an apartment?" she squeaked.

"This is yours, I take it?" She couldn't shake the feeling that his smile was slightly mocking.

She glanced around, mortified. "It's normally neater."

"*Liar.*"

"*Micah! Shut up, shut up, shut up,*" Lily willed him, knowing he couldn't hear her. "It's the apartment next door. Mrs. Chandler's. She went into a home." God, she was babbling like an idiot. She clamped her mouth shut to try and stop herself from making an even bigger fool of herself than she had already.

Sam grinned, that maddeningly sensual grin that made her body tighten in ways she couldn't ever remember feeling for anyone. Something inside her was melting, slowly, insistently, warming the ache between her thighs.

"Hey, I like the neighbours," he said. "Definitely a plus."

Lily laughed and offered the bandage in her hand but Sam held out his arm. The cut had closed. "All better," he told her.

"That healed fast."

"I'm a lucky guy. I had a great nurse." He laughed, brushing her concerns aside with a good-natured grin. "It just looked worse than it was. Mind if I look at this apartment before we go out? I really am in the market. I can call for you later. About eight?"

"Sure." It would give her time to change, freshen up, tidy up. "However long you need."

Sam paid for the apartment upfront, in cash, both the deposit and three months' rent. Not that it would take that long. To tell the truth, he had never encountered a woman quite so ready to be seduced. Lily's body hummed beneath his touch. He couldn't believe how easy this was going to be. For a moment he'd thought she was going to give it up right there in the laneway.

She wasn't what he had expected. Tormented by voices, yes, certainly. He could tell when one of them was trying to get her attention, the way that vague, distracted look came over her, the way her grey eyes drifted and the colour deepened. One of them had distracted her just when he would have kissed her. But when she said no, he backed off. Part of the rules, of course. Seduction did not involve coercion. It took finesse.

He stood in his new spartan bedroom, leaning back against the wall, listening. It was an old building, with thick walls, but that didn't hinder him. Next door he could hear her. She was humming to herself. The innocence of the sound made him hard all over again.

That was the other problem. She affected him in ways he hadn't expected. Sexual attraction, yes, but also...he couldn't put his finger on it. When he'd seen her pinned against the wall by that scum of humanity, something dark had erupted in him, and something dark for a demon was dark indeed. The first moments of attack were blurred and hazy, consumed with a distinctly undemonic, righteous rage.

Strange. So very strange.

It was almost as if he wanted to protect her.

Sam placed a call through to Chez Henri for a dinner reservation and waited another thirty minutes, just listening, waiting. She had gone quiet for a while, then he heard her again, talking in that lower, measured voice so he could not hear the words. One of her "friends", no doubt.

Easy, he reminded himself, it was going to be easy. Spirits tended to flee when a demon came on the scene, and only the most determined would stick around. Her spirit guide seemed determined indeed. Well, a small challenge was a diversion.

Sam flicked through the information the Nameless had implanted in his brain, assessing his tactics. Lily had no friends to speak of, an old schoolmate or two she never contacted, an ex-boyfriend who was a little too obsessed but seemed to have backed off. She had inherited a substantial amount of money at an early age and worked as a contract office admin if and when she felt like it, mainly for her own amusement. She was rich enough to be seen as eccentric rather than certifiable. Her family home was a long way out of town and so she rented here. Even though she didn't have to.

That was a mystery. Why not live as a recluse far from anyone else? When she worked so hard to hide here in the city, why not do it in the countryside where it would have been so much easier?

"Well," he said to himself. "Something to puzzle out after all."

Next door, Lily laughed. Sam jerked upright, his blood pounding through his body. And with it desire, hunger. He took a single ragged breath, calming himself by force of will.

Time to go, he told himself. His clothes shimmered and changed, re-forming to a simple black shirt and matching jeans. His unruly desires still left him on edge, but by the time he stood outside her door, he was sure he had that under control as well.

He knocked sharply, waited. From inside he heard her voice. Very faint, very quiet. Only supernatural hearing would pick it up.

"Yes. I know. But he isn't. Micah, you promised."

Micah?

Sam took a single step back, watching the door warily. A coincidence, surely. It had been a common enough name at one time. And she dealt daily with the spirits of the dead.

And yet, it would explain *so* much.

"I'm coming." Lily's voice sounded a little more shaky than immediately after the mugging attempt. Like she was hopping.

"Are you okay?" he called through the door.

"Yes, I'm just—" There was a thud, followed by a crash. "Ow."

The same panic rose up again, like a horse taking the bit in its teeth. Sam couldn't help himself. He brought the full force of his shoulder to bear on the door.

He was about to back up and run at it when she opened it. She wore only one shoe, the other dangling from her fingers. She limped as she tried to step back. Her coppery hair was dishevelled.

"What happened?" he asked.

"Nothing." But her face flushed red.

She dropped the shoe—a black stiletto—and wriggled a ridiculously shapely foot into it. Then she stood and pushed her hair out of her face.

She had wrought some kind of magical transformation in the time he had given her. Where before she had been dressed in shapeless casual clothes, this new outfit, a simple jersey dress, moulded the curves she had previously hidden. The shoes made her legs even longer and accentuated the line of her calves to a level of sensuality he had not expected.

Her scent carried a hint of jasmine and orange blossom, light and delicate. She wore a golden cross on a delicate chain around her neck. The tones of the metal married with the highlights in her hair. Unconstrained, it flowed down to the small of her back and it gleamed in the light.

"What?" she asked, a little unsteadily.

"Nothing. You—you look beautiful."

The smile that broke over her face was marvellous to behold. He had seen nothing like it in centuries, perhaps longer.

"So do you." And she blushed again, flapped her hand at him, flustered. "I mean handsome."

"Ah, well." He spread his arms wide, back on more familiar ground now and more comfortable for that. "I clean up well. I made dinner reservations at Chez Henri. I hope you don't mind."

Dinner was exquisite, but Sammael barely tasted a thing. All he could do was watch her. No spirits interfered. She smiled, she laughed, she spilled out hints about her childhood, her loneliness, information he could use. He flattered her, nudged her desire for him along, and tried to convince himself that the fact he wanted her just as much was merely a convenience. He took every opportunity to touch her hand or her arm, to walk closer on the way home.

By the time he reached the apartment building, he could hardly bear it. He twined his fingers with hers, brushed the ball of his thumb across the sensitive skin of her wrist and heard her gasp.

Without a word, he lifted her hand to his mouth, turned it over and, watching the frightened expectation on her face, kissed lightly against the throbbing vein just below the heel of her hand.

Lily's eyelashes fluttered and she sucked in another breath.

"Sam, this is all very fast..."

"Then no more this evening, I swear it," he said with an indulgent smile. Logic told him he could afford to be patient. His body screamed at him, offering a range of colourful suggestions of what he could do with his logic.

He walked her to her door and she stopped before she went inside, hesitating. Her heart was beating so loud he could hear it clearly, though they stood a foot apart.

Her lips parted, beautiful, tender and begging to be kissed.

But he couldn't rush her. To do that would be to lose her and if he lost her...well, the displeasure of the Nameless was not to be courted.

"Goodnight," he said. "See you tomorrow?"

She shook her head slightly and then seemed to catch herself. "Tomorrow?"

"When I move in. I'm your new neighbour."

The confusion melted to mirth, no, to joy. Ah yes, his chest swelled with well-warranted pride in his abilities. Yes, this was better by far.

"Well, that's nice." She stammered out the words, shifting from one foot to the other. But she didn't move inside. He stood very still, watching her, admiring her, and yes, wanting her, though he would never admit it out loud. "Sam..." Her voice trembled. "Sam, why are you here?"

His heart petrified the instant she said it, dropping heavy and cold inside him. Did she know? *How* could she know?

And that one overheard word came back to him.

Micah.

Swallowing down anger he dared not show her, Sam forced the sudden tension in his shoulders to relax. "Lucky, I guess," he supplied fluidly. "And my good deed of today is rewarded with both a home and a fascinating neighbour."

Lily hesitated again, her mouth opening and closing. She looked bewildered and still a little scared. And at the same time, her eyes softened, her fists uncurling.

Bringing up his knight-in-shining-armour routine was a stroke of genius, he had to give himself that. Her fears melted away at the thought of it.

Before he knew what was happening, Lily took those brief steps forward, rose on her tiptoes and pressed her lips to his. Her hands closed on his broad shoulders to hold herself up. Sam's lips parted to greet her, to claim her, and he gathered enough of his wits to return the unexpected kiss. As he slipped his tongue into her mouth, hers twined with it, darting around him. One hand closed on the small of her back while the other cupped her head, holding that small weight so he could take control of the kiss she had initiated. Her silken hair tangled around his fingers, and an image sprang unbidden to his mind, of Lara, kneeling before the Nameless, his hand knotting in her hair as he used her mouth.

The thought almost made him break away, but at that moment Lily made a noise deep in her throat, a small moan of need, or surrender, and pushed herself against him. Sam slid his knee between hers, parting her legs, bringing her closer so that she could not miss the hardness of his cock, the force of his arousal. She pressed in, her skin heated and turning wanton beneath his touch. His hand slid lower to mould the cheeks of her ass through the thin barrier of her dress.

Lily tore her lips from his and gasped his name as she struggled to breathe. And, though he had promised himself that he would wait, that he would make certain she was desperate and would do anything for him, Sam threw all his good intentions aside. He was a demon, after all. What place did good intentions have inside him? He kissed her chin, her throat, bent his head to run the tip of his tongue along her clavicle.

"Oh God," she cried out. "Please, not now, Micah." And she froze in his arms. Desire melted away from her, leaving...what? Shame?

Sam made his touch gentle again, put hurt confusion in his features. "Micah?" he asked with the innocence of a saint. "Who's Micah?"

"He's a friend. Just a—" Her face turned scarlet. He seemed to have a knack for making her embarrassed, though that didn't help him in his mission.

"I see," he said, as if he clearly didn't, and let his hands fall to his side.

Lily stood before him, devastated. Tears glistened in those gorgeous eyes. "It's not what you think, Sam. He's an old friend and he won't—" She dropped her head. "He's very protective, that's all." She sighed again, and her hands folded together, each finger worrying its counterpart. Was she going to tell him? Really? "There's something you should know about me. Please don't laugh. I'm a—a psychic."

He paused a moment, as if letting the enormity of the statement sink in. Most men would laugh, he realised. He wondered how many had. How many had laughed in her face and called her deluded, or mad? So he didn't. Hurting her would only damage his cause. He couldn't have that. He would be understanding, a believer. He would be her dream come true.

"As in 'I see dead people'?"

"Hear them, actually," she said hurriedly. "Most of the time. But Micah is my...my spirit guide."

I'm sure he is. Sam kept the knowing smile inside. It had to be him. There was no one else with the gall. And they would never leave someone like her unprotected.

Lily shifted feet again, her luminous eyes expectant. "Do you believe me?"

He hesitated for just long enough. Then he nodded. "I guess I do. If you do." He reached out and took her hand again, lifting it to his mouth so he could place a chaste kiss on her knuckles. They were white with tension, and her hand trembled. He smiled as his lips brushed her skin. Micah was here. And this had just got a lot more interesting. He wasn't hunting just one soul anymore, no matter how bright, but two.

And one of them was immortal.

Chapter Three

Micah watched Lily kiss Sammael, hardly able to believe she was the same woman who had left, so nervous that when she had been trying to put her shoes on and hurry for the door she had lost her balance and fallen. Those same shoes now lay by her bed and she was singing to herself, a beatific smile on her face.

I have to tell her. His heart sped up at the thought of such a transgression. *I have to. Her soul is at stake.*

Like the rustling of leaves in a gale, Micah sensed the approach of another of his kind. He froze, wishing he could escape before this particular confrontation. Once, he had stood high in the Holy Court but that was long ago, as his brethren never ceased to remind him, either intentionally or not.

"Micah, what are you planning?" asked Enoch. A warning hung in the voice, a hint of disapproval.

"It's Sammael. I can't just let her continue to walk blindly into his sphere of influence."

Enoch sighed. He acted as the Metatron, the voice of the Creator, but not in this instance. In this moment, he spoke as a brother, and his tones were both gentle and reproachful. *"If you do so, the Holy Court will be forced to remove you from her. She will have no protection whatsoever. If you tell her what Sammael is, what you are, you will fail and she will be damned. Are you willing to risk that?"*

"*No.*" Micah drew in a ragged breath and Enoch withdrew, a trace of satisfaction remaining behind like a smudge on glass. Micah opened his eyes to gaze on her. She looked blissful. And he hated himself both for resenting that and for risking her.

Micah tentatively made his presence felt again. He'd been so relieved when he sensed her outside the door that he'd gone to greet her, only to find her entwined with the bastard demon sent to seduce her. Her response had been to drive him back inside so he didn't know what happened next. Whenever she came within range of Sammael, Micah's awareness of her blurred. In fact, if he was not standing right beside her, it was difficult to discern her at all. Sammael seemed to overshadow her. A disturbing thought.

But if Sammael was here to seduce her then why had he left it at just an intimate kiss? Why was he not in here now with her, sprawled on the bed?

The thought of the two of them naked together sent an unexpected flash of pain through him. And something else. Something uncomfortably like arousal. Micah had been watching over her for so many years, but he still left her those moments of intimacy with her lovers. There had not been many, but some had brought her joy like this before they brought her sorrow.

He sat on the bed beside her and she must have felt the shift, or perhaps simply his proximity.

"Micah?"

"*Yes, my bright one.*"

She smiled. It pained him that she did. "I'm glad you're here."

A thousand answers came to mind, all of which were too petty to voice. "*I am glad you are here too.*"

"He wasn't like you thought he would be. He's wonderful."

"*He's dangerous. I know you don't want to hear it, Lily, but it's true, and however wonderful he seems now—"*

"Micah, anyone would think you're jealous," she said, laughing. "I'm going to take a shower. Keep talking to me?"

Jealous. That was what she thought? Not concerned for her welfare, or doing his duty to protect his charge. Not guarding her as he had guarded her for all her adult life. Jealous.

And he forced himself to admit that, yes, she was probably right.

And not just of Sammael.

In the ranks of Heaven, the touch of an angel was considered the highest joy, and what was a demon but an angel who had fallen? There he was, a fallen angel, so close, and even though he was the enemy, the eternal enemy, part of Micah yearned to see him, to touch him. To be near him.

No! It wasn't possible. It wasn't right. He had to keep Lily away from him before Sammael managed to win both her heart and her soul. He was already halfway there and if he continued along this path, Lily would love him unreservedly in no time. And then she would do anything to please him, even if it meant damnation.

The sound of the water in the bathroom drew his attention back to Lily. And then an image flared in his mind, of what she must look like, naked, water drizzling down her milky skin, beading on her firm, high breasts. Steam wreathed around her while she washed herself, the soap suds trailing between her legs and—

"You're doing this, aren't you?" His mental sending was part groan of need and, from near at hand—far too near at hand—he got his response.

"Just giving you a helping hand, Mike." Sammael's voice came to him, its mocking tone ringing clearly around his head. *"As I remember things, imagination was never your strong point. Thought a few well-placed images might help."*

Arousal surged up through him, from his groin to his brain. A gasp of air escaped him as he saw her again, on the bed, Sammael covering her, filling her. Her body arched and she cried out in wild abandon, clutching the sheets.

"It's going to be so much fun, Mike. You'll see. I'll make sure of that. Every little detail."

Abruptly the image stopped and Micah was released so suddenly that he staggered forward, gasping for air.

"And if you think that's good," Sammael teased, *"you wait and see what I do to her next."*

"Micah?" Lily's voice dragged him back to her reality. She stepped out of the bathroom wrapped in a towel, her long hair dripping glistening trails down her exposed skin. "You okay?"

Was he? Demons were demons, and Sammael's reputation as one of the most dangerous was well deserved. Micah struggled to bring his body back under control. His cock already stood erect and eager for her. How could he talk to her now, share the intimate contact of mind on mind, when his body, however ethereal, was hell-bent on betraying him?

"'Hell-bent'." Sammael laughed, his presence hovering around Micah like a shroud. *"That's funny, Mike. Real funny."*

When he didn't answer, Lily shrugged and let the towel drop. Micah's arousal turned to steel and he heard Sammael laugh out loud this time.

Next door. The bastard was right next door.

Lily brushed her hair and tied it into a plait, still wet. Micah drew back, trying to escape from the room yet unable to tear himself away from her. Somehow Sammael was holding him here, close to her. But if he spoke now, she'd know he'd been here, that he'd seen her naked.

His mouth went dry as she turned to face him and he beheld the full length of her.

"You've wanted that sweet body for so long, haven't you?"

Sammael said, and it was like breath playing on Micah's neck and ear. *"Tell me, Micah, do angels dream of sex with a woman like her in the way demons do? She's a light. There's nothing quite like one. It's almost as fulfilling as the bliss of Heaven, they say. Do you ache for her, my friend? Is it the innocence that attracts, or is it something else? Let's see, shall we?"*

Lily slipped a silken nightgown on. It tumbled over her curves, clinging to her breasts. It couldn't hide the erect nipples. Rather it emphasised them. As she climbed onto the bed, she brushed a hand over the swell of her breasts, and a shiver ran through Micah's body.

Anticipation.

"No," he told Sammael. *"You can't make me watch this."*

"I don't have to make you, Micah. You can't look away, can you?"

True, too horribly true.

Lily rubbed her palm across her breast, the material moving with her, and she sighed. Her other hand slid down to part her thighs, drawing up the bottom of the nightdress. The silk pooled like water around her as she slid a finger inside her depths.

Micah backed up to the wall, but he couldn't escape, not from Lily, not from Sammael.

"You want her, don't you?" Sammael said, and something gave Micah a little shove forward. *"Go to her, make love to her. You know you want to."*

"It's a breach of trust." Micah closed his eyes but it didn't help. Lily gave a little pleasure-filled moan and lay back on the bed, moving languorously against her own hand.

"Then allow me," Sammael replied.

Micah's eyes snapped open as Sammael materialised before him, naked and insubstantial as a ghost, so only Micah could see him. The sculpted muscles of his back flexed as he approached the bed, but Lily didn't look up. She couldn't see him, couldn't hear him. She didn't even know he was there.

This display was all for Micah. And he couldn't tear his eyes away.

Sammael's hand pressed Lily's chest and slid down. Her eyes opened, blind with need and hunger. Her hand moved more urgently and her breath quickened to a frantic pant.

Sammael's fingers joined hers and he smiled at the bewildered pleasure that filled her face. Leaning down, he pressed his lips to her mouth and she gasped, a sound so like his name.

"She's beautiful, Micah, magnificent. How have you managed to keep your hands off her for so long?"

Micah shook his head, riveted to the spot, and Sammael kissed a line between her breasts, pausing only to suck hard first on one nipple, then on the other.

Lily's moans turned more insistent. Her hips began to buck in earnest need. Sammael drew his finger from her, leaving her to her own ministrations and she relaxed a little, a small frown of frustration marring her brow.

The demon looked up and trapped Micah's eyes with his own. Slowly, very slowly, he slid the finger into his mouth and sucked her juices from it. He made a sound of pure pleasure.

"Ah, Micah. You should taste her."

Turning his attention back to Lily, Sammael moved to kneel between her taut legs, and bent his head. He licked slowly, insistently, his phantom tongue working in unison with her fingers.

She squirmed frantically closer to him, her head thrown back and her neck a long pale curve. An erratic breath broke from her lips as she came. Sammael grabbed her hips and rode out the orgasm, his tongue making it stronger and harder than masturbation would normally allow, milking cry after cry from her as she thrust against him.

Sated, Lily fell back, sleep claiming her almost immediately. Sammael's insubstantial form stood over her, watching her with satisfaction, her juices glistening on his face. When her breathing deepened and relaxed, the demon turned from her, and approached her guardian.

"*She's so eager, Micah. So willing. If you're going to have her, you'd better make a move soon. In a little while, she's going to be all mine. Understand?*"

Sammael's hands pressed flat against Micah's chest, pausing there as if trying to sense what lay beneath. They moved slowly, trailing through the light dusting of hair, tracing a line around his erect nipples before sliding down the ripples of his abdomen.

"*Tell me,*" Sammael's breath played against Micah's cheek, his face so close that if either of them turned, their lips would meet, "*do you always picture yourself naked around her?*"

With an oddly characteristic laugh, the demon evaporated and Micah was left alone, breathing hard and painfully aroused, in the darkness.

"Can I tempt you with freshly brewed coffee and a croissant?" Sam's voice made Lily glow from within. She opened the door, still bleary-eyed with sleep. Thank God she had gone on a blitz to tidy up the apartment. All she'd had to do was apply a little of the admin skills she brought to offices in chaos to her own life for once. Something she should have done years ago, if she admitted it. She'd bought files and bookshelves, new cushions and throws. It looked like a different place and she loved it. She loved being able to invite Sam in.

"That's three days in a row," she told him as she opened the door. "Careful, you're spoiling me. I'll be demanding this all the time."

The aroma of the coffee he had brought reached her and her mouth watered at the thought. It was a comfort, and one she had never expected. More than that, his company made her days easier, and even the voices seemed quieter when he was around.

As he stepped inside, Sam stumbled over a box left just outside the door. He recovered flawlessly, but he gave it an accusing glare.

"Bit early for mail, isn't it?" he said.

"Someone's dropped that," she said. "You collect mail downstairs. Did nobody tell you that?"

Sam shrugged, setting the coffee jug and the plate with the steaming croissants down on the table.

"To be honest I didn't follow too much of Cassini's tour, just got my keys. Well, except the storage room key. It's missing." He picked up a long box wrapped precisely with brown paper and tape.

"You can always use my space. There's some room. A little anyway."

"I don't have much to store." He handed her the box. While he poured the coffee, Lily opened it.

The box was full of pieces of paper. Shredded paper. Lily frowned, staring at it.

"Those look like my old telephone bills," she said. "And bank statements. I shredded them two days ago and threw them out."

Her fingers shook as she slipped them inside to comb through the strands and see what else was there. Her things, her papers, personal, intimate papers.

"*Careful.*"

Micah's voice came sharp and sudden to her ears. She stiffened. He'd been avoiding her, and the relief at hearing his voice again was only slightly marred by the concern in his tone.

Something jabbed into her finger. She gasped in surprise and pulled her hand out. Blood welled on her fingertip like a black pearl.

Sam's arms came from behind her, drawing her back against his broad chest. He caught her injured hand in his and before she knew what he was doing, drew it up to her mouth.

Her lips closed around her finger, suckling at it while he guided it deeper between her lips. The taste of blood filled her mouth and his other hand tightened around her waist, stroking her stomach through the silk of her nightdress and wrap. Sensations fluttered through her: hunger, desire, shock, and need. Her heart raced and as he drew her hand away. She released her finger with a faint pop, and he raised it to his own lips, placing a kiss on the very tip.

"There, all better," he said. "Now what the hell is in there?"

She shook her head, aware of the pounding blood between her thighs. Squeezing them together did nothing to alleviate it. Sam released her and tipped the box over so the contents spilled out. Shredded paper fell away and inside were half a dozen dead roses, shrivelled and black, one of the thorns glistening with her blood.

"Lily, there's danger here."

"I know," she said. She'd be a fool not to realise it. Sam just looked confused.

The expression made her want him even more.

"Have you received these before?" he asked.

She shook her head. She hadn't received them. But she knew someone who had.

She heaved in a deep breath and slowly let it release. "Just a prank, I think. A friend of mine got some. She's psychic too. It's some kind of sick joke, but no one knows the punch line."

She hadn't heard from Rachel since that happened. She needed to give her a call. But she'd been—she took a long look at Sam again. She'd been distracted.

Sam snorted and picked up a small piece of paper which had been wrapped around the shrivelled stems.

"*M'khashephah lo tichayyah,*" he read. "It's old Hebrew, Exodus 22:18."

A chill ran through Lily's body, chasing away the arousal. Other arms encircled her, Micah's presence enveloping her in an effort to comfort her. It almost worked. If he had been real, she would have burrowed into his arms, to hide her face in his chest.

"*Oh, Lily, my bright one. It isn't true.*"

Sam was eyeing her as if he didn't understand. But how could he not know the translation if he could say the words so perfectly? It was a phrase every psychic heard eventually and Lily dreaded.

"*Thou shalt not suffer a witch to live,*" she said, surprised that her numb lips could form the words.

Sam seized the box and thrust the contents back inside. "Sit down," he told her brusquely. "Let me deal with this." He strode from the apartment, the offending articles beneath his arm.

Lily sank back into the chair, and could have sworn she felt hands take hold of hers, as if someone knelt before her.

"Micah?"

"*Yes Lily, I'm here.*"

"Where have you been?"

"*Around. I'm always nearby. You know that.*"

"Why would someone send that?"

"*I don't know, my bright one. Some people are not right. They don't recognise the Creator's gifts when they see them and—*"

"And they think I'm a witch? Oh God," she said. "Isn't it enough that I hear voices and can't lead a normal life, but this has to happen to me again? Isn't it enough, Micah, that I had to

44

leave home once already?"

The sweet cinnamon scent of him came closer and Lily closed her eyes, the better to sense him. Micah's breath played on her cheek. He released one hand, still cradling the other, and stroked her hair, so gently it was like a warm breeze. His lips brushed against her and her body reacted. Not as it did for Sam, although there was an element of that, which she had not expected. Her heart seemed to blossom, and ripples of desire ran through her. Not lust. Nothing so simple. This was deeper, stronger. This was as old as time.

"Cassini doesn't know who dropped it," Sam said, slamming the door behind him.

She jumped, her eyes opening wide, expecting to see two men before her instead of the one, who watched her carefully.

"Lily?" he asked after a moment. "You okay?"

"Yes." What could she say? Micah's arms still seemed to encircle her, holding her carefully against a body she could not see, but longed to. "I'm fine," she told them both. "Really. It's just a sick joke or something."

"Well, sick joke or not, it's getting reported. Cassini's on the phone already and the cops will be here to take a statement. You might want to get dressed."

She nodded and tried to move. Micah held her for a moment longer and then, reluctantly, he released her.

"I don't know, Sam." She forced mirth she didn't feel into her voice. "I've known you for three days and this is my second police statement."

Rachel's house phone rang out, and the mobile went straight to voicemail. Lily frowned and tried the studio.

"*What are you doing?*" Micah lingered nearby.

Reception answered and when Lily asked for Rachel, she was connected to another voice immediately.

45

"This is Rachel's co-host, Todd Lane. Can I help you?" Rushed and urgent, hard words and harder tones.

"I-I'm a friend of Rachel's. I'm trying to get in touch about a story of hers."

"You haven't heard? Rachel's missing. She hasn't been seen in two days."

It felt like the world dropped out from under her. Lily leaned on the table, tried not to fall, tried not to cry. "She said she had a lead. She said she knew who sent her the flowers."

"The flowers?" She heard the noise of typing, rapid, frantic typing. "Listen, what do you know about them?"

"I got them too." Her voice sounded empty. If Rachel was missing, if her suspicions had been right—

"You're psychic too?" He swore, then rapidly apologised, but he sounded more scared than angry. "Was there a note? Anything personal?"

"Yes. They were wrapped in personal papers. They had a note. In ancient Hebrew."

"Hebrew? You're sure." More typing.

No, but my new neighbour is. She didn't say it. Couldn't. What on earth would it sound like? "I think so."

"Listen love, you need to talk to the cops. Understand? This guy is dangerous."

"I will. Someone's already called them. But I wanted to check with Rachel..." Her voice failed her. Rachel was missing. Rachel, who'd had the same sick gift she had.

"*Hang up.*" Micah's voice calmed her, as it always did.

She shook her head. "Todd? You know what Rachel thought, right? That she was being targeted? What if it wasn't just her?"

"It isn't. I got them too. It's like a game. He's one sick fuckhead. Talk to the cops."

"I will." Repeating herself felt like a punch to the guts. Was he even listening? "Todd, have you talked to them? Told them everything?"

"Everything? Of course." But she knew journalists, knew the way they worked. They only told what they had to until they had the story. She'd worked with Rachel, sorted out her office. She was more than a chat show host, more than a celebrity psychic. She'd been the only person to understand what Lily went through every day. Of course, Rachel, being Rachel, had begged her to come on the show, and Lily had run a mile. But Rachel hadn't been put off. Somewhere along the line they'd become friends.

A chill slithered up her spine. Whoever sent her the flowers had Rachel. She just knew it. "Todd. Be careful, all right?" She hung up and her strength deserted her. She wilted onto the sofa and began to cry as if she would never stop.

Sammael knew he had to take her mind off the dead flowers. All Lily seemed to want to do was sit at home, hide and try to push the delivery from her mind. Talking to the police had left her broken inside and so very afraid.

"Come on," he told her shortly before lunch. "Let me take you out."

"Out?" She turned a dazed look on him and something twisted inside him.

"Out," he said firmly. "Let's go for a drive."

"Do you have a car?" Her voice sounded terribly distant, lost. He'd never seen her like this. It unnerved him.

"I have a great car," he lied. Well, not quite a lie. By the time they walked down to the garage he would have a car, a great car. He just didn't know what it was just yet.

Lily's face remained unmoved.

"I know almost nothing about you, Sam." She wrung her hands together. "I run into you on the street and the next thing

47

I know you're living next door, we're—what is it we're doing? Dating?"

He struggled to mask the growing cold inside him. Instead he put on a hopeful smile. "If you like." He stretched out to touch her face, but she flinched back.

Damn, this was bad. This was seriously bad.

"We're dating. Suddenly we're dating and then I start getting deliveries of dead flowers from someone stalking another psychic I know. Rachel's missing now. The cops say he's dangerous."

"You can't think it's me," he protested, trying to edge nearer.

Lily's shoulders tensed. "I don't want to but I know nothing about you, Sam. And Micah—Micah says *you're* dangerous."

"Does he now?" He couldn't keep the growl out of his voice. "The disembodied voice in your head who refuses to identify himself thinks *I'm* dangerous?"

"I've known him for years. He's closer to me than anyone else in my life." She exhaled slowly and Sam forced himself to calm down. She wasn't stupid. No one could ever accuse her of that. She was smart and quick minded. She was—

She was special. A light.

That was why he was here, after all.

"Look, Lily." He reached out again, pausing before touching her, letting her come to him. She hesitated and for a moment he thought it was all lost, that he had failed for the first time ever, that he might never touch her again, press his lips to her lips, slide his skin along her skin. The cold wave of despair was both unexpected and unwelcome. True, he would be punished if he returned to Hell a failure. But that hardly mattered right at the moment. Nothing else mattered to him when faced with the prospect of losing her and, deep inside him, something tore itself apart. "Lily, please listen, I can't explain why I'm here now."

"*Why not?*" Micah hissed. "*Why not tell her you're more of a danger to her than any human could possibly be?*"

Sam shut him out, but he saw Lily flinch and knew that Micah was saying something similar to her. He winced, but didn't withdraw his offered hand.

"Please, Lily," he urged. "Please trust me. If nothing else, I can protect you from whoever sent those roses, if they decide to go further. Maybe that's why. It's fate, or whatever you want to call it. Maybe I'm here to keep you from harm."

He closed his eyes, his brow creased with pain and stress.

Then, impossibly, he heard Micah again, and his voice sounded completely different. No longer antagonistic, not a trace of anger. Rather he sounded almost plaintive.

"*Do you truly believe so? You can protect her if he comes here?*"

Sam shook his head. "*If* who *comes?*"

"*Answer me, demon,*" her guardian snapped. "*Tell the truth for once and don't twist your words.*"

"I will not let any harm come to you, Lily," he promised solemnly, surprised to find that he didn't just believe every word, he meant it. He meant it as if the promise was carved on his heart. "Not while we live. I swear it."

"*So mote it be,*" Micah chimed, using the old words, the powerful words, and for a moment the world of the supernatural lurched around him. Sammael drew in a shuddering breath in an effort to centre himself, but felt something else instead, something that buoyed his spirits again.

Lily took his hand, her fingers entangling with his. "I believe you."

She leaned forward to brush her lips against his. She tasted of coffee and the salt of her tears, but he didn't care. As her lips parted beneath his, Sammael wondered who was tempting whom, and what side of this war of light and dark he had suddenly found himself on.

"Let me get changed," she said slowly. "Then we can go out. I'd like that."

She walked away from him and he couldn't tear his eyes off the sway of her perfectly formed rear.

"*I may not believe you,*" Micah said, "*but that was an oath and I will hold you to it. You won't harm her.*"

Sam waited for him to depart as well, and then sank back in relief. He was shaking from head to foot.

Harming her had never been his intention, not physically anyway. Her soul was another matter but he'd managed to get away with it, by the skin of his teeth.

But now, sitting on the floor of her apartment, waiting for her in a most undignified stance, he swore to himself that he had meant that oath. Every word. Whoever this stalker was, he would not harm a hair of her head.

Chapter Four

Tying Sammael to Lily had been the last thing Micah wanted, but then again, what else could he do, other than make himself corporeal and guard her himself? The aura of evil intent surrounding the box of dead flowers had been so potent he was surprised Sam hadn't felt it, but perhaps it seemed commonplace to him.

Watching them together, Micah was forced to admit that Sam made her happy. That galled him indeed, and yet it attracted him. He couldn't help but watch. She smiled. She laughed. She was playful, expressed delight and relaxed into her pleasure.

Sam's seduction continued relentlessly but slowly, carefully. Micah knew it for what it was, and yet it seemed sometimes that the demon courted him as much as his charge, keeping, for the time, a respectful distance.

But Lily still whispered Sammael's name in the darkness, during the night. And Micah turned away, unable to watch her arch up from the bed, even if he felt every shudder of pleasure that coursed through her.

It couldn't go on. Somehow he had to stop her from seeing Sammael. But to protect her, to keep her safe from whatever was stalking her, what better protection could there be than a demon?

Micah knelt by her side while she slept and prayed for

guidance. A few millennia ago, the Voice would have been there for him in an instant, the Word filling him with love and light. He had been created for just that purpose, to be a vessel for the One. Whatever he had done wrong, so long ago, all was silent. He didn't expect it anymore. Even the angels looked down on him. Not shunning him, exactly, but he sensed their pity and it grated. The Holy Court was not a place which had much sympathy for those on the verge of falling, and Micah felt himself sliding nearer to that edge every time he looked at Lily.

He was going to fail as her guardian. He knew that. But it didn't mean he had to doom her as well. And if Sam could keep her safe...

Sam. Such a simple name for such a complicated individual. Sammael had not fallen with Lucifer and the others during the war in Heaven. He had not been cast out. He had merely absented himself. He'd only been made a demon in retrospect when it was discovered that he was already in Hell serving the Nameless.

Micah sensed him next door, awake and waiting, a frisson of anger vibrating through the air. Micah had managed to avoid being in the same area alone with him so far. But that was something else that couldn't continue. They needed to talk. And Sammael was not going to forgive him for binding him in such a way. No beast appreciated a collar.

Micah slipped through the wall between the two apartments and found Sammael gazing out of the living room window, with the city lights laid out before him. He had acquired some furniture now—neat and chic, shades of brown leather complementing the cream carpeting. It wasn't an apartment designed to be lived in, like Lily's, merely to impress. Everything about Sammael was designed to impress. He wore the finest clothes, his body was every woman's dream, and he moulded his character to be best suited to the object of his seduction. In this case Lily. Micah knew as well as anyone that

Lily needed someone understanding, full of compassion and goodwill, so for her, Sammael had become just that.

But Lily wasn't here now.

"You took your time." Sammael's voice was a low growl, a threat in and of itself.

"*I didn't know you expected me.*"

He whirled around, his eyes flaming in the darkness. "You fucking well know I've been waiting for you. And you can cut the ethereal crap too. I know what you are. Show yourself."

It took a surprising amount of effort. For so long Micah had remained on the spiritual plane that to become corporeal now took a moment or two of determined concentration. But he did it.

Sammael stared at him, drinking in his appearance. How long since he had seen one of their kind as once they all were? His face took on a parched look, for just a moment. Then the same slow and vicious smile spread like an infection across his expressive mouth again.

"Not bad. I see angels keep themselves in shape in between the harp practice and the songs of adulation."

Micah didn't react to the dig. He appeared as he had always appeared. He wasn't going to change that for Sammael.

Except that he had made sure to remember clothing this time.

"You're angry, Sammael." It wasn't a question. There was no doubting the simmering rage beneath the perfectly tailored exterior. "You offered your word."

"And you made sure I was bound by it."

"Didn't you mean it?"

"Oh, I won't let a human with his own personal God complex hurt her. *Thou shalt not suffer a witch to live?* Rest assured, whoever sent her those cursed flowers will find out all about suffering if I have any say in the matter. But you—" He stalked forward, his very stance dangerous. "You had no right."

Something perilously close to pride swelled in Micah's chest. He allowed himself a small smile and Sammael froze, outraged.

"I'm her guardian. That gives me the right. She's special. You know that, it's why you're here, to win her for your master, to corrupt her and ultimately take her soul. And now you can't hurt her."

"*Physically* hurt her. That doesn't count souls, or emotions or—"

Micah tipped his head to one side, unsure of what he was seeing in Sammael's anger. Something more than a demon bound, certainly. Something far greater than a loss of control. Not a loss at all, in fact, but something found.

"Sammael? Do you have feelings for her?"

The demon shuddered, a deep line forming between his eyebrows, beneath his frown. "I don't know what you mean." The words were clipped and threatening.

And lies.

Now that was interesting. For all the temptation Sammael was making sure Micah felt, it seemed that some temptations were riddling his own dark soul, and not the ones a demon welcomed.

"Do you think she's another Eve?"

Sammael bared his teeth. "That was a long time ago. A *very* long time ago."

It was unmistakable. The demon was only a foot away from him, and tears glistened in the corners of his eyes.

"Not so long for the heart." Micah stared at Sammael in fascination. "She's a light, the next spiritual step for mankind. If—"

The punch took him completely by surprise. It felt like his jaw exploded and the force of the blow hurled him to one side.

He barely managed to keep himself on his feet.

"Get out, you bastard," Sammael snarled, and all trace of softness evaporated into flames. "You want to see what I'm capable of? I'll show you. I won't harm her, don't you fret about that. I'll bring her more pleasure than any human has ever known. I'll make her plead and beg for more and then I'll take her there. I'll fulfil her every desire. And then we'll see where she ends up, won't we?"

"Sammael, you cannot hurt her."

"I won't." The demon seized Micah's shirt and pulled him in so they were face-to-face. "I'll let you do that."

With a single push, he hurled the guardian from him. Micah struck the wall with a backbreaking crash and slid down. He staggered back to his feet, his anger finally breaking loose. He balled his hands to fists and prepared to throw himself at Sammael, to finish this for once and for all.

But before he could, a terrible scream rent the air.

"*Lily!*"

Her terror, blind and incalculable, descended on him and, Sammael forgotten, Micah shed his physical form and evanesced to her side.

It was a dream. Just a dream.

Lily struggled against the cruel hands holding her, against the duct tape that sealed her mouth. The shadows had her. They pulled her down into the darkness, onto the cold wet ground, and he loomed over her, a shape black and endless, a silhouette of hatred with no substance but a million ways to hurt. He had no features, nothing but a shadow, and as he threw her down, he laughed at her muffled cries.

This isn't happening. I'm at home in bed. This isn't real!

The shadow man grabbed a fistful of her hair and dragged her to her knees.

"You've been accused of witchcraft, how do you plead?" His voice grated over her body. *She trembled, tried to speak, but the duct tape was still there.*

"Your silence aids you naught. You'll face the trial of water then."

The shadow man slid behind her and, before she knew what was happening, his foot slammed into her back, pitching her forward, and she was falling.

"Micah! Help me! Please, Sam, Micah!"

The water hit her like a hammer blow and she sank, hands tied behind her back, feet similarly pinioned. Struggling, fighting, trying to wriggle free, she descended the depths, silver bubbles of air blinding her. Her hair swirled around her like water weeds, leached of colour in the half light. Her lungs strained, burned, and then the water came, water all around, flooding her, freezing her until the bubbles ended and the shadows closed in.

Lily wrenched herself free of the vision, her own will pulling her clear and back into reality.

She lurched up from the bed, screaming, the sound tearing itself out of her. Instantly, Micah was there, holding her, trying to calm her.

"It's okay, Lily, it's me. Can you hear me? What happened?"

She sucked in breath after breath, staring wildly at the shadows dancing on the wall. There was no light. How could they be moving when there was no light?

What had she just seen? It wasn't a memory. It wasn't a spirit. Was it...was that a murder?

"He killed her, Micah. I...I saw...felt him kill her. I was right there, in her! Micah!"

His presence closed around her as if he were trying to hold her against his chest and stroke her hair, as if he was a lover next to whom she woke in terror.

A thunderous banging on the front door almost made her

scream again.

"*It's Sammael,*" said Micah. "*It's just Sammael.*"

"S-Sam?" The word came out halfway between a sob and a hiccough and she tried to get up.

Micah held her just for a fraction too long and she paused. "What is it, Micah? What are you trying to keep from me?"

His ethereal arms fell away and he gave a clearly audible sigh. She felt his breath rush across the skin of her shoulders.

"I need to hold someone, Micah. Someone flesh and blood. Someone real." As soon as the words left her mouth she wished she could have taken them back. A chill filled the air and she felt him withdraw, not just his ethereal self, but everything, his emotions, his friendship, his love. "Micah? Micah, I didn't mean it as it sounded. Micah?"

Sam banged on the door again and called her name. He sounded scared, worried for her.

"Micah," she yelled, "please, talk to me!"

But he didn't answer. Lily stumbled forward, tears streaming down her face, blinding her so that in the darkness she crashed into an armchair and almost fell over the coffee table.

She felt cold, empty. She had never been alone, not like this. Micah had always been there, ever since her psychic awareness first burst into terrifying life.

Yanking the door open, she fell into Sam's arms, her chest heaving out sob after sob.

"What is it? What happened?" He pulled her against him, pressed her face into his chest so his shirt soaked up her tears. He held her as Micah might have held her, if he were real. If he were really real.

But he was gone.

Jesus, he had been real, hadn't he? Twenty years she'd known him, trusted him, loved him. He had to be real.

Sam steered her inside the apartment, kicking the door shut behind him, and he sank onto the couch, still cradling her.

"What happened, Lily?" His fingertips ran over her hair and from somewhere she found a trembling reed of a voice.

"I had a dream, a nightmare. I saw a shadow man. He kidnapped me, tied me up and taped my mouth. Said I was a witch and he drowned me." But that wasn't the worst of it, not anymore. How did she explain about Micah? How did she tell him that?

"And then?"

"Micah—Micah's gone."

Sam breathed calmly, quietly, his chest rising and falling beneath her. His questing hands moved to her shoulders, massaged the tension there. "But you called him your spirit guide. How can he be gone?"

She shook her head, the tears starting up afresh. She couldn't catch her breath, couldn't seem to stop. "He's not. I hurt him. I just said—"

She looked up suddenly to see his face gazing down at her, handsome, even more sculpted in the darkness of her living room. His dark eyes were almost black and in them she could see more than concern. His mouth looked grim and stern.

"What?" he asked. "What did you say to him?"

"That I...that I needed you."

He let out a sigh, but that same smile drifted around the edges of his mouth. "Lily, this probably isn't a good time to..."

A good time? When was there ever a good time?

She moved before she could think about it, before she could regret it or let common sense talk her out of it. Rearing up, she captured his mouth with hers, kissing his with all the passion she had ever suppressed. Sam fell back beneath her, so shocked that he didn't respond.

Lily's heart stuttered inside her and then shame welled up,

a flaming wall of embarrassment moving up through her body. She tore herself back and looked down on him, this handsome God-sent man, and her heart gave way to the agony waiting for it.

He didn't want her. He didn't want her any more than Micah did.

"Oh God." The two words scraped off the inside of her throat.

Sam's hands closed on her upper arms, holding her to him. His grip was like iron, like stone, and he stared into her face with those darker-than-dark eyes.

Then he kissed her.

He didn't let her go, but held her close and his lips captured hers. His tongue slid across her lower lip, teasing her and slowly, so slowly, his grip on her arms gentled. He ran the palms of his hand down her bare skin, sparking little thrills of erotic pleasure in his wake. He caught her hands and rubbed the centre of her palms with his thumbs, a strong, firm motion that stirred the rising heat at the base of her spine. And that heat, an ache, a hunger, spread.

Lily lifted herself and parted her legs, sinking down so she could sit astride him, the silk of her nightdress and his clothes the only barrier between them now. She rocked her hips forward, feeling his hardness against her, wanting him.

Sam let out a low groan, his eyes still feasting upon her. He let go of her hands, but he didn't release her. His fingers trailed back up her arms, stirring up the delicate hairs as if he trailed static behind him. She shuddered, her eyelids fluttering closed.

"Look at me, Lily," he said. "I want to look into your eyes."

She obeyed, wanting the same thing, wanting to gaze into the deep darkness of his eyes, wanting to see them cloud and blur with pleasure.

He flicked the narrow straps off her shoulders and the

nightdress fell, uncovering her breasts. Cupping them, he ran his thumb over the nipple, watching it grow erect, ready for him. Lily sucked in a breath as he rolled the little bud between his fingers. Needles of pleasure shot through her skin, down through her stomach and straight for the welling depths of her womanhood. She pressed against him, his hardness stimulating her while she rocked back and forth.

"This isn't going to be slow." His voice was hoarse with need.

She nodded, unable to form words. She didn't want it to be slow. She wanted him now, hard and fast, with all the hunger damned up inside.

In answer, she pulled open his cotton shirt so she could touch him as he touched her. Sam moaned and his mouth closed on her breast. He sucked on her nipple, leaning her back, taking control. Turning beneath her, he flipped her onto the sofa, shedding his clothes with frightening ease. Naked, he was breathtaking. Not muscled per se, but toned. She could sense the strength beneath that olive skin, could see the muscles tensing, struggling for control.

And there was no doubting his arousal.

He knelt before her, grabbed her thighs and pulled her towards him. The nightdress slid down the length of her legs to pool around her feet. He lifted them so he could retrieve it and held it up to his face, breathing in her scent, watching her all the time.

He laid it aside like a sacred artefact and slipped his hands between her knees, pushing them relentlessly apart, tracing a path up her thighs to the glistening pubic curls. She watched him lean in close, pause and inhale. Slowly, with relish.

His fingers combed through her pubic hair, teasing and testing, parting her honeyed lips, using a single fingertip to circle the edges, moistening the skin around until he reached her clit. She gave a broken cry and his mouth closed on her, his tongue darting deep inside.

He licked her with a calm determination, with deliberate intent. Lily's body squirmed against him and she grabbed his head, knotting her fingers in his hair.

It was too much. She didn't want it to be over yet. Didn't want this to be finished. Yet her body was betraying her. Sam's wickedly sensual tongue darted into her, drew back to lathe her clitoris and then entered her again. His lips caressed her and his hands held her down. She couldn't move, not even to press herself against him. All she could do was push his head down, harder and harder while all the time the pressure built, and the rippling in her stomach grew. Her body convulsed, contracting inside as if to hold him with her. She cried out, shouting words that might not have even been words, and reality exploded around her.

Sam continued to lick, holding her down and drinking from her as if she was the elixir of life. When her orgasm lulled, she lay, spread out before him, her arms stretched across the back of the sofa, her nails digging into the leather.

When he looked up, she smiled, dazed and sated, but one look told her he was far from finished with her. A frisson of fear trembled through her and her sated euphoria evaporated like morning mist.

His eyes were so dark, like the endless dark of a starless night. And within them, she saw flames dancing.

"Come to me," he told her.

She released her grip on the sofa and slid forward, down to sit astride his kneeling form, taking his iron-hard cock deep inside her with a single movement.

"Oh God," she exclaimed as he filled her. "Sam, please. Oh God."

Taking hold of her hips, he pushed her down, forcing himself deeper, and she gave another stuttering cry. Sam kissed her, claiming her mouth with a searing kiss which she returned with matching passion. Quick, sudden bursts of pleasure, timed with the flex of his supple hips, enveloped her. She leaned back, her head and shoulders supported by the sofa. Sam dipped his head so he could tongue her breasts again, nipping the flesh, sucking hard as she met his thrusts.

His hands filled themselves with the globes of her ass, his fingers teasing the delicate area between them, and she could stand it no longer. With a moment of blind panic, her body slammed down on him, the walls of her vagina clamping around him. Sam's face went rigid and then his orgasm was upon him. His grip turned possessive, holding her against him while his body poured itself into her. Lily cried out his name, coming again so fast and hard that she lost all sense of the world beyond them. All that mattered was Sam and the wondrous things he did to her. All that mattered was Sam, buried deep inside her, coming so hard that his body glistened and the muscles beneath turned to stone.

Afterwards, Sam kissed her forehead, her nose, her chin. He fluttered light kisses over her lips and then he lifted her, his cock still nestled deep inside. It didn't seem possible, but he held her as if she was weightless and carried her into her bedroom, let her down onto the bed and thrust into her again. As she lay beneath him, slowly, so very slowly, he began to make love to her once more. And Lily's body began to respond, all over again.

Chapter Five

Sam lay awake listening to Lily's deep and even breathing. A magical sound, a mixture of exhaustion and total satiation, he could listen to it for hours, until the urge took him again. With other lovers, he would wake them, yet for some reason with Lily he just listened. Contentment never came easy to him, but this was close. This was perilously close.

He stroked the silken skin where her back curved, feeling the vertebrae through it, marvelling at the texture. Her hair spilled across the pillow like strands of polished copper, such an unusual colour, captivating. Had it been so long since he had lain with a woman? Time was relative to all demons, but it felt like an eternity since a simple seduction had felt like this, had brought him this much pleasure.

Lily had matched him stroke for stroke, desire for desire. She was voracious, and inventive, and revelled in her pleasure. She was magnificent.

Asleep, she looked so childlike, though her body belied that impression instantly. Sam couldn't believe he was doing this, lying here with her, thinking the way he was. The rage Micah had drawn from him earlier had evaporated when he thought she was in danger. For a moment every instinct had told him to tear his way through the wall to reach her, but some shred of sanity remained and he had raced for her door.

"Is she sleeping?" Micah asked hesitantly.

Sam narrowed his eyes, looking into the corner of the room where a flickering light grew. Lily wouldn't be able to see it, but he knew at once her guardian was back.

"I should thank you, Mike," Sam said. "I thought you wanted me to stay away from her, but then you throw her into my arms."

"*She needed you.*"

He couldn't hide the laconic tone of his triumph. "She got me."

"*You said I'd hurt her. I can't think even you expected it to happen so soon.*" Micah sounded desolate, lost.

Sam smiled. Yes, it was cruel, but then, he was a demon and cruelty could be a pleasure as well. "I can't say I did. But thank you for being so prompt." He glanced down at his sleeping lover. A frown ghosted its way across her face, just for a moment. When he stroked her cheek with his hand, it vanished. But he couldn't deny what he had seen. "What did she dream?"

"*A murder.*"

"Whose?"

"*I don't know yet. But we'll find out. That spirit won't rest until she sends it into the light. It needs her.*"

Wandering spirits were never good news, neither for Heaven nor Hell. People like Lily were special because they could direct them, above or below as they saw fit. They were rare beings, created for a purpose, closer to angels than even the angels would admit, designed by the Creator for an express purpose. Lily was special. He sighed; Lily was special for a hell of a lot more.

"*Sammael, when you're near her you block the other spirits, don't you?*" Sam nodded slowly, wondering where this was going. "*You have to stop doing that. It's like damning a river without giving it any means of draining off an excess. Eventually the energy will grow so strong it will burst through that block and overwhelm her. Like tonight. The dream was so powerful, so terrifying that it was real to her. She died in that dream, drowned by a madman. Do you understand? If you care about her."*

Care about her? Since when did Micah imagine demons cared about anyone?

Since when did a demon allow himself to care?

A low growl rolled up through his chest and Lily stirred. He forced himself to stillness, glaring at the place where he sensed his adversary.

"Why put her through it, if I can drive them off and give her some peace?"

"Because I tried once and she had a breakdown. Please, Sammael, that would avail you naught. You have to let her visions continue."

Sure, it was his fault. That figured. The angel would say that.

Problem was, the angel was right. A breakdown and subsequent medication and treatment would only hinder his mission.

"All right, I'm listening. What are you proposing?"

"A truce."

Sam laughed out loud. He couldn't help himself. Lily squirmed against him and he forced himself to be quiet again. "A truce? Are you insane?"

"It's the only way."

"I'm not giving her up, Mike," he hissed. "I will not stop. It isn't in my nature. I live to seduce, to pleasure a woman like her. Why can't you get that through your thick head?"

Lily stirred again. This time, she woke. "Sam?" She lifted her head and looking at him with heavy eyes. "You all right?"

Sam pushed thoughts of Micah from his mind. "'Course I

am, sweetheart. Shh, go back to sleep."

But Lily rubbed against him, like a cat demanding attention. She all but purred. "Not sleepy," she lied.

His smile tugged at his mouth and he cupped her shoulder briefly before moving down to her breasts. They filled his hands as if they had been created for his attentions.

"Not sleepy, eh?" he teased, and she shook her head, her hair tumbling into her face. She pushed at it ineffectually, so he laid her back on the pillows and did the job himself. While he was up there, he nudged his way between her long, shapely legs and felt them rise to wrap about his waist, drawing him into her again. Her scent enfolded him, sweet and musky, the perfect enticement.

Sam's smile broadened. "Lily, I'm starting to think you're insatiable."

"I could say the same about you." She grinned up at him, more awake now, her hand closing on his erect cock to guide him to her.

She sheathed him, warm, wet and welcoming. Her inner muscles gripped him, rippling down his length. Damn it, she didn't even have to move and he would come for her.

Light dappled the wall above his head, reflected light, bouncing off the mirror and between it, flickering shadows. Micah was still here. He was watching them.

This time, Sam's smile turned truly demonic.

"Do you want me, Lily?" He circled his hips, rolling his cock deep inside her.

"Yes," she gasped.

He fixed her with his most domineering glare. "Tell me."

"I want you, Sam."

"Are you listening, you holier than thou bastard?" He got no response to his sending, but the light that only he could see didn't dim. *"Still here, you angelic peeping Tom? You like to*

watch, do you? Well, watch this."

"Reach down, Lily. Make yourself come for me. Now."

She slid her hand between their bodies, finding her clitoris with the unerring accuracy of womankind. With the centre of her pleasure already slick from his penetration, she began to stimulate herself, holding him deep inside her. She gazed up into his shadowed face and smiled for an instant before her features took on that studied intensity that meant she was succeeding in her task.

Sam's arms trembled as her knuckles brushed the base of his cock and his body coiled, ready for release. The weight in his balls was incredible, a familiar but always revelatory sensation. Her muscles closed on him, gripping him, and he stayed as still as stone.

Lily's breath came in a burst and a low moan rippled up from deep inside her, originating where they joined and rising to his ears like a song of salvation.

"That's it, sweetheart," he said. "That's it. Now, come for me, Lily."

She cried out and her body slammed into his, her vagina squeezing him hard so that he couldn't have held back if he wanted to. With a cry of triumph, Sam's body convulsed and she milked him, her muscles undulating all around him, holding him without hope of escape. He collapsed on top of her, pinning her hand between them, shocked by the severity of his reaction to her.

For a moment he wondered if he was still breathing, if she had ground all his immortal life out of him. Beneath him, Lily was laughing, running her free hand through his hair. She kissed him savagely and rolled him onto his back so she could nestle against him, still kissing him, still gripping him deep inside those velvet walls.

"Weren't you expecting that?" She giggled, nipping at his lower lip.

He didn't answer her. He couldn't. The light was gone. Micah had departed. At least he had that, Sam thought. One small victory. And now it felt ridiculously small.

Lily nuzzled into his neck, and Sam stroked her supine body, distracted. Not for the first time since he had arrived, he had to wonder, who was seducing whom?

Micah could think of no choir of angels as beautiful as the sound of Lily singing quietly to herself in the grey light of early morning. She brightened the day, called the sun to rise and filled his insubstantial body with such light that he thought he would ascend back to Heaven without a divine summons.

Perhaps this was part of the reason he was stuck here, with her. Unlike the Nameless and his demons, the Creator gave no guidance to those he sent to the earth. He relied on them to know, to intuit their path, and to act accordingly. But Micah had never felt so lost.

Like a ghost hovering on the edge of her world, he lingered by her because he couldn't leave. Even though he knew she wanted—no, *needed*—Sam, even though she called for him the moment she left the demon dozing in her bed, Micah didn't answer. He didn't know what to say.

Lily busied herself in the kitchen, flicking on the TV for noise and singing along with the commercials and jingles while she opened the orange juice and cooked pancakes. She had always loved pancakes, a comfort from her childhood, she claimed. Of course by the time Micah had appeared in her life that childhood was well and truly gone. Her parents were terrified about the changes in their beautiful little girl, when she transformed into an unstable, moody, angst-ridden young woman. Pancakes were the last thing on their minds then.

Standing there now, controlling the light that emanated from his body in a beam of sunshine, Micah watched her. No matter how much harm Sam would eventually do—and the demon would do harm, there was no avoiding that—the pleasure Micah felt looking at her now made his heart lurch inside him.

Lily sipped her glass of orange juice. It made her lips glisten for a moment, before her tongue licked it away.

Remembering what he had seen last night, Micah groaned, trying to push other, more intimate images from his mind.

"The top story again," said the cheesy voice of the newscaster on the TV. "A gruesome find down by the docks this morning has authorities baffled. More about that after this break."

The morning news jingle floated through the air, and Sam appeared in the doorway from the bedroom.

"Have I died and gone to Heaven?" he asked with a smirk directed towards Micah's hiding place. "What is that smell, sweetheart?"

"Coffee, juice and pancakes." She didn't turn away from the TV. She gripped the spatula in her hand like a weapon, staring at the adverts. Her other hand, holding the glass, began to tremble; minute vibrations ran down her arm and made the juice slosh against the sides. Just a little. Just enough for them to notice.

A chill passed through Micah's body and he moved towards her. Sam beat him to it. As always.

The demon slid an arm around her shoulder. Lily leaned into his strong embrace, but said nothing.

A wall of air rose around Micah, keeping him from her. Sammael's doing, no doubt. No doubt at all given the look the demon turned his way.

"Sammael, something's wrong with her. Can't you sense it?"

Sammael just grunted and nuzzled the curve of her neck, his lips teasing the sensitive skin there. But Lily said nothing, gave no response, much to Sammael's chagrin. She didn't even move.

The sense of nervous anticipation swelled. Micah tried to force his way closer, but Sammael flicked his eyes towards him and the barrier became even stronger.

Micah pushed, trying to force his way through, and saw Sammael's arrogant smirk. He'd won. They both knew it. He was stronger and every intimacy with her just increased his powers. It was only a matter of time before he would be able to make her do whatever he asked. And then she would be his forever.

Anger exploded inside Micah and he raised his fists, ready to fight his way through, preparing to call on light and love to aid him. He was stronger than a demon. Always had been, though he chose never to use such power. But this time, this time he would.

Lily drew in a breath and the air turned icy cold. Micah stilled, staring at the dawning horror on her face. It came just seconds before the TV picture changed, showing the dockside, several cops and a large swathe of yellow crime scene tape. The reporter stepped into shot, a young woman, perfectly turned out, with a tightness in her face.

"The scene here this morning is grim. While the body retrieved from the water is as yet officially unidentified, it would appear that the killer who calls himself the Witchfinder has indeed struck again. Still missing, Rachel Deveral and now her associate Todd Lane. Both known psychics, with something of a celebrity following." Images flashed up of a dark-haired woman and a younger man. Micah recognised the woman, had been with Lily when she worked with Rachel, had listened to her talking to Todd on the phone. Rachel was her friend, or the closest thing she had to a friend. She'd understood Lily in a way few others could. And Todd had followed her leads, leads he hadn't shared with the police.

"*Sammael,*" he tried, more urgently, "*Sammael, this is bad. This is really bad.*"

But Sammael wasn't paying any attention to him now. All his attention was fixed on Lily.

"Rachel," Lily breathed. "It's Rachel."

"Who?" Sam asked, running his fingertips down her spine. She didn't react. She looked like she was rooted to the spot.

"It's Rachel." Her voice was thin and drained. "He killed her. He murdered her, Micah!"

"Shh." Sam's breath stirred the sensitive hairs at the edge of her hairline. "It was just a dream, sweetheart."

The glass slipped from her hand, crashing to the floor where it shattered. Juice and shards of glass flew everywhere. Sam swore, jumping back, curses falling from his lips as he danced away from harm.

But Lily just stood there. The trembling started in her legs. Her sob was a bark of pain and grief. She wrapped her thin arms around her chest, digging her fingers into her arms.

"Lily?" Sam called, trying to reach out for her, trying to stop her before—

She stepped forward, straight onto the glass, but she didn't stop, didn't even cry out.

"Lily, stop!" Sam shouted over the dreadful crunch of the glass. The volume of the TV lurched up to deafening levels.

"Bound and gagged, then drowned," boomed the reporter. "The pattern is identical to the murder of Claire Redgrave three weeks ago."

"Lily, you have to stop!"

"Rachel Deveral was abducted from her home on the evening of the twenty-ninth, after she returned home from her successful afternoon chat-show spot."

Sam dived for the cable and wrenched the plug out of the wall. The sound died abruptly and in the moments of silence,

Lily gasped for air, her mouth working to form words she couldn't quite bring out.

She bent in two, clutching her middle, and she screamed. A heartbreaking sound.

Micah threw himself against the barrier, but it repelled him yet again. *"Lily! Damn it, Sammael, let me out of here. Let me out! She needs me."*

And at the same time, Lily's howl became coherent, became a single word. "Micah!" Light burst within his chest like fireworks.

And the walls of air tumbled down.

Micah caught her as she fell and lowered her to the ground, quelling the convulsions that racked her. He smoothed his hand across her forehead, poured his light into her body and fought to calm her, fought to bring her back.

"Get something for her cuts," Micah snarled at Sam. The demon didn't argue for once. The first-aid kit appeared in his hands in a curl of shadows.

"Here. What is it? What's wrong?"

But Micah didn't deign to answer Sammael. He was focused entirely on Lily.

"It's me, Lily. I'm here. It's going to be all right. Can you hear me?"

She struggled briefly and then fell still, her dove grey eyes fixed and glassy, staring past him, right at the ceiling.

"He took her in the night, right from under her family's nose. He locked her away in the darkness and he tested her. *Summis Desiderates, Malleus Maleficarum,* the *Hexenhammer.* He wouldn't let her sleep, wouldn't let her eat, wouldn't let her sit, but he asked her over and over and over." Her voice dropped to a low, gravely rasp, scraping off her throat. *"Are you a Witch? Are you a Witch? Confess it and be spared. Confess it and be saved."* Lily gasped for air, her face distended and bloodless, like a corpse, like a drowned corpse left in the water.

"No way," Sammael hissed, his eyes narrowing. "Witch trials? Witch trials in this day and age?"

As if she heard him, Lily's voice started up again, and though Micah tried to soothe her, tried to make it stop, the words kept coming.

"He pricked her with needles, he pricked her with knives. Then he tied her up and took her to the water. Said if she'd renounced the water of life, then the water would renounce her and she'd live, and he'd know. Know what she was. Know her for a witch."

"*Lily, enough now,*" Micah pleaded, rocking her back and forth, his eyes locked with Sammael's. "*Please, my bright one, let go of her now. Show her the light and let her go to peace.*"

Lily jerked in his arms once more, locked her frantic eyes with Sam's and snarled, "I know you. I know what you are!"

Micah caught her face in his insubstantial hands, turned her towards him and kissed her. Light blossomed beneath her skin, and every pore glowed. She slumped beneath him, exhausted, bleeding, but peaceful at last.

Micah gathered her against him, holding her close.

Sammael was staring at him, waiting for an answer, an explanation. "The spirit of the dead girl?"

"*Yes, or what remained of her consciousness after days of torture and cruelty. Tell me, when the witch trials were in full flight, how many turned to your Master during their ordeal? How many swore fealty just to get out of it?*"

Micah already knew the answer. Sammael shrugged. "Thousands. But here, now?"

"*The one who sent the flowers, I'd wager.*"

"You're not allowed to wager," Sammael said distractedly, kneeling down opposite him, staring at Lily. "It leads to sin."

Micah stroked the side of Lily's face. "*So do many things,*"

Sammael."

Micah held her while Sammael doctored her wounded feet and removed the glass. Micah poured healing energy through her so that the lacerations closed. He even removed the potential scars. She was, as she always was to him, flawless.

"Leave us," Micah told Sammael. *"Let me see to her now."*

To his eternal amazement, Sammael obeyed.

It shouldn't have affected him, but it did. Sammael stumbled back into his own apartment. He slammed the door behind him and leaned against it. But his legs wouldn't hold him up anymore and he sank to the floor, his whole body trembling.

"That's an odd place to find yourself, Sammael," said Asmodeus. The demon was sitting on the sofa facing the door, a sly grin on his broad face. "Problems?"

Sam jerked himself upright, glaring at him with venom. "Nothing I can't handle."

Asmodeus hummed to himself, shaking his head slowly. "Doesn't look that way, now, does it?" He rose to his feet, towering over Sam, his head almost scraping the ceiling. "You had her, Sammael. You were in her bed, screwing her royally, I might add, and then, what? You just hand her back to the angel?"

Sam bristled. "What else was I to do? I couldn't help her. And she's no good to us in that state."

"Was that your opinion or the angel's?" Asmodeus snapped his fingers and a coil of shadows appeared between them. From it fell a thin, fragile body which slammed down fully formed onto the carpet. A female, naked, shivering, with a mane of golden hair spilling around her. She lifted her pale face, her violet eyes looming huge with fear as she saw not one demon but two.

"Please, no," Lara whimpered, curling in on herself. "Please, please not again."

Sammael tried not to let distaste show on his face. "What?" It was barely a question.

"The Master thought you could use a reminder of what happens to those of us who don't please him. And of what you're meant to be doing. That's why I'm here."

"What are you going to do, show me how to fuck her? I know, already."

"It's not about fucking, Sammael," Asmodeus admonished him. "It's about lust. It's about what someone will do when they are consumed with it."

He grabbed Lara's shoulder, pressing his fingers into her bare and bruised flesh. Pain flashed momentarily over her features and then the transformation swept over her. Her eyes widened and then turned glassy. Her full lips parted and her tongue darted out across them, leaving a glistening trail behind it. She breathed in deeply, her chest heaving up, and a flush of heat stained her skin.

"Please, my Lord." Before Sam knew what was happening, she dropped to her knees before him, her quick and clever hands working to open the zipper. In spite of himself, his cock stirred and as she slipped her cold hand inside to draw it out, he sucked in a breath.

"Stop it, Lara. I don't want this."

But his commands fell on deaf ears. She opened her mouth, swallowed his cock down and worked its length with tongue, lips and hands.

"Fuck." Sam couldn't pull away from her. Lara moaned around the length of him, pressing her body against his legs, writhing beneath him as she gave him head.

"Oh, she wants to," Asmodeus laughed. "Even though Lara hates you, hates all of us, screams and cries and wakes in terror, she wants to fuck you. That's how I won her, a vessel, a light, just like your target. That's how I stole her away from her angel and became a King of Hell. I made her want to fuck." He stepped closer, his shadow falling on the woman who groaned even louder, those sounds muffled and distorted by Sam's cock.

Sam could barely think. His mind kept throwing images of Lily doing the same thing, Lily's mouth, Lily's hands, Lily's dexterous tongue curling around him, sliding over the glans.

Asmodeus's hand fell on Sammael's shoulder. "And you want her too."

The lust was instant. It burned through his body, searing the blood in his veins to boiling point. A demon's lust. A demon's hunger. He grabbed Lara's head, forcing himself deeper, hearing her choking and not giving a damn. His demonic self revelled in the abuse, breaking free of the constraints he had placed on it, tearing away the veneer of civilisation he wore. He withdrew from Lara's mouth, his cock huge and ready for her, the head already beading with pre-come.

"Turn around," he commanded and Lara shivered, turning around to raise her pert ass towards him in readiness.

"No," said Asmodeus.

An invisible force hurled Sam back against the wall. Chains snaked out of the ceiling, entangling his wrists in bands of iron. He was hauled up until his feet barely touched the ground and his arms strained in their sockets. He struggled, almost wrenching his muscles in his contortions, but to no avail. He couldn't tear himself free.

Lara bowed her head and sobbed, the lust dissipated now, her despair taking control again. Her eyes filled with shame and she hid her face from him.

"That was too easy." Asmodeus snorted a single laugh. "I expected a little more resistance. Your human prey must have quite an attraction. I can't wait to meet her. Now listen to me,

Sammael, and listen carefully."

Sam burst into frantic violence again, but Asmodeus remained just out of reach. He laughed as Sam fought, trying to regain some control of the boiling lust flooding his body.

"This is just a warning. You're going to spend a day and a night here contemplating your failure, locked away where no one can hear you. Don't worry. The spell will wear off in the morning, but it'll make you more the demon you are meant to be."

"It'll drive me back to savagery," Sam hissed. "It'll turn me into some kind of monster."

He'd seen it happen to countless number of his kind. It had happened to him. Being denied the pleasures of the flesh for too long while under Asmodeus's ministrations had driven him to do unspeakable things throughout the fifteenth century once they had released him. Whole countries still bore the scars.

He had to get out of this. If he didn't, there was no telling what he would inflict on Lily once he was free. He'd launch himself on her like some kind of animal, thinking only of sex and blood, thinking only of sating his body, driving himself into every orifice over and over again. He jerked forward, using the agony running down his arms like steel wires to regain some semblance of self-control.

"You know she has an angel," he told Asmodeus. "I can get him too."

That got his attention. The demon king lifted his head and fixed him with a piercing glare. The lust abated slightly, though Sam could still feel it there, coiled around his cock, teasing his balls with its weight. At least his head had cleared. At least he could think halfway straight.

"An angel?" Lara uncurled, looking up at him again with wide, red-rimmed eyes. "I had an angel once, one to watch over me and keep me safe. You can see how good he was at his job. I fell, but not him. No, he was away as soon as I reached the edge. You pride yourself too highly if you think you can snare such an adversary, Sammael. He'll leave her. They'll make him."

Asmodeus ruffled her hair affectionately. "Let him speak, Lara dear. Sometimes it's good when they try to bargain." She wilted beneath his touch.

Sammael drew in a shaky breath. "She has an angel, but I can get him too. I can get both of them."

There was no reading Asmodeus's expression.

"Go on," he rumbled.

"That's it. I can get them both. He loves her. She loves him. I can use that to make him fall. Think of it, Asmodeus. Think of what the Nameless will say."

The floor beneath them rumbled ominously. Asmodeus tilted his head to one side as if thinking hard, but Sam knew that was none too likely. No, Asmodeus was listening to other instructions. Thinking had never been his strong point.

"Very well, our Master agrees. But there's a time limit. A week, Sammael. And you must bring us both."

Lara's violet eyes lit up, half insane. More than half. "An angel? We'll get to play with an angel?"

She surged to her feet, pressing against the whole length of Sam's body. Her hands framed his face, stroking him, maddening him.

Asmodeus grabbed her by the hair and threw her to the ground. "You don't get to play with anything, bitch. Not without permission. And you'll wait your turn like everyone else." He waved his hand and Lara vanished in the same coil of smoke as she had arrived. The chains holding Sam evaporated and he landed heavily on the floor, the impact jarring his whole body.

"Remember this, Sammael," said Asmodeus. "And you had better not stumble again, or I really will give you something to remember."

Chapter Six

Lily awoke to a blinding headache late in the afternoon. She lay in her own bed, and her stomach churned as she tried to sit up.

"*Hush now.*" Micah's voice came to her, booming around her head. When she winced, he dropped the tone and his voice became a ripple in her mind, a breeze. "*Better?*"

"Better," she agreed. "I thought you'd gone. I thought I'd lost you and then...then I couldn't make it stop." Tears stung the corners of her eyes and across the bridge of her nose.

"*I'll never leave you. I'm sorry I made you think I had.*"

She felt his arms around her, and for a moment his cinnamon scent was laced with something else, something entirely more earthly.

"I shouldn't have said what I did." Her throat tightened. "I don't need Sam more than I need you. Just differently."

Was it her imagination or did he sigh? It sounded like regret. Or even heartbreak.

"Micah? I can...sometimes, I can feel you. Your touch, I mean."

"*Yes, Lily.*" It felt as if phantom fingertips brushed against her forehead, as if trying to smooth her frown away. It was like the touch of a warm breeze.

"Can you—can you do more?"

The touch withdrew and Lily's heart lurched. It was too much, a request too far. She had pushed him and done it again, scared him, hurt him, whatever it was she did that kept driving him away.

She was about to say something, to apologise for asking when the unmistakable feeling of a pair of lips brushed against hers. The contact was feather light, the touch of butterfly wings, and her breath escaped in a gasp. She heard an answering sigh. Right in front of her, her own breath misted and danced with light and, for a moment, just a moment, she thought she saw a face.

Handsome, golden, glowing with inner light, sensual lips, a cleft chin, and a strong jaw. It was only a glimpse. Then it was gone.

"*I only wish I could do more,*" he said. The touch of his lips returned and lingered against hers for another long moment like static electricity. But moments couldn't last.

"Why? Why can't you?"

"*I can only love you, Lily. That's all I can do. Anything else is...it is forbidden.*"

The tears started to escape, no matter how hard she tried to hold them in. "That isn't fair, Micah."

His invisible hands cradled her face, gently framing it, while his thumbs brushed away the tears that trickled down her cheeks. She closed her eyes, and suddenly it was all real, solid. She could picture him, holding her just like this, feel his touch so distinctly. He was real.

The headache was gone. She had never felt so alive.

Micah kissed her again, and this time she parted her lips for him. His surprised breath filled her mouth, sweet and light, a zephyr flowing down within her, washing away the shadows her vision had left. He still held the sides of her face and she got the impression that he was staring at her. She knew his eyes were blue, the colour of harebells, so pale and delicate and yet blazing with an inner light. She lifted her hand and touched skin, soft, smooth skin, lightly flecked with silken hair. She could taste him on her tongue, cinnamon again, cut with a hint of salt.

Heat rose within her, unbidden and all-consuming. It welled at the base of her stomach, and her body turned to liquid honey beneath his touch. Dampness rose between her legs, melting her with need.

"Micah," she breathed and leaned forward. "Micah."

"*This has to stop, Lily,*" he told her, and his voice held eternal sorrow. "*It can go nowhere. It would only hurt us both.*"

"It can't. It won't. Micah, I need you. You know I need you."

His voice sharpened, unlike his usual tones. "*Like you needed Sam?*"

"Yes, like I need Sam."

His presence lurched back from her and she almost sobbed in frustration. But he didn't leave. Not this time. Her body ached, her clitoris throbbing and her heart racing.

"*He's dangerous, Lily.*"

"Yes. But he hasn't hurt me."

"*No. That seems to be my role in this. But Lily, he cannot be trusted. He cannot help himself or his nature. Don't you see?*"

She shuddered and goose bumps rose all over her skin, a prickling down her spine that only served to send the arousal that plagued her even further out of control.

"And what are you, Micah? My invisible friend? My poltergeist tormentor? What?"

"*Just your friend, your guardian and guide. I never meant to hurt you, my bright one. And I will not allow him to do so. And I will not allow you to doom yourself, no matter what it means for me. I love you, Lily. You know that, don't you?*"

Her guardian? He was more, so much more, and suddenly, in a flash of inspiration she understood what he was, what they both were.

"I know, Micah." She wished it wasn't true. Because knowing, she couldn't leave it like that. She refused to let him leave it like that. She had to change his mind. To force him to admit that there could be more.

And then to make him take that step.

She knew only one person she could rely on to help her do that, only one person with powers equal to his.

"You want me to *what*?" Sam stared at the woman standing outside the door of his apartment in the evening shadows as if he had never seen her before. Certainly it wasn't something that Lily would ask, not the Lily he knew. But it looked like her, sounded like her, even smelled like her.

Lily pursed her lips and said it again, as if she was talking to someone hard of hearing or, failing that, particularly stupid. "I want you to help me see Micah."

"Micah?"

She nodded eagerly, a swift motion that made her breasts jiggle beneath the light fabric of her blouse. With the remnants of Asmodeus's lust spell still running through his body, in spite of several hours and a couple of cold showers, his cock leaped to attention, instantly and painfully ready for her.

He struggled to keep his voice even. "Micah, the voice in your head?"

Her face fell to uncertainty. "But he's not just a voice in my head, Sam. He's something more. I almost saw him today."

Down the corridor, a door opened and their neighbour Mr. Hopkins stepped out, sending a glare of disapproval towards them both. Sam shifted to a more aggressive stance before Hopkins moved on, muttering to himself. Sam caught Lily's arm and pulled her gently inside. The door clicked shut behind her and, in the unlit interior of his apartment, Lily shivered.

Not so certain of herself now, it seemed. He let his hand drop away from her and left her standing there in the dark. After a moment she moved towards the light switch.

"No," Sam barked and she froze. Another shiver, not of unease this time. Something else. He could smell her arousal. A game, perhaps, but whose?

"Sam? I can barely see you."

"It's late to be knocking on someone's door, Lily, especially to ask them to help you 'see' someone else. What brought this on? I thought Micah was your spirit guide?"

"Yes," she said, though she didn't sound so certain. "But I think he's something else too. Something more."

Sam leaned back against the wall, watching her carefully. His balls felt uncomfortably heavy and his cock twitched again. She looked so vulnerable, standing there in the dark, depending on him, asking for his help. A slow smile spread over his face as the sense of power set the demon part of him racing.

Well, if this was a game, he could play too. And if it wasn't he could easily make it into one.

"And how do you think I can help?"

He projected himself towards her, running invisible fingers down the line of her back. Lily jumped, turning towards the touch, but when Sam chuckled to himself, she stopped, staring at the location of his voice.

"Why won't you turn the light on?" she asked, her voice a lot more shaky now.

"I like the dark. And you haven't answered my question, sweetheart. Why ask me for help?"

"Because Micah said..." She shut her eyes, breathing harder as his invisible hands cupped the firm globes of her ass.

"What?" He sent his voice so it was right against her ear. His breath moved the fine hairs behind it. She gasped and tilted her head back towards the imagined mouth but found nothing there but air.

"He said you weren't human." She blurted out the words.

"And yet you're still here."

She shivered again but didn't answer. Her arms closed around her chest in a defensive motion. He wondered if she realised it also pushed her breasts together and upwards, offering them to him in an ageless gesture. He let his awareness drift close, inspecting them under the material. Her nipples were pinched with arousal, hard points ready for his touch, his mouth.

"What do you think I am, Lily?"

She shuddered and closed her eyes. "A demon."

Clever girl, clever, clever girl. "What makes you think that?"

Lily swallowed hard and opened her eyes again, grey and sharp as knives. They looked inside him, knew him. Oh yes, she knew him. "The way you move. The way you are. The things you do. And the way Micah hates you."

Sam chuckled and she flinched. "Yes, Micah hates me."

"Because you change things around me. You stop the spirits coming through. You make me feel safe and so terribly *unsafe* at the same time."

"And what does that make Micah?"

"An angel." She didn't even hesitate.

The world around them shifted. For a moment he feared that an imbalance threatened, but she had worked it out herself. No one had told her. The seconds slid by and nothing happened.

Dammed-up blood pounded in his head. Sam took a deep breath in and then slowly let it out. It rippled across the space between then, touching her intimately, stirring her arousal. Her eyes flew open, clear and bright, the grey of polished silver, frightened and at the same time aroused.

Sex and danger made for interesting bedfellows, as Lily was

just starting to find out.

"He's right, isn't he?" she asked. "I can feel you. Even though you're standing all the way over there. I can feel you up against me, touching me, inside me. Help me, Sam. Please."

Words like that were his weakness. He loved to hear a woman beg. And more. He would give her everything she was begging for, whether she knew what that was or not.

"What's in it for me?" he growled, letting the right hint of danger bleed into his voice.

"What do you want?" she asked, her nerves ringing like bells.

And at the same time, he sensed her arousal intensify.

"Take off your top," he told her.

"Sam?"

"You heard me."

Lily hesitated, and then, with hands shaking so hard she could barely undo the buttons, began to obey.

Damn, she was naturally good at obedience. Nervous, sheltered, hiding from the world, from her gift, from everything, she stepped into the role with incredible ease. Sam had already made love to her, but this was something more. Much more. This was his first step.

The material dropped to the floor where, hours earlier, Lara had knelt, sucking him off.

"And your bra," he continued without missing a beat. Lily's hands moved deftly to release the back, and the wisp of lace slid down the length of her arms and onto the top of the blouse.

She wrapped her arms around herself again and this time the view of her breasts was even better.

"Sam, we can just go to bed," she said tentatively. "If that's what you want."

"Be quiet. If you want my help, Lily, you're going to be silent. And you're going to do what I tell you. Everything I tell you. Then we'll discuss terms. Do you agree?"

She swallowed hard, and the pulse in her throat leaped a little faster. She was so beautiful. So incredibly beautiful. At the sight, Sam's body strained, aching for her. Damn Asmodeus and his lust spells. Damn them all for sending him here, to do this, and more. And Sam damned himself most of all.

"For how long?"

That brought another smile to his lips. She was a smart girl, one he could not afford to underestimate. Tempting as it was to step in and take total control right now, she'd flee and find some other way to get to her angel. No, he'd be patient. Careful. Dominant, yes, but also giving.

"Two hours." He'd make them both the longest and shortest two hours of her life, he promised himself. He'd make her curse when the time was up.

Lily nodded.

"Do you agree? You need to say it out loud, Lily."

"I agree, Sam." The words were sweeter than the song of the heavenly choirs. "I'll do whatever you want for two hours, if you'll help me."

"Take off your jeans."

Lily unbuttoned the fly and slid the indigo denim down her long legs, kicking them off with her shoes. She stood there with only a wisp of lace covering her sex. Her creamy skin glowed for him in the darkness.

"Turn around," he told her.

She moved at once, turning her back to him so he could admire the perfect sweep of her side, the flare of her hips and the way her hair hung down, teasing her spine.

"Put your hands flat on the door in front of you."

She had to lean forward a little, which pushed her shapely ass out towards him. She stood with her feet apart, waiting for his touch, breathing hard in anticipation.

Sam took his time getting there, watching her body as he approached. She was afraid but ready, so unbelievably ready, both for this and for him. Questions were buzzing around her head, but she stayed silent. Her breasts, thrust out by the angle, trembled. Sam shed his clothes with a single thought and brought his hands around to cup those perfect breasts, filling his palms while at the same time fitting his body against the entire length of her. Lily's breath escaped in a single cry which she bit back.

Sam ran his fingertips down her skin, across the slight curve of her stomach and over her ass, using them to circle her pelvis slowly against the iron of his cock. She needed to know how ready he was for her, and that he was prepared to wait so that this could be more than simply good for them both. She needed to know that it would only be hers when he was ready.

She pushed back against him and Sam took a step away, out of her reach.

"I didn't tell you to move, Lily. Stay still. No matter what."

He thought he heard a frustrated sob, but he let it go. There was no way she would stay completely silent. Not yet. That took training and it was early days.

Yes, this was going to be fun.

Slipping his hand down the front of her panties, he combed his fingers through the curls, deftly parting her lips. She was ready for him. Slick and honeyed, skin like velvet melting beneath his touch. He slid a finger inside her, working it within her for an endless moment before withdrawing. She shuddered against him and he smiled, pressing his lips to the skin of her shoulder, his cock pushing against her ass, caught in between the cheeks, cradled there.

He pressed that same finger against her clit. It was aroused and hard, throbbing against his touch. But he moved on. He swirled around it, teasing her without touching, without the hope of release. All the time the implied threat of his cock against her anus made the trembling deep inside her grow.

Oh, you're ready, Lily. You are primed and ready. But not yet. I want so much more from you, sweetheart.

He withdrew his hand but kept his pelvis hard against hers. Gripping both sides of her panties, he slid them down, only lifting the pressure from his groin long enough to drag the lace by. It teased the length of his cock before snapping down. He let it fall, discarding it on the floor.

"Part your legs," he instructed huskily. "Wider, Lily."

She stepped out at once, her balance now entirely reliant on her hands pressed to the painted wood of the door and his hold on her. Her breasts hung down, free of her ribs and he took them in his hands again, playing with them absently. They were full and ripe. Part of him wondered how she'd react to nipple clamps or piercing. The thought set his heart racing harder, and the hunger almost took him. He recalled the sensation earlier in the day when all he wanted to do was grab Lara by the hips and fuck her until he came or she fell apart beneath him.

He pulled on Lily's taut nipples, pinching them, and she bucked against him, her teeth hard on her lower lip in an effort to keep her silence as instructed. Good girl, he thought, and gentled his touch once more. Yes, she'd respond well to clamps. But not now. There was time enough to come. Tonight was just the beginning.

Stepping back from her, Sam heard her sigh. Teaching her to keep quiet might actually be the most difficult part of all. To everything else she responded instantly and with vigour.

"I'm not going to fuck you yet, sweetheart," he said in a gentle voice that surprised even him. Carefully, taking his time, he reached around her trembling hips and parted her pubic hair again, trailing his fingertips across the glistening labia. "But I'm going to make you come." Before she could gather her thoughts or begin to protest, he thrust one finger deep inside her, right to the hilt. Her inner muscles spasmed, gripping him.

Oh yeah, she was ready.

"Stay still for me now," he reminded her and dropped to one knee so he could look up the length of her. He fingered her hard and fast, deliberately, first with one finger, then two. Above him, her breasts danced and her mouth opened. She made a single quick and desperate sound before clamping her teeth down on the swell of her lower lip again. Sam watched, captivated, as she struggled to obey him in spite of his best efforts to make her lose control.

Sam curled his fingers and brushed against her G-spot. Then, with so studied a movement that it was almost mean, he brought the pad of his thumb up onto her throbbing clitoris, pressing it down hard. She stiffened, her whole body going rigid, her face stretched with desire. Her nails clawed against the door and she came, jerking against his hand. Her knees buckled, but he held her up, flexing his fingers deep inside her and feeling the responding aftershocks.

Sam drew his hand out of her slowly, giving her clitoris another massage as he did so. He lifted himself so he could suckle on her dangling breasts, one after the other. With the nipple and areole in his mouth he sucked hard, flicking the top with his tongue. From deep inside her came a groan, which she struggled to suppress, and he chuckled to himself, his laugh rippling through her.

"Stay there," he told her again. "Don't move. And close your eyes. Keep them closed."

Getting to his feet, he watched her struggle to obey again. She was trembling, exhaustion and reawakening desire working their combined magic on her.

Sam held out his hands, palms up to the ceiling, and summoned a glass dildo, long and slender with a raised ridge spiralling around it, red where the rest was clear. It felt cold to the touch, so very cold in his heated hands. He pressed the tip against her wet cunt.

She bucked, startled by the coldness, by the hardness, but before he could make a move, she thrust herself towards it.

"Greedy girl," he admonished her and then slid it into her.

Lily moaned and rocked forward to take it all. Sam knelt down in front of her, using one hand to steady her hips, the other to move the dildo in and out. Heat skimmed the surface of her skin. He couldn't resist it anymore. He reached out with his tongue to lick her clit, swirling the tip around the pulsating nub while the dildo stimulated her inside.

At the same time he reached out with his mind to touch hers, to stimulate it in the same way as his body stimulated hers. She opened to him, welcoming, hungry and ready. At his first touch of consciousness to consciousness, she wrapped herself around him. Deep inside she was a riot of emotions, her body merely a reflection of what was going on in her mind. Images flashed before him, what they were doing now, what they did the other night. Like a strobe in a sex club, he saw himself above her, behind her, filling her and taking her. His mouth made her pant, made her body writhe against him and the cold of the dildo stretched her and filled her.

Sam felt it like his own body, as if he was the one penetrated and succumbing to the dominance of another. He shuddered as he tongued her and that movement transferred to her, setting her off again. This time she fell, no longer able to hold her own weight, but he caught her, holding her up while her orgasms shook her body. He recalled the sensation of her inner muscles closing on him last night, trapping him, milking him, using him for her pleasure.

It was not going to be that way. He pulled her down to the floor, on her knees before him, and pulled out the dildo, casting it aside. She sighed as he did so, in both regret and expectancy. Beyond rational thought now, Sam moved behind her, parting her ass, teasing her with his dexterous tongue. He loved the way she responded, the way her tiny anus panted for him, as hungry as the rest of her.

Soon, he promised himself, so soon.

But now he needed to fuck. Asomodeus's lust was a faint ember compared to the fire she sparked inside him. He seized her hips, lifting her and sinking deep into her body. His mind still coiled around hers, he felt her welcome the savage entry, knew she didn't want or need gentleness now. Anything but. She wanted him animal, savage. He shoved her head and shoulders down to the floor. Carpet rasped against her breasts as he took her. This time she couldn't help herself. She fought for silence, for obedience. Her mind struggled to suppress the need to voice her pleasure and release, but it was like trying to hold quicksilver in her hands.

Sam slammed his body into hers, his balls slapping off her pubis, his fingers digging into her skin. Lily's cry was ragged and broken. It bounced off the ceiling and walls and spurred his body to come. He froze, only his hips in motion, pumping in and out of her, spilling all he had for her.

From a sweaty tangle of limbs, he lifted his head to find her slumped beneath him. Her eyes were glassy with sated lust and he grinned at her lazily, wondering if he started again right now, would she react. Silly question. She had proved herself just as eager as he. More so perhaps, because she was the one who wanted to fuck the angel. He'd seen it in her mind, her desires, her love. She wanted Micah in every conceivable way.

And so did he.

Sam nipped at the cheek of her ass. She gasped and the arched her back. "Are you ready to make that deal?" he growled against her skin.

"Make the deal?" She lifted her head, confused. "I thought—"

"No, sweetheart," he laughed throatily. "That was just an appetiser."

"What else do you want?" Her lips were plump, bruised by her own efforts to keep quiet at his command. They'd never looked more kissable. Or more fuckable.

What else did he want? Everything. Everything she had, everything she was. For some reason he couldn't get enough of her. Like a drug, an addiction. Even the little he had taken so far just made him hungrier. Like some kind of ravening wolf.

"You want Micah, yes?"

She nodded, her eyes very wide. Oh yes, she wanted him all right. Desperately. She longed for the matchless touch of an angel, even if she didn't completely realise all that entailed. But she would. Once she got what she wanted, she'd know him for all he was. And it would blow her mind.

To touch her mind during sex had been exhilarating, increasing the experience for both of them. To touch another mind, an angelic mind like his own, one which could touch back, to be a mortal like Lily caught between two such minds...

They had all been angels once.

"Then you shall have him, Lily," he said as he kissed her skin again, licking away the salt of her sweat, trailing his tongue up her spine to the nape of her neck. She panted as he pressed her hard against the floor, undulating beneath his weight.

They had all been angels once, before the war in Heaven, before the Fall, before they had been separated. They had lived, mind to mind, body to body, in constant love, in heavenly never-ending wave after wave of bliss.

"You are going have him all to yourself. And then, you'll share him with me."

He pressed his cock deeper inside, claiming the G-spot, holding himself there while he circled his hips, pressing her down against the carpet, grinding her into it. They lay there, body to straining body, sweat and tears mingling.

"Is it a deal?" he asked, barely able to keep from shouting the question, demanding the answer. Knowing already what it was.

"Yes," she panted. "Yes, yes, yes!"

Chapter Seven

Micah paced the room, knowing where she had gone but not sure why or how long she would be. How could he know? But he could fear. He could dread. Her desire, her arousal, was tangible on the air and he struggled to close himself off from it. Sammael had shielded himself and his bolt-hole from the moment he had arrived. When Lily walked in there, Micah felt the shields grow stronger.

But the demon couldn't entirely hide her from Micah. He had been attuned to Lily for far too long. It made him weep to feel what she was feeling now, and to recognise the pleasure Sammael was giving her. Raw, animal pleasure.

He pressed his hands to the wall and tried to will light and life to her, only to feel it rebound, wasted.

"Lily, come back to me."

No answer. Nothing. She was gone and he had failed. Micah pressed his forehead to the wall. He had failed. Through all the years he had but one task, to keep her safe, and he had failed. Worse than failed. He had handed her over to the enemy.

His skin tingled with light, his senses ringing like bells, and he turned to face the column of fire which materialised in the middle of Lily's living room. "Back again, Metatron?" he said, inclining his head.

The flames flickered away to reveal a young man in jeans and a classic Rolling Stones T-shirt. His shaggy hair hung down over ageless blue eyes.

"And in the flesh. I'm honoured." If the sarcasm registered, the angel before him gave no sign of it.

"I still prefer Enoch," he said, his voice like ethereal music. "Despite the elevated title." He grinned, but when Micah gave no answering smile, the expression faded. "I've come to take you home, Micah."

After so long? Denial and suspicion warred with the surge of mindless delight. Enoch was the closest thing he had to a friend among the Holy Court, and even he regarded Micah as some kind of outcast. There was only one reason they would bring him back now. "She knows I'm an angel?"

"Yes. So it's time to leave, before you endanger yourself."

"I can't."

"You're too close to her. And she's lost to us."

"I don't believe that."

Enoch crossed to the bookshelf, trailing his hand along the colourful spines of the paperbacks. He paused at a picture of Lily smiling in a ray of sunlight and then he sighed.

"A loss. A great loss. But no need for you to be dragged down with her." He turned around, holding his hands out to the angel. "So, are you ready to go?"

"I'm not going anywhere." Micah stood where he was, rooted to the spot. "I can't leave her, Enoch. Not now."

"But she's gone, Micah. The demon has her. She went willingly, knowing what he is, what you are. Contrary to popular opinion in Heaven, our mortal charges figure it out in the end. It's their doom. Every step is inevitable now. Just like every time before. The same thing all over again. We've lost a light and that is a tragedy, but—"

"No!"

Enoch evanesced, shimmering like a heat haze and vanishing, only to reappear right in front of Micah, face-to-face.

"You should reconsider," he said. "Patience is divine, but unlike us, not eternal."

Struggling to control a most unangelic surge of anger, Micah swallowed hard. Enoch's body shimmered with light, with joy made flesh. He was an angel, one of the highest of angels, scribe of the Holy Court, spokesman for the Creator Himself.

And he stood uncomfortably close.

"I can help her," Micah said in a faint voice. "I know I can help her. We can't just give up."

Enoch frowned, reaching out to stroke a finger along the line of Micah's cheekbone. His skin shivered in its wake, static sparking between them. The surge of pleasure was unmistakable.

Micah closed his eyes and let his breath escape in a long, low hiss.

"We love you, Micah," said Enoch, though his voice was something greater all of a sudden, rippling through the air, filled with the power of roaring wave and grinding earth, shimmering against his skin like heat. "We feel so close to losing you. And that causes us to fear, for your loss would grieve us greatly."

"But I can't just let her go."

"And we cannot just let you go. Especially not to follow her path."

Micah dropped to his knees, bowing his head. "Please, *Abba*. Please."

Enoch's hands were warm as sunlight on Micah's hair, his fingers threading the strands. He sighed and suddenly Enoch's voice was his own once more, that other presence departed.

"Very well. But be careful, Micah. Please be careful. You're very close to the edge. One misstep and you too could fall. One step too close to this woman, and she will drag you down with her."

Micah lifted his face to see the eternal sorrow in Enoch's expression. "No. Not Lily."

Enoch rolled his eyes to the ceiling. "She's special, Micah, but she is just a mortal."

"There's no such thing as *just a mortal*. And yes, she is special. You have no idea."

"But I do." Enoch gripped his hands and pulled him to his feet. "You can only have a week to save her or let her go. No more than that."

"A week? But this is the work of a lifetime."

"Yes," Enoch said. "A week." Fire roared from his feet to his head and he vanished, as if he had never been there.

Micah stood alone in Lily's home, staring at an empty space where the other angel had been.

"Enoch? What does that mean?" he shouted, but there was no answer.

Lily's key scratched around the lock before it slid in. The door squeaked, high-pitched and grating to the ears. Micah listened to her stumble in, exhausted and smelling of Sammael, of pure and unadulterated sated lust. Tears sprang like needles in his eyes. Nonetheless, he watched her, every movement until she curled up in her bed alone and sank into a deep and dreamless sleep.

Once he was certain she would not sense him, would not feel his presence as she always did, he sat by her side and stroked her hair.

Why only a week? What was going to happen in a week?

He could guess the answer. And that chilled him more than he could possibly say.

"Mother of God!" Cassini yelled, his voice sounding outraged and disgusted even muffed by the distance to the hall outside. "What sort of person does these things?"

Lily struggled to wakefulness, her body protesting with the dull tired ache of too much sex. Too much? God, was there such a state? It had been mind blowing. And more, the dominance, the promises, the intent. Had Sam really meant it? That he wanted Micah too? Her angel and her demon, both of them... It sounded so wrong, so deliciously wrong, that for a moment her mind was consumed. A spike of desire shot through her, followed by a languid heat.

Cassini continued to curse in rapid Italian outside, so she pulled on her robe and went to the door. Opening it, she saw him bent over right outside, a cloth pressed to his face.

"What is it?" she asked. "What happened?"

Then the smell hit her. Stale milk. Not just stale, rancid. Her stomach flipped and her throat closed convulsively.

Cartons of milk had been left in a pile outside her door. Milk congealed on the floor, globs of it clinging to the carpet.

"Oh my God," she exclaimed and flung her hand over her mouth.

"Go back in, Lily. When I find the *bastardo* who did this, I'll—"

Sam's door opened and he poked his head outside. Damn him, even half asleep and assaulted by this stench he looked hot. "What's going on?"

"Sour milk. Another gift." Lily's humour drained away as she saw what was under the pile of cartons.

"*Madonna*," said Cassini. "I'll call the cops. Go back inside, Lily."

A picture of Rachel lay underneath, the milk curds clinging to her face. Not Rachel as she had been alive, a starlet in the making. Her skin looked cold and grey, her lips blue. Her wet hair clung to the side of her face. This was Rachel's corpse after it had been recovered from the docks.

The world lurched around Lily, speckles of light dancing right in front of her eyes. Her stomach buoyed up through her while the rest of her body fell away. Strong arms caught her before she hit the ground. As her vision cleared, she saw Sam holding her, cradling her against him.

"It's all right," he said softly, "I've got you."

"It's from him, isn't it?"

"Probably." He nodded to Cassini, who was eyeing them with a concerned expression. "It's okay. I'll take care of her. Just call the cops." Sam kicked her door closed behind him and set her down on the sofa. The same sofa where he had—

Oh God! Lily's mind balked at the thought of what they had done now. There was a killer pursuing her, sending his sick little messages, taking the lives of others, and all she could think about was sex—sex with a demon and sex with an angel. All she could think about was the way her body responded to them both.

Sam opened the window wide. The breeze caught the light curtain, setting it billowing inside.

"Where's Micah?" he asked, his voice darkened now they were alone.

Lily reached out with her mind, but there was no apparent sign of her guardian. "I don't know. Will I call him?"

"Seems like a good idea. That was left for you, wasn't it?"

Was it? Well, for who else? Rachel's killer had his sights on her now. Lily wondered where Todd Lane was, what was happening to him? Her whole body went cold, from the inside out.

"Micah?" she whispered. "Micah, please, I know you're angry, but I need you."

His presence fell around her like a sheltering cloak the very instant she called. "*I'm here.*"

He didn't sound angry. More sad. Heartbroken. Lily bit the

tender skin of her lower lip. She'd broken his heart.

"Where do you go when you aren't with me?" she asked tentatively.

"Not far. There are just some things in your life that I don't need to see."

She had always considered it that he allowed her some privacy, a personal life. She had never imagined it was because he couldn't bear to see her with another man. Now it was suddenly clear. She glanced at Sam. Was it him? Did his presence make her guardian so transparent to her?

"What did he say?" Sam asked, suspicion narrowing his dark eyes.

"He knows damn well what I said," Micah spat. *"He only has to listen."*

Lily gaped at the air before her, wishing she could see him. She'd never heard such venom in Micah's voice.

"He's upset, Sam. That's all. Worried."

"About your being with me or the new gift from your stalker?"

"The what?"

Lily told Micah quickly, ignoring Sam's attempted barbs. She felt his anger lessen, but not depart. It simmered, beneath the surface. She'd never experienced anything like it. Calm, considerate, her rock to cling to, Micah had never, ever shown anger before Sam had arrived. She tried to probe closer with her mind but felt him immediately withdraw, like some kind of exotic flower, curling in on itself at the first sign of intrusion.

"Cassini's calling the cops," Sam said, his words sharp and succinct, like a soldier giving a report. He stiffened, his eyes suddenly distant. Were they talking to each other? Was that even possible? Sam glanced at her and his face hardened.

"Whatever you two have to say, I want to know," she growled suddenly. She didn't even know where the commanding tone came from.

Sam's mouth fell open. Then he smiled. "That does seem fair," he conceded. "Look, how about a coffee and then we can all discuss it?" The sudden softness didn't fool her. Even as she nodded, his face went hard again.

"*Yes, fair,*" said Micah. "*Forgive me, my bright one. That was rude.*" His invisible hands touched her shoulders, massaging away the knots of tension. She wished he'd just make himself visible to her. Sam assured her he could.

And now they were both lying to her. In an effort to protect her, it seemed, but a lie was a lie.

She hung her head, letting his touch work magic on her tense body. "What did he say to you, Micah?"

"*Just exchanging information. It is quicker than forming words.*"

"What? You just step into each other's minds?" Like Sam did to hers last night. And for a moment her body trembled with desire. For a moment she imagined them both doing it, both of them within her and around her, together.

Heat flared up the length of her back and her core melted with pleasure. It throbbed with her pulse. From behind her, she heard a sound, a gasp that was almost a moan.

"Micah?" She hardly dared to move.

"He's still with you," said Sam. "You startled him. That's all." He knelt in front of her and took her hands. Searching her eyes with his, he smiled, a genuine one this time. "Your physical reaction to his touch. Not your thoughts."

"Did you see my—?" She flushed red as embarrassment swept through her. Sam would want to do it. Sam would do anything, given half an opportunity. And she had promised... But, oh God, if he could see into her mind...

"No." He laughed. "Neither of us can. Not unless you want us to."

His words licked up her body and she leaned back, feeling Micah's strong support.

"*He's tempting you, Lily. Stay strong, my bright one.*"

Oh Micah, she thought, keeping it locked deep inside her mind. Not just me, my love. And God help me, I'm his ally in this seduction.

"I need to get dressed." She forced herself to her feet. Sam stayed where he was, running a palm down her calf, and behind her she felt another wave of mistrust and anger from Micah.

Sam felt it too. How could he fail to?

"Get a grip, Mike," he sneered.

Leaving them to it, Lily went to get dressed.

"*One week?*" Sam asked mind to mind. "*They told you one week too?*"

The angel looked impossibly flustered. It made him seem vulnerable for the first time since Sam had laid eyes on him. And all the more attractive for it. The thought made Sam smile, but Micah pushed by him. Sunlight touched his hair, making it gleam like old gold.

"*One week. That was all I was allowed. They think you've won.*"

Sam sat back on the sofa, folding his arms. "*I have. Didn't you notice your girl didn't come home last night?*"

Micah turned on him, his eyes blazing with indignation. "*They gave me more time. So it isn't over.*"

"*Please, there's only one way you'll win her back now, and you won't risk that. So your week is worthless.*" The time frame gave him pause again. One week. That was too precise. From both courts. "*What's going to happen in one week?*"

The light died in the angel's perfectly chiselled face. He closed his eyes and pain rippled over his features, draining them of life. He looked like one of Michelangelo's sculptures, tortured and lost. "*I think she's going to die.*"

"Well screw that," said Sam out loud, so startled by the revelation that he couldn't help himself. Screw that indeed, but how was he going to stop it if both Heaven and Hell believed it to be inevitable.

Chapter Eight

The smartly dressed woman who came to the door introduced herself as D.I. Reid. Her team worked almost silently on the mess in the hall, while she spoke in a calm, confident voice about what they knew so far.

Lily listened to a frighteningly short speech, which had been crafted to put her mind at ease and practiced once too often.

"We'll have a uniformed officer outside the building at all times and three surveillance personnel backing them up. I'm on constant call. Really, there's no need to worry."

Sam gripped Lily's hand a little tighter. "And was there any reason for Rachel to worry?" he asked in a tight voice. "No one is coming near Lily. I can promise you that."

Reid regarded him placidly, with eyes that betrayed a lot more going on behind her cool exterior. "Yes, Mr. Mayell. I understand your concern. Please understand we are doing everything within our power to bring this man to justice."

"It's definitely a man," breathed Lily.

"Yes, all the profiling indicates—"

"No. That wasn't a question. It's a man. I rang your department several days ago to tell you what I saw. I left a message."

Reid frowned. "I wasn't aware of that," she said stiffly. "I'll look into it as soon as—"

"Great," Sam growled, his antagonism even more apparent now. "You don't even believe in psychic abilities and you're heading up the investigation?"

Reid stared him down. Lily revised her opinion rapidly. Whatever she was, Reid was both an expert at her job, and she believed. "On the contrary, Mr. Mayell, I have the greatest respect for people like Lily. My brother was a psychic. And Lily helped me on a case not so long ago."

That surprised Lily more than anything so far. "I did?"

"Yes." Reid smiled then. "You hadn't moved then. You rang the local PD with a report of seeing a missing child. Didn't they take you seriously?"

Lily winced. Yes, she remembered that. She remembered Sergeant Graham's laughing response. *I'm not calling on a special task force with some cock-and-bull story you've dreamed up this time, Lily. You've no business trying to interfere. Next you'll be looking for money to perform your damned parlour tricks.*

She let out a long sigh and Reid hazarded a smile.

"But he did report it. In his way. He mentioned it as a joke to one of my colleagues. They passed it on to me and I followed it up. Led me right to that little girl. I tried to contact you, but you'd already moved away."

Lily blushed, curling her fingers around Sam's. She found it hard enough to dredge up her memories of those days, let alone talk about them. "Home became difficult, after that. People didn't take kindly to my gift, or my interference. It seemed like a better idea to move here, to gain a bit of distance. And privacy."

Reid nodded in understanding. "I appreciate that, Lily, but if you can, will you help us here? He knows who you are and what you can do already. If you could help us to find Todd Lane? He's killed two victims so far. I don't want Todd to be number three. Or you to be number four."

"And what's in it for her?" Sam asked, his voice unconvinced. His nerves caused his unfair hostility. His own sense of helplessness. Sam wanted to attack something, but there was nothing available. Nothing but Reid.

Lily squeezed his hand again, like squeezing a stone, and he sat back, growling under his breath. Great. Just what she needed. An irate demon ready to attack the only person to take her seriously for years.

"Hopefully, my life," she said calmly. "Sam, could you go and get some coffee please? I'm sure we'd both appreciate it. Maybe you'd call Mike and let him know what's happening. I'm sure he's worried too. Tell him I'm fine and see what he thinks."

"Mike?" asked Reid.

"An old friend," Lily said confidently. "Let me describe what I saw the night Rachel was killed."

Once Sam was gone, Lily described her vision, the nightmare of Rachel's death while Reid took detailed notes, her pen scratching on the page of a little notebook.

Sam clattered and crashed his way around the kitchen, and she could hear him muttering, talking to Micah, she presumed, or venting his anger at being dismissed. That was going to be trouble later on, she could tell. When she sighed heavily, Reid cocked her head and smiled.

"Boyfriend trouble?"

"Something like that." Lily smiled. "He's feeling powerless. He doesn't like it much."

"Most men don't."

Lily was about to reply that Sam wasn't like most men, when it occurred to her that in many ways he was.

"Have you known him long?"

"Not terribly long, no. But he's not—" Oh God, did Reid think Sam was the killer? Lily balked at the thought. How on earth could she explain that he wasn't? That he couldn't be because he wasn't even human.

"It's okay." Reid smiled. "I checked him out before I came." She put down the notebook. "New neighbour moves in, right before this begins? I'd have been a fool to leave that uninvestigated."

A crash came from the kitchen and Lily winced.

"You'll want to watch him though," Reid added smoothly, picking up her notebook again. "He has the devil's own hearing."

Micah leaned against the kitchen doorframe unseen, gazing at the two women and the light that danced above them as they talked. Two souls, their brightness feeding the other. They could have been friends, in other circumstances, in other lives. She had lacked that, a female friend, a confidant. No one would get near to her once her abilities started to manifest. And she would allow no one near her after that.

Reid slid her notebook into her jacket pocket. "I'll be in touch, but if anything comes up, anything at all, ring me directly. Right away."

They shook hands and Reid left. Lily looked bereft.

"Are you all right, my bright one?"

She just nodded and crossed to the window. "Who do you think it is, Micah? Could it be someone I know?"

The problem was, there weren't many options. Given her solitary lifestyle, she had few friends.

"I doubt that, Lily."

"Then you're too gullible by half," said Sam, carrying two mugs of coffee out of the kitchen. He handed one to Lily and then cast a glance over his shoulder towards Micah's location. "I'd offer you some if you'd deign to join us. No?"

Micah breathed in and out carefully, watching them. The mood changed, just with the arrival of the demon back in the living room. Lily sipped her coffee, her gaze fixed on Sam. For a moment Micah could have sworn she was smiling, but her mouth was hidden. He couldn't tell for sure.

And that disturbed him more than anything.

"No." Sammael sighed and turned back to face Lily. "He doesn't want us to lay eyes on his physical form. He fears it would corrupt him, you see?"

"What? Us seeing him?"

Sammael's chuckle flowed through the air. It shivered its way across Micah's skin, like a caress. "What we'd do. An angel is so beautiful, Lily, that mortal women, and some demons, have been known to lose all control at the sight of their bodies. So he hides from us, without realising that what cannot be seen can be just as alluring."

Sam put his mug down on the coffee table, then took hers and put it side by side with his own.

"*Don't do this,*" Micah tried to say. He wasn't sure if the words reached them or not. "*I can't watch again.*"

Sam didn't respond, and Lily didn't seem to hear. So Micah watched, against his will, as their mouths joined, and their fingers entwined.

"He's still watching, Lily," Sammael said. Without hesitation, Lily stepped away from him and pulled off her form-hugging T-shirt. Her skin was the colour of cream, her breasts clad only in contrasting black lace.

"Stay, Micah," she said. "Please. Show yourself to me."

The temptation made his blood run so hot, he couldn't breathe, not in the calm and mannered way to which he aspired. She maddened him. So did Sam.

"I can't."

Lily's mouth fell open at the sound of his voice, not in her mind but against her ears. She took a step towards him, and Micah jerked backwards. Only to find Sam standing right behind him.

"You want this," said the demon, his voice like liquid chocolate. Micah froze, trapped between the two of them, caught like a bird in a snare. "You know you want this."

Sam reached for him, body and mind, and Micah could do nothing to avoid his touch. Sam's hands slid into him, fingertips trailing through the motes of light that made up Micah's arm. Sam's mind brushed against his and it felt like all the joys of reunion, all the wonders of a friend long gone returned. Micah shuddered as Lily approached him, her tongue tracing a gleaming trail along her lower lip. She still couldn't see him, he was certain of that. Or almost certain.

Hands caressed him, Sammael's hands, so close to an angel's, so close to hers, surprisingly gentle. Lily stood right before him now. It would only take a single effort of his will to render himself corporeal and be with her, be with them both.

"Micah," she whispered. "Please."

Sammael's laugh rippled through his body, chasing his apprehension ahead of it, driving out his reticence.

And that scared him more than anything.

"*No!*" Micah broke free of them, tearing himself away. The effort almost shook him to pieces. He fell onto the carpet, and with a brief, remorseful glance at their bereft faces, he fled to his sanctuary.

The main upshot of D.I. Reid's visit was not what Lily expected. Sam refused to let her out of his sight and Micah had vanished to whatever bolt-hole he hid himself in. Lily tried not to be disappointed. Sam was a considerate and exceptional lover. In that sense she was falling hopelessly in love with him. But she had always loved Micah. Always. Now she was afraid he would never come near her again. Sam tried to comfort her but when she told him her fears, he just laughed.

"No, sweetheart. He can no more leave you alone than I can."

She tried very hard to believe him. Sam took her shopping and encouraged her to pick out all her favourite foods. He added a bunch of roses to the shopping basket as they reached the till. When they got back to the apartment building, twilight was creeping up the edges of the horizon. Tired and depressed by the events of the last few days, Lily was ready for nothing more than a meal, a shower and a good night's sleep.

Sam, on the other hand, seemed to feel a need to cram everything possible into the day, like he was afraid it would end too soon. He cooked *pollo alla diavola*, poured two glasses of Burgundy, melted chocolate over raspberries for dessert and kissed the nape of her neck whenever he walked by.

There was no sign of Micah.

"For a guardian angel, he's very good at the disappearing act," Sam sniped when she mentioned it.

Lily pursed her lips to silence a retort. Petulance actually suited Sam. It knocked away some of that raw appeal, made him seem a little more human, with feet of clay. Sam was sulking too, it seemed, and not with her. Once again, he took it out on the only person present.

"You've seen him," she said. "What does he look like?"

Sam snorted, setting his wineglass down on the table. "Like an angel, of course. Beautiful. Perfect. The type of face that looks best when it's suffering. He gets this sort of noble stoicism, especially around the eyes."

Lily stared into the deep red wine, trying to picture that while her own reflection stared back. "And do angels love?" She glanced up at Sam. He wasn't smiling now. His expression was unexpectedly sombre. "Do demons for that matter?"

"Yes." The single word was a whisper.

Lily let her breath calm before she asked another question.

She needed to be calm for this. "Do you?"

"Yes," he said again. But nothing more.

"Are you evil, Sam?"

The twitch of his lips might have been a smile, or something else. She marked it though and filed it away for later consideration.

"Sometimes," Sam said. "Sometimes I'm very evil indeed. It's in my nature, Lily. That doesn't mean I don't love, or feel, or want."

"And why do you want Micah?"

Sam sighed and pushed his chair back from the table. He gazed at her levelly, with those endlessly dark eyes that seemed ready to devour her at any instant. He was like an animal, a big cat at rest, just a heartbeat away from action, from violence. Her heart beat faster and, inside, her body clenched in anticipation. He aroused her effortlessly.

"Angels and demons were the first children of the Creator. We were the same then, one thing. We lived in complete harmony. Our lives, our hearts, our minds, everything was open and there for the taking. We loved each other without reservation, and everything we did was joy. Then came mankind. Few of the angelic host understood that move. I mean, he had us. What did he need you lot for? The Morningstar, highest among the angels, forged a knife to kill the Creator, but his brother and equal, the Eveningstar, refused to join him. They fought and the Morningstar fell and became—"

"The Devil?"

Sam winced, shifted as if suddenly uncomfortable in his skin. "We prefer to simply call him the Nameless and leave it at that. With the Fall that bliss of union and proximity to the Creator was lost. I can't explain it to you, Lily. Not in a way that would make sense. Imagine that moment of orgasm. Imagine it continuing forever. Imagine the comfort of unrestrained

111

intimacy, sharing everything, your touches and caresses returned without reservation. Then imagine that it stopped and you couldn't get close to it ever again. Not for more than a few brief moments. That's what happened. We knew eternal ecstasy and then it was taken away."

"When you fell?"

"No, not just demons. All of us. The angels too. When some fell, and others were cast out, we all lost that sense of union. Only those kept in the Holy Court can still experience it, because they're still connected to the Creator's presence. But the rest of us, Micah included, have just the memory and the loss. When we come into contact with our own kind, our lost brothers, it rekindles. As small an echo of the full sensation as is possible, but it is there. It is real. When I see him, when I touch him..." He closed his eyes and his face relaxed for a moment. "He's trapped here, you know? Can't go back. One of them even came to take him, and he refused. He wouldn't leave you."

It came as an unexpected shock. Wouldn't leave her? From the way Sam described it, he would give anything to return to the Holy Court. But Micah had refused, for her.

"Then where does he go? When he's not here? Where does he hide?"

Sam shook his head. "Somewhere close by. Somewhere that reminds him of home. Quiet, high up, peaceful."

"The roof," Lily said, knowing it on some intrinsic level. "The roof garden."

Sam opened his eyes, and the peace was gone from them. The hunger was back. She recognised it now, like an addict craving a fix. He'd do anything, anything at all to get what he wanted. Cold fingers dragged down her spine at the thought. "Then that's where we need to go."

"Sam, you're scaring him off. You do realise that, don't you?"

He stood up, towering over her, dinner forgotten. "What?"

Lily took another sip of her wine, using the moment and the alcohol to quell the sudden fear that leaped up inside her. "Let me do this. I made you a promise. I will keep my word."

Sam glowered at her, obscuring the light. His face fell into shadows. Only his eyes were visible, points of light, far away. Lily opened her mouth to speak, but then the world turned black.

The light overhead sparkled, dancing with the movement of the surface. She reached for it, but her hands and legs were bound. Struggling, she tried to tear herself free, but the knots were too good, professional. Her lungs ached, but she knew that if she tried to breathe she would die. She wriggled again, and this time something gave. One arm was free, then the other, and she tore at the ropes, striking out for the surface, for safety. Breaking the dark water, she gasped in a lungful of fresh air. Safe. She was safe!

Lily swam to shore, collapsing on the shingle of the riverbank, her body spent, drawing in breath after desperate breath. Stones bit into her skin, but she didn't care. She was alive. She was free. She was...

A shadow fell across her, huge and black, the face lost in shadows. Only his eyes were visible, points of light reflecting the moon. "The water, by which man was baptised, rejects you. Which means, warlock, that it will be the flames." Something heavy crashed down against the side of her head and the unconsciousness rose around her like black tar, sucking her down into its embrace.

"Lily? Damn it, Lily, answer me!" Sam sprawled on the floor beside her, cradling her against him. As she opened her eyes, he murmured something in a language she couldn't understand and pressed his cheek against hers. His relief washed over her, ridding her of the darkness and the fear. Tears scalded her skin, her tears, Sam's tears, slick between their faces. "Are you

113

okay?"

"Yes." Her voice came out in a throaty croak. Red wine pooled on the carpet next to her. It drenched the front of her top and dripped down the leg of the table like blood running from a wound. "It was him. Todd Lane."

"Is he dead?"

"No. Get me the phone. Quick. I have to ring D.I. Reid."

"*Lily?*" Micah's voice burst into her mind, fuelled by anger and afire with rage. "*What has he done to you?*"

Before she could respond, something sleek and golden barrelled into Sam's body, tearing him away from her and hurling him to the ground on the far side of the living room. A leonine figure stood over the demon, head lowered in challenge, shoulders squared, hands fisted at his side. His toned muscles rippled beneath the sun-kissed flesh.

He was naked, beautiful, angelic, every idealised image of a man rolled into one.

"Micah?" she ventured, pulling herself up onto her knees. She couldn't make herself rise any further. Micah glanced over his shoulder with eyes the colour of lapis lazuli. Lily sucked in a breath, her mouth hanging open in wonder. There was more than anger in those perfect eyes. Quicker than her pitiful human senses could follow, he bent down and seized Sam by the throat, hoisting him into the air.

"What have you done?" Micah growled, and the air trembled around him. No trace of the gentleness she knew remained. This was her guardian enraged, an avenging angel.

"She had a vision," Sam gasped, struggling to breathe. In the end he just gave up. His eyes glowed again, that taint of crimson infecting the brown. For a moment he became the demon she knew him to be, menacing and dark, secretly thrilling. "You're going to have to put me down eventually, Mike. I haven't hurt her. I can't, remember?"

"Micah, I'm okay," Lily said. "He's telling the truth." Slowly, like an expert trying not to spook a wild animal, she got to her feet. She approached warily, one footstep carefully placed and grounded before she took the next. He was real, corporeal, and so beautiful it made her heart ache.

Reaching out her hand, she tried to still her trembling fingers before she touched him. They vibrated in the air, millimetres away from his skin. She felt his warmth, like sunlight, emanating from him to brush her flesh.

Oh God, she thought, *he's actually real. He's actually here.*

Lily laid her hand on his shoulder. Beneath the silken skin, his body was iron hard. The muscles shifted in response to her touch, tightening, and her hand tingled. The sensation travelled up her arm and her throat closed in sympathy. She tried to breathe on a dry mouth but her chest didn't seem to be working. She just couldn't get enough air.

"Micah." His name was a prayer, a song on her lips. His head lifted, tilting back. His eyes closed, his lips parted, he shuddered from head to foot.

The spasm reached his hand and he released Sam, who slumped to the carpet at his feet. Neither Micah nor Lily moved, the contact between them rooting them to the floor.

Getting up, Sam brushed himself off, like a cat who knew someone had seen him tumble accidentally into the dirt. Lily only afforded him a brief glance. She couldn't look away from Micah. Not now. Not when he might vanish again and then try to deny he was ever real and corporeal. She knew it now. She could feel him beneath her touch. His skin felt warm and smooth. The echo of his erratic heartbeat ran through her. His chest rose and fell, the air rushing in and out of him. He was real. She could touch him. She didn't want to stop.

"Lily?" Sam asked warily. She wasn't entirely sure what he wanted but she recognised the question in his voice.

"What?" she breathed and Micah trembled again, like a

caged lion, held captive by her touch alone. Even though a moment earlier he had been wild, untameable, her fingers on his skin held him still.

"It's your choice," Sam said, with shades of warning in his voice. His desire swirled in his eyes. He wanted them both, she knew that, had made no bones about it. But not now. Not this time. She'd waited twenty years for this. Ever since Micah had first come to her shortly after the nightmare of her twelfth birthday, she had wondered what he looked like, had fantasised about the feeling of his skin against hers. This feeling. This moment.

"Later, Sam. I need you to go."

"But Reid, Lane..."

Damn, no! Breath stopped in her throat and her fingers stiffened. If she moved, if she focused on something else, would Micah vanish? Only the thought that Sam had hurt her had brought him here. Only the fact that he had lost his temper, had given in to his anger and fear, had made him visible to her.

Sam's voice came again, rich and sultry, more certain of his position once again. "Micah won't go, if that's what you're scared of. Will you, Micah? It's time you two had this out, after all. Twenty years is a long time for a human. You owe her, angel. What do you say?"

Micah hung his head again. He hadn't opened his eyes, not since her touch stilled him, but now the lids parted a little. She saw a sliver of blue, so bright. Sam was right, though it pained her to admit it, suffering suited him more than she could say. He looked like a true martyr. Now, when he knew it was over, that the thing he feared had come to pass, he accepted the turn of affairs with noble stoicism, just as Sam had said. And he was so, so beautiful.

"I shall abide," he said in broken tones like a series of minor chords. "Until Lily bids me leave."

"And me?" Sam asked, teasingly.

The fire of anger flashed through her angel again and his muscles tensed. "You have nothing to do with this, Sammael."

"Ah, but I do, Mike."

"Stop calling me that."

"What? *Mike*? But I think it suits you."

"Enough," Lily told them, finding more strength in her voice than she expected. To her surprise they both fell silent, watching her. Two perfect faces, as different as day and night, as beautiful as each other. Like Sam, Micah towered a head and shoulders over her, and yet she was the one who held him still with just the touch of her hand. "Micah, please, will you stay? I have to let Reid know what I saw. And we need to talk. Please."

He nodded, but he didn't voice his agreement. Well, he was an angel so she would just have to hope his word was his bond, and that a brief nod counted as much. Lifting her hand was the hardest thing she ever had to do. Micah trembled as she released him, but didn't move away. Her hand stayed warm, as if some trace of him came with her.

She brushed her fingers against her palm. She could almost feel it, like gilded dust, or the finest silk, lingering in the afterglow of touching him. She lifted her hand to her face and there it was, the unmistakable scent of warm cinnamon and sugar, Micah's scent, one she had known all her life.

"Sam, the phone," she said, unsure where this new commanding Lily had come from. She'd never felt so strong. Sam cast her a surprised look, but did as she instructed. He transferred his scrutiny to her while she dialled Reid's number. Micah took a few steps forward, until he could turn. He leaned against the wall, watching her in a less speculative fashion. It was more like dread.

Taking a deep breath in case she chickened out, Lily turned her back on them. Everything in her screamed that this was the wrong time, that if she didn't act now she might lose Micah forever.

117

A male voice answered. Reid was out of the office. Could he take a message? Quickly, she spilled out what she had seen, hearing his grunts of acknowledgement grow less enthusiastic as she continued. Finally, she ran out.

"Yeah, I'll—aah—I'll let her know. Thank you for calling." The line clicked and went dead. Lily stared at the handset. It felt wrong. Even with everything that was going on, even with what waited behind her, Lily's instincts wouldn't let her step away from this.

"What was her mobile number?" she asked faintly.

"Let me," said Sam. In her hand, the phone began to dial, a rapid series of beeps and then a ring tone.

This time Reid answered. She sounded distracted, but listened intently to what Lily said. Even about the message. "At the office? That's strange. Must be someone from another division. I'll check it out. Thanks Lily. I'll call you in the morning, okay?"

Click, dead line. Time to turn around, Lily, she told herself. Time to face him. For the first time in twenty years.

And her own anger flared, warming her chest, making her heart pound against her ribs. Twenty years. Hiding from her. Pretending to be what he was not. Twenty fucking years.

"Sam," she said, her voice trembling. "I'd like to talk to Micah alone."

Sam looked like she'd just told him she'd send him a bill for the dry cleaning or something. If she pushed him, she wondered if he would fall over. Micah on the other hand might have been one of the Renaissance statues to which Sam had likened him, petrified, or carved from stone in the first place.

"I need you to go, Sam. Now."

"Go? Lily, I don't think—"

"Now!" she snapped, unable to tear her eyes off Micah's placid face. If he sensed her sudden anger, the angel didn't show it. If anything he looked ready for the worst.

Sam let out his breath in a long hiss. "Just remember what you owe me, Lily."

She clenched her jaw, the threat in his voice raking against her nerves. "And if you don't do what I say now, you'll never collect, do you understand?"

He laughed, a low chuckle, far too knowing a sound. "You're learning, sweetheart. You're definitely learning."

"I had a good teacher," she told him, not even bothering to keep the snark out of her voice. "Go away, Sam. Now."

Sam rolled his shoulders back, forcing his body to relax, though she could still see the tension around the edges of his dark, dark eyes.

"All right," he said as if it didn't matter at all. "I'll see the pair of you tomorrow. Try to keep the noise down, won't you, Mike? Some of us will be trying to sleep."

Chapter Nine

The door to the apartment clicked shut with the finality of a key turning in a lock. Micah's skin jumped around his frame with the sound, but he didn't move.

"Lily, this has to stop." He tried to keep his voice patient and calm.

Lily took two steps towards him and slapped his face, hard. The pain was unexpected, and in some ways a relief. The bite of blood in his mouth brought him back from the spell of her touch, the hold she had over him.

"How dare you?" she said, her voice dangerously low. "How dare you, for so damn long?"

"How dare I what?"

"*He* lies, *he* hides the truth, *he* manipulates people. Not you. Not you, Micah. I always believed that, and yet here you are, in the flesh after twenty years of letting me believe that you couldn't't."

He backed away, even though he was taller, broader and stronger than her. Lily didn't become angry easily, he knew that, but this little whirlwind of rage and resentment was something entirely new. She had ordered Sammael out of the room, commanded him to leave. He'd never seen anyone in thrall to a demon able to do anything of the sort. But Lily had.

His sense of pride soared.

Until she stepped in again and raised her hand against him

once more. Micah caught her arm before it could fall and stared into her face. Tears formed in her eyes, matting her lashes as if netted with diamonds.

"You lied to me, Micah. All these years. I have loved you. Only you. No one else could compare. And you could have been with me, could have loved me back."

Her free hand curled into a first and hit his chest.

"Lily, I couldn't." He cradled her face with his hand, tracing the line of her high cheekbone. "You were a child. It would have been wrong. So wrong."

"I wasn't a child, Micah. Not once dead people started turning up in the night. Not once I heard their voices and felt their deaths. I wasn't a child. And I'm not one now. I'm a thirty-two-year-old woman. I needed you. Back then and now." Her voice dropped, the anger leaching out of it as he gazed down into her face. "I need you."

"I can't." He was holding her too close. He knew that. Naked as he was, in human form, his body couldn't help but react to her, to long for her as his mind longed. She was beautiful. His brightest light. His beloved Lily.

"Yes, you can." Her hand pressed flat against his chest, fingertips grazing the light scattering of golden hair. His nipples tightened, and so did his chest. His whole body did, to tell the truth. With her so close, he was uncomfortably aware of the growing erection.

Lily's eyes trailed downwards, then lifted to his face. She nuzzled into the hand resting against her cheek, turned towards it and pressed her lips to the heel of his hand.

Micah drew in a breath and pulled back again, trying to escape her, even when he didn't seem able to let go of her arm. His fingers were welded there, and no matter how hard he tried, he couldn't make them uncurl. The wall came up behind him, hard and cold. And beside him, the door to her bedroom. There was nowhere else to go.

121

Rhiannon Leith

And Lily closed on him again, drawn after him by his grip on her, by her grip on him. Like dancers, he thought absently. Like dancers who needed each other, just as she said.

"This must stop, Lily," he said, his gaze filling itself with her lips, the delicate line of her nose, the sparkling eyes. Her mouth opened and he found himself leaning towards her, pulling her towards him. "We have to stop."

Her lips parted. Her soft grey eyes fluttered closed.

"Stop," he tried for the last time, his mouth brushing against his, their lips interweaving. "Please make it stop."

She groaned as he claimed her mouth with his own, pulling her towards him and crushing her hand between them. His fingers threaded her hair, like strands of silk, like everything he had ever dreamed. She smelled of orange blossom and jasmine. And Lily, the sweet scent of Lily he'd known for so long. His grip slid down her arm to her shoulder and, free once more, she caressed his face.

Her body pressed against his groin, maddening him and she moved slowly, her tongue curling around his, drawing the kiss out and sending ripples of desire running through every vein in his insubordinate body.

Her clothes came away beneath his hands. He didn't even know what he was unbuttoning or pulling free. There was no conscious thought about it. Only need. He gave in to it, forsaking what he thought he knew for what he could feel.

Her breasts were full and high. His hands cupped them, lifted them, and when he brushed his thumbs over the nipples, she cried out softly, her voice smothered by his mouth.

Her own hands were not idle. They roamed lower, trailing the ridges of his abdomen, teasing the sensitive skin of his upper thighs until his breath turned ragged. One snaked down to close around his hard and ready cock. It pulsed beneath her touch, and as she slid her hand and naked body along the length of it, his own need rumbled up into his voice, right from

122

the depths of him.

"Please Lily," he groaned, no longer sure what he was pleading for, "please, my bright one."

She rocked against him and he moved with her, his hands roving across her velvet skin, her hips, the downy hair between her legs. She was wet, glistening, the moisture between her legs like warm honey.

Micah pressed a finger home and she cried out, her fingers working along his cock, trailing down to cup his balls and back up the shaft.

Lily breathed his name as he twisted his finger inside her and then withdrew it. Her scent filled the air, confounding him, sending his blood pumping even faster. It pounded at the base of his brain, driving all sanity from him.

With strong and certain hands, he lifted her from the floor taking her lips once more. Eager for him, she wrapped her legs around his waist, trapping his cock against her. But Micah just kissed her, his mouth devouring her, taking control as he had wished to so many times.

He carried her into the bedroom and laid her on the bed. She stretched out for him, welcoming him to her, arching up to greet his body with her own.

"Please Micah," she begged, "please, please Micah." The two repeated words were a litany, a song of pleasure and need. He parted her legs and knelt between them, gazing down all the wonderful length of her.

Every instinct told him this was wrong. Everything that made him what he was, what he had been created to be, told him to stop, to dissolve himself into light and flee from her. But he couldn't. Hadn't he said as much to Enoch? He couldn't leave her. And if they were right, if this week was all she had, then how could he pretend it didn't matter? How on earth could he just let her go?

"Ah, Lily," he groaned. "You'll damn us both, my bright

one."

Before she could answer, he bent low and ran his tongue up the line of her labia, parting them so he could press it deep inside her and drink down her essence. Lily gave a stuttering cry and her hips lifted from the bed. His hands cupped her ass, holding her up and she squirmed against him, shouting out his name in ecstasy.

"Now, Micah. I need you. Please."

He lifted himself and she smiled, her eyes distant and blurred with desire. Her hair spread around her face and she rocked her hips towards him.

He couldn't resist any longer. Lifting himself over her, holding himself up on his arms, he let her guide his cock to her. He stopped, poised there, savouring the forbidden, the look on her face, his own rising hunger.

Is this what it is to fall? he wondered. If so, no wonder so many of his kind relinquished their hold on Heaven.

Micah hung over her, gazing into her face for a moment longer.

"Lily," he said and she smiled. All the world brightened when she smiled. Releasing his last reservations and regrets, Micah plunged into her depths, moving with her, his body ravaging hers and hers claiming his as her own. She closed around him, her legs wrapping around his hips, her mouth taking his once more. She tangled her fingers in his hair and came with a cry that rang through his body and his mind.

He buried himself in her, his hips bucking as he came. A ragged cry tore itself out of him and he released himself, and all that he was, to her care. He emptied himself into her, sobbing as he did so.

He might have lain there a minute or a lifetime, spent in his surrender. Lily's body moved around him, and her inner muscles drew him deep inside her again.

He rolled onto his side, but she came with him, face-to-face, side by side, her eyes heavy with desire still.

"You've made me wait far too long, Micah." Her fingertips skimmed up his body and he shuddered. The movement echoed deep inside her and Lily gasped.

He smiled, relishing the power she had over him, the power he had over her. Wrapped together, entwined on her bed, they were one, if only for a little while. He kissed her, savouring each movement, each taste, each tiny breath of pleasure as he started to move within her again.

"I promise, Lily," he breathed, "I will never make that mistake again."

Sam closed the door behind him with a combination of regret, dread and triumph.

And jealousy. That was the last thing he was expecting, and yet it was there, a spike of envy for both Micah and Lily. It shouldn't affect him. It shouldn't matter to him that they would finally face each other, that they would make love as they longed to. He could make Lily want him. He could make her come, scream his name, beg for his touch, do anything. But she loved Micah.

His hand shook and his key skidded across the surface of the lock.

Lily loved Micah.

It had never been more obvious to him as it had the moment she had told him to go. He'd covered the shock but he couldn't hide it from himself. No more than he could quell the lust that rose in him at the sight of the angel in corporeal form. As an ethereal he was beautiful, enchanting, a wonder of light and shimmering air. In physical form, "breathtaking" came to mind. Sam closed his eyes, conjuring up that image to torment himself with. The idea of them, of the two of them together, Lily's creamy skin against the gilded tones of Micah, her

125

coppery hair spilling across his golden curls.

Sam sucked in a breath and his pulse jumped.

He could almost see them. If he reached out with his mind he would be able to sense all they felt. But he couldn't do it.

The apartment was dark, empty and soulless. He stepped inside and closed the door behind him. He didn't need the lights and he didn't feel inclined to see the world anyway.

From the next apartment his preternatural hearing picked up a gasp. The quintessence of pleasure, condensed to a single sound. He wasn't sure which one of them it was. It didn't matter. His chest tightened and his cock leaped inside his jeans. He reached in to adjust it, and found his hand refusing to move out again. Maybe his mind didn't want to be involved. His body had other ideas.

The button fly opened and he eased back the denim. Running his hand along the length of his cock, he shuddered and leaned forward, one hand on the wall to support himself, fingers splayed. He rocked forward and curled his palm around the shaft. In his mind, he pictured them. No matter that they probably hadn't got beyond a touch or a kiss next door. He imagined Lily on her knees while Micah thrust himself into her mouth, deep into her throat. Or Lily, tied spread-eagled on the bed while her angel fucked her, his taut buttocks tensing with each flex of his hips. Or Lily sitting astride Micah's face, her hands on the wall just opposite his, throwing back her head as she came.

"Well, this is charming," Asmodeus's voice mocked. "Ineffective, I'd wager, but just charming."

Sam spun around, a snarl on his face, but he was too slow. Few demons in all of hell had enough power to stand against Asmodeus, a King of Hell for so many centuries now, and Sam was totally unprepared, defenceless.

With a derisive flick of his fingers, the lust demon called forth the same serpentine chains. They coiled around Sam's arms and legs, hauling his back to the wall. Stretched like an *X*, like a crucified man, Sam struggled helplessly as the metal shifted to thick restraints, cold against his wrists and ankles. His clothes melted away to shadows and he stood there, writhing in a vain effort to free himself, more from pride than belief that it was possible.

Asmodeus ran his hands through his long black hair. He took the role of demon seriously, far more so than Sam did. Asmodeus revelled in it. No victim claimed was insignificant, but to trump a rival, he had once told Sam, was the sweetest victory of all.

"Let's see now. We left it here earlier, didn't we?"

"I got more time," Sam growled.

"Yes. But we felt using it to bring the lovebirds together was a misuse of that time. So for every mistake there's a punishment. And this will be yours, Sammael."

"He wasn't going to come to me. She's the honey trap, you idiot. She's the bait to bring him to me."

Asmodeus laughed. "Do I look like I care? I've been given a task here, Sammael, and I'm going to do it. Not play games. I abhor games." He smoothed his broad hands down the front of the leather vest he wore. "Our master feels you need an incentive, something to remind you of your task, something to goad you a little. I said I'd be happy to provide it."

"But I—"

He didn't stand a chance. Asmodeus grabbed the back of his head, yanking his hair sharply. Sam opened his mouth in shock and rage and the demon kissed him. It was a vicious, unfeeling kiss, a branding of one by the other. Teeth and tongue battered him, and with his head held in place and his body pinned to the wall, Sam could do nothing, which just made it even worse. At the same time Asmodeus pressed his hand to Sam's abdomen and power flooded him.

Lust tore at his body, his muscles hardening to iron, his

127

blood surging and breath sawing in and out of him. His lungs worked like a bellows as he strained against the bands and the demon holding him. Sensations swamped him. He wanted to fuck. Needed to fuck. He almost screamed with the suddenly palpable and all-consuming necessity.

Asmodeus stepped back, smug and victorious as Sam twisted this way and that, trying to escape.

"Don't worry, little brother, it isn't forever. You talked your way out of it so prettily the last time, we thought it better not to give you the chance on this occasion. You'll take your punishment. Then you'll do your job."

"You can't leave me like this," Sam howled, trying to find some way to stave the mounting desire, trying to turn his body or think his way to the blessed relief of orgasm.

"No, you're right." Asmodeus reached into his pocket and drew out two lengths of black material. "You'd make too much noise. Don't want you disturbing the neighbours, do we?"

"Asmodeus, don't do this. Please."

The demon closed his glowing eyes, inhaled deeply as if savouring the aroma of a favourite dish. "Ah, Sammael, I love it when you beg." He reached forward and securely gagged Sam with one length. "But this time you need to be quiet. There's more to this than leaving you in the torment of unfulfilled lust, or driving you to madness with your desire. Looking at it another way, it's a gift."

He ran his hand down the side of Sam's face, following the line of the gag towards his mouth. He left behind a burning trail. As his finger approached, Sam snapped at him, but Asmodeus pulled back just in time. He took the other scarf, wrapped both ends around his hands and pulled it taut, so sharply that it made a snapping sound. "I'm going to let you experience everything your lovebirds experience tonight. You'll feel each kiss, each caress, every single orgasm. You won't come, Sam, but you'll go through everything they go through.

Without the release. So next time you be more inclined to make sure they include you. Understand me?"

Sam cursed him, the words mangled by the gag, but not the sentiment. Asmodeus listened to him, still grinning, loving every moment of it.

"Now, now, a gift remember? And an opportunity to learn. To study your prey. I thought you prided yourself on doing just that. And this—" he snapped the material again and then lifted it to bind Sam's eyes, "—is just so that nothing can distract you while you're at it."

The world turned dark, silken and erotic. The material blinded him and made the rising sensations even clearer. The chains held his body still so that he could do nothing about the unadulterated lust coursing through him. Lips touched his, soft and gentle, questioning. Other lips responded, hesitant but filled with need, with desire. Lily's scent encircled him and hands that weren't his hands, for all they felt like his, caressed her. Micah groaned. The sound echoed through Sam's body, shaking him to his core.

"Night night, Sammy boy," Asmodeus drawled, and then he was gone.

Invisible thumbs brushed over his nipples and he cried out mournfully, his voice smothered by both the gag and Micah's mouth. He knew it was Micah's mouth, because he felt Lily's too, her soft lips hungry and demanding, her body arching as his arched, her fingertips teasing the sensitive skin of his upper thighs until his breath turned ragged. One hand snaked down to close around his painfully eager cock. It pulsed beneath her touch, as she slid her hand and naked body along the length of it.

It wasn't her, he tried to tell himself. Or rather it wasn't him. He was the interloper here, the phantom whose presence was a secret, a spy, a ghost. Lily's scent filled the air, confounding him, sending his blood pumping even faster. And

Micah's cinnamon musk trailed after hers. It pounded at the base of his brain, driving all sanity from him.

Micah's mouth devoured his, his strong arms lifted him. Their voices whispered through the darkness, an enticement, drawing him into their intimacy against his will, against his better judgement.

"Please Micah, please, please Micah."

"Ah Lily, you'll damn us both, my bright one."

The angel's tongue caressed Sam's balls, and his mouth filled with the sweet taste of Lily. He drowned in her, in them, his own identity slipping away as Micah thrust into her depths, into his own depths. Sam's body lifted from the wall, straining to tear himself free of his restraints, and of the touch of two lovers who didn't even know he was there. His body pulsed, vibrant with need. Micah cried out, his voice ringing through Sam's mind as he came with a cry of deliverance.

Sam fell back, his chest heaving in agonized gasps, still feeling the sensations of Lily's spasms of ecstasy, her moans of release. His cock strained away from him, hard as iron, pulsating with need. No release for him. The irony of feeling what they felt, his own private torture. He let out his breath in a ragged groan which shuddered through his sweat-slicked body.

Sam hung from the restraints, his head sinking to his chest. The corded muscles of his arms wrenched as he tried to tug himself free. It was a feeble effort, pointless, but he had to try. Already, they were stirring again, Micah still hard inside her, Lily determined not to let him escape her again. Moving slowly, intimately, wrapped around each other, unaware that they were also wrapped around him, in his mind, in his flesh.

A drop of cold sweat trailed down his neck, across his chest, and down the ridges of his abdomen, like a teasing tongue, like a lover. Lily whispered and Micah laughed. Their voices in his mind just made it worse.

Chapter Ten

Lily stretched out, catlike, luxuriating in the feel of Micah's length beside her, hard muscles and smooth skin, his flat stomach and strong legs, the warmth of him. It made her feel like purring as she rested her face against his broad chest and listen to the steady thunder of his heart beneath.

"You're alive," she said.

He laughed, a low, exhausted chuckle. "I am, my bright one."

She looked up, surprised, to find a curious combination of peace and resignation in his bright blue eyes. He blinked, golden lashes brushing his cheeks, and then tried to smile. It didn't quite make it all the way to his eyes.

"Micah—" She pushed herself up on her elbows.

"Don't," he said abruptly and closed his eyes. Strain etched his features, drawing two lines between his eyebrows.

She reached up with a trembling finger to smooth them away. "Are you sorry?"

He caught her in a grip both frighteningly strong and perfectly gentle. His long fingers circled her wrist, and he slipped his legs under hers moments before he turned, flipping her onto her back. Looming over her, the light from the streetlamp outside illuminating the edges of his silhouette, he smiled. This one did reach his eyes. It made them glow an even more vibrant blue and she sank down beneath him, bewitched.

"Not for a second, my bright one. How could I be?"

He bent to kiss her and she drew him to her again, trailing her fingers along the muscles of his back, the hard planes and curves.

"Are you sorry?" he asked, his lips brushing hers.

"Not for a second," she said without hesitation. He deepened his kiss, his tongue dancing with hers. Lily sighed, her hips rising to meet him of their own volition.

"*Where am I?*"

The voice echoed through her head, sudden and unexpected. She flinched and Micah rose, confused.

No, not now. Please.

"*Where am I? What happened? I was in the—*"

"Lily?" He drew back, pulling her covers up around her. "Voices?"

She nodded, worrying her lower lip with her teeth in an effort to block the spirit.

"Help them," Micah urged.

Tears stung her eyes. "Not now." She rolled onto her side, curling into herself. "Not when I'm with you, Micah. It's not fair."

He smoothed her hair, brushing it back from her face. "I know. But they can't wait, Lily. Please."

Her body lurched with grief. He was right, she knew that. But for just a while, just for a short while she had thought herself free.

"Go to the light." She tried to visualise it for the wandering spirit who had found her. "They're waiting for you, in the light. Go on now." She felt like someone shooing a child on its way. And inside her, her heart cracked.

She was alone again, all alone.

"Lily?" Micah nestled behind her, his body warm against the length of her, a cloak, a shelter.

132

"Why now, Micah?" she whispered into the empty shadows before her. "Why would they come back now?"

He nuzzled the back of her neck, his breath tickling the sensitive hair there. His kiss was so gentle. It shouldn't have hurt. It shouldn't have made tears leak from behind her clenched eyelids and slide down her face to wet the pillow. But it did.

"Sam was blocking them. That's why the visions came through, I believe."

"But the visions were of deaths, or near deaths. There were no spirits to be guided on, Micah. It was different."

"Shh." He wrapped his arms around her. "It's okay, Lily. It will be okay."

She shook her head, but said nothing. What could she say? For a brief moment she had everything she had ever wanted. Then the very thing that defined her, that made her what she was, interfered again. Sam could make it go away. Micah would not.

"Close your eyes." Micah kissed her neck again. His hands massaged her shoulders, easing the tension out of her with a skill she had never suspected he might possess. Inside her something uncoiled, warm and wicked, and she found herself wet for him once more.

A deep groan sounded through her mind. Not Micah's. Not her own. It sounded like—

"Sam?"

Micah jerked against her, his whole body stiffening at the sound of the demon's name on her lips.

"What about Sam?" he asked warily.

Lily rolled onto her back and glanced at his face. His eyes were very bright, full of concern. "You don't feel him?" He shook his head, his lips forming a grim line. "I do. He's suffering, Micah. Something's wrong."

"Where?"

"I don't..." She closed her eyes again, trying to find him again. There was nothing. Not a trace. "Damn it. If only I could use this instead of it using me."

Micah rested on his elbow, gazing at her for a long moment. "There's a way," he said at last. He didn't look too happy about the idea. But the sound of Sam's despair haunted her.

She didn't hesitate. "Show me."

"Close your eyes and open your mind to me."

She obeyed him, trusting him as she always had. If she couldn't trust Micah, what hope was there for her?

The blend of warm cinnamon and musk that always accompanied him encircled her mind. Like a drug on her senses, it brought with it relaxation. She released her grip on the conscious world and let herself slip deeper and deeper. The darkness was complete, but with Micah cradling her, she wasn't afraid.

"*Do you remember how your visions started?*" he asked.

Pain, usually, she realised, shock and frozen panic. Not this. Not this safety and comfort.

"*Well, that's not a good thing to induce. We'll have to try another way.*"

What kind of other way? She wasn't sure if he would hear her thought or not, but to her surprise, Micah's soft laugh ran through her.

"*Visualise a single point of light, a distant star or a candle flame. Then take yourself through it. Think of Sam as you do it. Think of that last contact. Like this.*"

A light flared before her, like the flare of a struck match in the night. She seized it, pushed herself towards it. Breath exploded from her lungs and her body twisted.

He was naked, his arms and legs chained, his muscles corded with pain. She smelled something chemical, sickening.

"Lily?" *Micah was still with her, cushioning her from the worst of the suffering. But she could feel it all the same, as if his beaten body was her body. She couldn't see his face. It felt more like she was inside him, or struggling alongside him. He'd been tortured and it wasn't over. He struggled weakly, pain lancing down his aching limbs. Lily shied back at the touch of nightmare in his mind.*

"Stay calm, my bright one. You can't be hurt with me here. Remember that. No matter what." *Micah's lips touched her shoulder. It helped, and for that she was grateful, truly grateful.*

"Where are we?"

The body housing her coughed and heat seared the skin of his feet.

They weren't in a room. The sky opened above them, dotted with stars. Leaves stirred as the breeze travelled through them. And beneath him...beneath him...

Flames leaped to life on the petrol-soaked wood. They seized the body and he screamed, his voice a howl of agony. Lily screamed with him and Micah enfolded her, dragging her back to him.

"Wake up, Lily!" Micah yelled, and the fear in his voice shocked her back into the real world. She gasped for breath, arching off the bed.

"He's burning, Micah! Oh my God, he's burning! He's tied up and—there's fire—petrol—"

She threw off the covers and tried to get to her feet, but her legs gave way. Micah's arms caught her. He was always there for her, always ready to catch her when she fell.

And Sam—Sam was burning.

"Put on some clothes," Micah said curtly. "He's got to be next door. Otherwise he's back in Hell." He wound one of the sheets around his waist, looking more like a living sculpture than ever. "Come on."

Lily struggled into a pair of jeans and a T-shirt while making for the door behind him.

The hall outside the apartment was dark. They stopped outside Sam's door and she knocked, praying he would just appear, sleepy, irritated, but unharmed. There was no answer.

Lily pressed her ear to the door. "Sam?"

It was very faint, a groan, exhausted, agonised. She looked up into Micah's eyes, indigo in the shadows.

He swallowed hard, his throat working and he nodded. "Step back. Stay behind me."

"Micah, he's in there, isn't he? But I saw the sky, the trees. I saw fire."

He nodded but didn't answer. Instead, he pressed his hand to the keyhole and closed his eyes. His brow furrowed in concentration. There was a loud clunk and he pushed the door open.

"Sammael?" he called. "Can you hear me?"

A soft growl came from the darkness. Animal with arousal, it rumbled through Lily's body, loosening the tension inside to a flood of desire.

Micah stepped inside, feeling for the light switch, but as he flicked it, the bulbs only flickered dimly. It was enough to see Sam gagged and blindfolded, his body pinned to the wall by iron bands. His breath came in urgent gasps, his cock straining out in front of him, his skin drenched with sweat, glistening in the erratic light.

"Oh God." Lily started forward, pushing past Micah. She stopped before Sam and his head turned sharply, like a predator smelling prey. She tugged off the blindfold and Sam burst into frantic struggles, trying to free himself. The material came away in her hand and his eyes blazed with fire, wild and dangerous. She gave a cry as she fell back and landed heavily on the floor.

"*Let me go!*"

Sam's voice invaded her mind, but it hardly sounded like Sam anymore. This was the voice of a demon, a creature maddened by desire and the need to sate itself in flesh.

"Lily, get back from him." Micah stepped between them.

"What happened? What is doing this to him?"

Micah cocked his head, listening, as Sam grunted in thwarted rage and rolled his head back against the wall. Sweat dripped from his chin.

"Asmodeus. Demon of Lust. One of the Kings of Hell. It's a punishment. Asmodeus filled him with desire, with lust, and then let him feel..." The angel's face hardened in disgust. "They let him feel everything we did. Everything. As if we did it to him."

Lily struggled to her knees, grabbing Micah's leg for support. "Oh God, that's—"

Micah sighed. "Demonic?" As if she wasn't there, he stretched out his arm and laid his tapered hand flat on Sammael's chest. Sam shuddered, and a groan tore its way from him again. His heavy balls contracted and his cock jumped.

"We have to help him," Lily insisted, rising to face him. "Can you make it stop?"

Micah shook his head, but didn't remove his hand. "It will wear off. Eventually. But it will leave him changed. More the creature he was. Less like your Sam."

"Micah, we have to do something," she insisted and reached out with her own hand. Sam froze at her touch. His chest stilled. His skin was on fire. "Let him go."

"There's only one thing we can do, Lily, and that's try to make it bearable for him. If we let him go, he'll attack. Right now the only thing on his mind is sex and he'll take it willing or not. He won't be gentle. He won't consider you at all. You'll be a thing to use. Something to fuck. We can't let him go."

Her mouth went dry. "You want me to, to what?"

"Trust me."

She glanced at him. It took effort to tear her gaze away from Sam's but what she found in Micah's face didn't inspire trust. It wasn't quite hate. Despite what he was saying, there was no sign of pity. The closest thing she could discern there was a need for revenge.

"Micah?"

"Shh." His left hand glided up her arms to her shoulder. He drew her hair back from her neck like a skein of silken threads and lowered his lips to her skin. Feather light kisses drugged her senses. Without realising it, she leaned back against him, her eyes fluttering closed with desire.

Sammael moaned. The noise ran through her and Lily opened her eyes to see his tortured expression. Micah's hands described the curves of her body, raking her T-shirt up to expose the naked breasts beneath. He cupped them, as if offering them to Sam, offering her.

"Micah, don't, please."

"Do you think he'd listen if you pleaded, Lily?" Micah lips brushed the curve of her neck.

Lily shook her head. Micah rolled her taut nipples between his fingers and thumbs, the delicious pressure making her resistance melt into blind need. She ripped the T-shirt off and cast it aside, twisting around to capture Micah's mouth.

Sammael arched away from the wall, his muffled curses strained with despair. Micah rolled his hips against hers and tugged down her jeans, filling his hands with her ass, his grip driving her out of her mind with need.

"Turn around," he said in a low, dangerous voice. "Look at him, Lily. I want him to see."

"But it—it isn't—"

Micah took her shoulders, turning her gently so he was pressed against her back and she faced Sam, could see his torment. Pleasure coursed through her at the expression, at the corded muscles, at the sheen of sweat glistening on the hard planes and angles of his magnificent body. Micah's hard-on pressed against the small of her back. As he moved against her, she felt herself succumb.

Fair. She had been about to say fair. But Sam didn't care about what was fair, or right, or anything like that. Sam cared about pleasure. His pleasure.

Sam tried to close his eyes. Was it easier with the blindfold, she wondered? Did it hurt to look at her, to see her with the angel?

Micah's long elegant fingers dipped into the wetness between her legs, smoothing back the intricate folds of her skin until they came to rest on the pulsing nub of her clit. Her legs went weak and she gasped as he caught her, controlling her fall, lowering her to her knees. He knelt with her, his every movement the epitome of grace. She parted her legs for him, and Micah's cock nudged at her opening, surging into her from behind, stretching her, filling her.

Lily looked up to find Sam watching her. He had fallen still, his eyes no longer blazing. As Micah thrust into her, his fingers working their magic on her clit and on her breasts, Sam's body rocked back and forth, and tears glistened in his eyes. His cock danced not far from her face, a drop of pre-come shining on the head. Her mouth watered at the thought of its taste, at the idea of leaning forward and taking him in her mouth while Micah's thick cock shafted her. Sam's gaze flickered over her face, longing, pained. Was it his idea or hers? And did she care either way?

"Come for me first," Micah instructed huskily.

How could she let him down?

Blood rushed through her, pushing her to that final

glorious moment of ecstasy. She cried out Micah's name and Sam jerked back, his buttocks slapping against the cold wall. Her body clenched, stiffening, and then her passion crested, burst forth from her with a trembling cry of liberation.

Micah roared as he released himself inside her, holding her hips and pounding into her. Lily fell forward onto her hands and thrust back to meet him stroke for stroke.

Sam groaned, his body clearly aching for her, for them.

"Did he feel that?" she asked. "All of it?"

"Every iota of sensation, my bright one."

"And before?"

"Since this spell was cast, probably since he left us."

Lily rose up on her knees again and rested her hands on his thighs, where the muscles strained beneath his olive skin. Skimming through the lustre of sweat, she described whorls and spirals. Sam's chest tightened again and she watched, almost distractedly, as his balls contracted still further, his cock bobbing up and down with need.

"Do you want him, Lily?" Micah began to massage her shoulders. "If you want him, take him."

Sam's body stiffened even further. Outrage, she thought. And why not? To be offered like this to someone whom he thought to take. To be treated like some sort of slave. It killed him. It had to.

So why was her arousal building beyond bearing all over again?

"Are you sure you don't mind?" She licked her lips.

Micah laughed, a chuckle deep inside him that rolled through her body. It was almost as if they had changed places, Sam and Micah. And she was still caught between the two of them.

But somehow she ceased to care.

Lily glanced up the length of Sam's exquisite body. It shone for her, his chest heaving, each line of muscle the work of a master sculptor. His tears had soaked through the material of the gag and his eyes were closed now, resigned. *Noble stoicism* personified.

With the tip of her tongue, she licked away that glittering pearl of pre-come that taunted her so. Sam drew in a shuddering breath. Lily curled her tongue around the swollen glans and brought her hands in to tease his balls. They were tight with need, so tight she had never seen the like. Pity surged inside her. Sammael was all about sex, she knew that. He lived it, breathed it, it was his reason for existence.

But he'd never been so helpless in the face of it before.

She knew that instinctively, and it hurt to think that she had put him here. Not directly perhaps. But it was all because of her.

Lily closed her mouth around him, drawing him into her mouth, grazing the sensitive tip with her tongue, which she then curled around the length. She worked his shaft with a gentle but determined hand. He thrust towards her, pushing himself deeper, and she let him, swallowing him. Her hand strayed to the sensitive line of flesh behind his balls and he shivered against her.

Behind her, Micah's hands stroked her hair, brushed her sides and then withdrew, leaving her to her self-appointed task.

Sam moaned, his voice clearer now. She flicked her eyes up to see that the gag hung around his neck like a black noose. His mouth hung open, pleading wordlessly.

She worked her mouth more quickly, tightening her grip on his shaft. The sounds he made became more desperate and his hips jerked towards her.

Suddenly his voice was smothered again. She heard the sound of a kiss, mouth to mouth, tongue to tongue, hungry and demanding. She glanced up again to find Micah kissing Sam. It wasn't gentle, or loving. Micah gripped Sam's face and light

141

sparkled between their lips. Sam moaned into Micah's mouth and his trapped hands stretched out, flexing and uncurling.

She didn't know what did it, her mouth on him, or Micah's, perhaps both together. Sam's body convulsed suddenly and he came, hard and fast. He bucked against her face, but she grabbed his hips and slammed him back against the wall. Taking his cue from her, Micah overpowered him, still kissing him with unabated passion. He held the demon down while Sam groaned in blissful agony and flooded her.

The bands of iron melted away and suddenly the two of them were the only things holding him up. Gently, with the greatest of care, Micah and Lily released him, but didn't let him go for fear he would fall. He sagged in their embrace as they lowered him to the floor.

Sam opened his eyes, looking up into their faces with eyes dark and haunted, and now entirely human looking again. His voice was harsh, broken. "Thank you," he groaned.

"Rest now." Micah smoothed back Sam's sweat-drenched hair from his forehead. "Later, we'll talk."

Chapter Eleven

Sam came to in Lily's room rather than his own, tucked into her bed, her comforter pulled up to his armpits, his arms laid out at his sides on the top. Like a corpse or a coma patient. He struggled to sit, but his body ached, his head swam and he fell back down with a snarl of frustration.

Micah appeared in the doorway wearing a pair of black jeans and a white T-shirt, looking just like any human being. Well, not just *any* human being. He leaned on the doorjamb, training that penetrating blue gaze on his face. "How are you feeling?"

A dozen smart answers sprang to Sam's mind, but he didn't voice them. "I've felt better. Where's Lily?"

"On the phone. The police called."

"D.I. Reid?"

"Yes. There has been a development. Another death. Todd Lane."

Sam swore and pushed back the covers. He'd never been ashamed of nakedness. He felt far more comfortable in his own skin than in clothing, to tell the truth. But as soon as he felt Micah's gaze on him, he froze.

Images of the previous night surged to the forefront of his mind, the two of them together, Micah's lips on his.

Sam pushed them away, concentrating on the facts at hand, on the death. "She saw it, didn't she?"

Micah nodded slowly. "Thought it was you. That's why we went in there." His eyes ranged over Sam's body.

Sam stretched his arms above his head, extending his spine, rolling his head from side to side. Muscle and ligaments protested but if it meant giving the angel a full view and watching his Adam's apple bob up and down in his throat, it was worth it.

"Which of you came to my rescue first?"

Micah gave a brief and bitter laugh, hardly more than an expulsion of breath. "Yeah, that was me. Charged right in there, of course."

Sarcasm. Well, Sam could deal with sarcasm. It was more comfortable than a lot of other forms of expression.

Lily appeared behind Micah, her face pale, dark shadows under her grey eyes. A far cry from the vibrant creature who had knelt before him last night and saved his sanity. She looked frail, washed out, hurting. Her eyes locked with his and she ran to him.

Lily's body hit him hard, almost bowling him over. As it was, he had to take a step or two back to keep his balance. She held him as if her life depended on him. Slowly, he lowered his arms around her, drawing her closer.

"He's dead. Todd's dead."

"What did Reid say?" asked Micah.

"That he was burnt alive. In Jericho Park, last night. About the same time as I—"

"As you saw it happen," Sam finished for her.

She nodded, her cheek rubbing up and down against his chest. Her lips pressed closer for a moment, a kiss.

Damn it, what did she think? Did she expect something in return?

Micah watched them, his expression unreadable. "But Lily thought it was you. After all, we went looking for you, not

Todd."

"Looking for me?"

"Visualisation. Lily was worried about you so we—"

Sam stiffened, alarm spilling up through his body. "Are you insane? Don't you know where I could have been? Where you could have taken her?"

"I was there." Micah lifted his chin, firming his jaw as he clenched his teeth. "I was always with her. She would not have suffered any harm. I will never allow that to happen."

Sam stroked her hair. She shivered beneath his touch.

"D.I. Reid wants me to look at the crime scene for her, see if I can't pick up something else about this lunatic," said Lily.

"You said no, didn't you?"

She pulled back, looking up into his face in amazement. "I said yes. Sam, if he's coming after me next I want to give the cops everything they need to catch him. They're sending a car for me."

"For us," Micah corrected just ahead of Sam. She looked just as startled at that. "We're coming too, Lily. You aren't going anywhere on your own."

She disentangled herself from Sam, standing between them as if she wasn't sure which one to explode at. "I hardly think being with Reid and all her people constitutes being on my own, Micah."

"It's the only way I can watch over you, Lily. I've done it for twenty years. I'm not about to stop now. So, we're coming." He cast that brilliant blue gaze briefly in Sam's direction. "You'll need clothes, Sammael."

He tried to summon them but he was too weak. The image spluttered and died. Micah didn't react to the failure.

Thank heavens for small mercies. Or whoever.

"They're next door," said Sam.

Micah left the room and Lily stormed after him. "Now you

145

just wait a minute, Micah—"

Her voice cut off in the sound of a kiss and Sam froze, just listening to them. The angel was kissing her thoroughly enough to drive all other thoughts from her mind. Sam's lips burned as the memory of last night returned, of Micah's mouth claiming his in just such a kiss. A bizarre combination of hard and soft, of give and take, while Lily, saviour of his sanity, Lily had given him a blow job he would never forget.

He sat back on the bed, resting his head in his hands. His body was already reacting again. He could pretend it was just the after-effects of Asmodeus's touch, but it wasn't. It was the thought of Lily and Micah, of both of them together. He let out a ragged breath. If he failed, last night would be playtime in comparison to what the Nameless would put him through. If he failed.

Sam drew in another breath and let it out again, commanding his body to get control of itself. Micah was just an angel and Lily was just a mortal. There was no special magic about them, and that feeling of sublime grace when they touched him had just been desire. That was all. The bliss of fulfilled desire. He had to keep it together.

"Here." The clink of a mug settling on the bedside cabinet nearly made him jump out of his skin. Lily flinched back, but didn't retreat. She looked down at him with something frighteningly like love in her eyes. "You okay, Sam?"

Okay? No. Definitely not okay. How had she even got that close to him without his knowing? Weakness, that was the problem. He was worn out from last night. Bloody Asmodeus.

The aroma of coffee filled the air, one of the truly great inventions of humanity, but Sam couldn't be bothered about it now. Lily's fingers touched his hair, trailing through the dark curls, whispering against his scalp.

"What are we going to do, Sam?" she asked.

He caught her wrist in a firm grip, not hard enough to hurt,

146

but secure enough that she couldn't pull away. He pressed the side of his face into the palm and then bit, even so gently, on the mound of tender skin below her thumb. Her startled breath ended in a moan.

"Don't forget about me, Lily." He didn't intend for the words to come out in that way, a touch of self-pity seeping through his guard. Damn. Hardening his voice, he tried again. "We still have a deal?"

Her eyes were closed, her mouth open just enough so that he could see the pink of her tongue. She drew in her breath, exhaled and her fingers flexed against his face. "Yes, Sam. But—"

He rose to his feet, sweeping her into his arms, burrowing one hand into her hair so she had to look at him, the other tight on the small of her back, pulling her hard against his body. The first flicker of fear reasserted itself in her eyes. That was better. He needed her to remember what he was, what he intended.

He needed to remind himself.

"No buts, Lily. There were no buts when you agreed, were there?"

She opened her mouth again to speak, but then the spark faded in her eyes. She pressed her soft lips together, the lips that were still bruised from taking him last night, and she shook her head.

He couldn't help himself. He had to know her thoughts. "What were you going to say?"

"Not against his will. I won't do it if it's against his will."

Sam bent his mouth to hers and kissed her, savouring the taste of her. Not too many minutes ago Micah had done the same thing and he smiled against her lips at the thought of reclaiming what the angel thought he had won. Turning around, he sat her down on the bed and bent over her, still kissing, twining his tongue with hers, lips and teeth stirring the current rising between them. She had to lean on her hands to

147

keep from falling and she was his, trapped, at his mercy. He just had to keep reminding her of the fact.

Sam sank to one knee and ran his hands up the length of her thighs as he broke the kiss. She gazed at him, startled, shell-shocked, beautiful.

"Not against his will," he agreed, keeping his voice low and intimate. "But it won't be, sweetheart. You'll see. He'll want it as much as you and I. You saw him last night, didn't you?"

"Yes, but—" Her eyes darted up, widened, and Sam could guess what she was seeing. Ever so slowly, as if it were the most unimportant thing in the world for him, he glanced over his shoulder to see Micah in the doorway holding a small bundle of clothes. Sam shot Lily an encouraging smile as he got up and faced Micah's grim face. Not so giving now.

"Clothes," he growled.

"Thanks." Sam sauntered towards him, unashamed and undeterred. "My colours too." He took them from the angel who quickly snatched back his hand. "You know, Mike, you weren't so coy last night."

"Last night, Sammael, we acted to save your sanity, and this city from having you unleashed on it like that time in Budapest."

Sam blinked, trying to remember a time in Budapest. True, much of the fifteenth century was a blur, but he didn't recall Budapest as being any worse than—images flickered through the back of his mind, like watching a light box, and some of his self-assurance bled away. He gazed into Micah's face, searching it for more, but the angel might as well have been made from stone.

No, despite his assurances to Lily, this was not going to be easy. Not at all.

The cop driving the sedan didn't look too thrilled about

having all three of them crowd into the back but, quite frankly, Micah didn't care. He had no intention of either letting her sit alone in the front, or of leaving her in the back with Sammael. And from the look on his face, Sammael was thinking precisely the same thing. Lily squirmed between them and their driver eyed them suspiciously in the rear-view mirror. As they travelled through the lunchtime traffic, the car weaving between lanes, Micah tried to ignore the press of her thigh against his, and the way her breath increased and her skin flushed. When he did look her way, he noticed Sammael's hand stealing between her knees.

"Stop it."

Sam just gave a snort and sat back, his hand stroking her lower arm instead. Lily closed her eyes and edged a little nearer to Micah. For that at least, he was grateful. But Sam's power was strong, so strong that Micah knew it was affecting him as well.

Sam sat on the other side, immaculately dressed despite the rush in black denim and a charcoal silk shirt, open at the collar. His colours indeed, flattering his olive-toned skin and dark hair, even though Micah had just reached blindly into the wardrobe and grabbed the first thing that came to hand.

The car passed through the park gate, waved on by the uniform cops securing it. They lurched over the uneven path and down to an area of open ground alive with cars, lights and people in uniforms, in white coveralls, in neat suits, all swarming around a tented area. A light mist of rain was starting to fall.

Reid was right in the thick of it, barking orders. She gave Lily a grim smile when she saw her, but as her eyes alighted on Micah's face, her jaw sagged. She hid it well, but her eyes were too easy to read.

"This is my friend, Mike," Lily offered quickly. "And you remember Sam?"

149

Reid shook Micah's offered hand, still staring at him. "Mike. Right, Lily mentioned you." Her eyes darted to Sam and back again. The demon treated her to his most rakish grin. For a moment, Micah wondered if she was going to stand there staring at them until night fell, but suddenly she drew her shroud of professionalism back around her shoulders and took Lily's arm, leading her towards the tent. "Are you sure about this, Lily? I mean, it's not pretty."

Lily drew the corners of her lips back as she tightened her mouth. "I've seen it already, remember?"

As Micah and Sam approached the tent, Reid turned. "It's a bit cramped in there, boys. If you don't mind waiting out here, you can be sure she'll be safe with us."

There was nothing they could do. Lily was swept inside and Sam and Micah were left standing there in the drizzle.

"Well, this sucks." Sam traced lines in the mud with the toe of his designer shoe. "Don't suppose you brought an umbrella, did you?" Micah ignored him, studying the tree line off to the right. "What about hoisting up those wings and giving us a bit of shelter?"

"I don't have wings when corporeal, Sam. I thought you might have noticed that."

Sam barked out a laugh. "I was a little distracted last night."

Lily re-emerged, looking even paler, with Reid's hand on her shoulder. Both her guardian and her seducer moved as one towards her, but a quick glare from her made them stop.

"I want to just walk around the area," she was saying to Reid, "see what I can pick up first, okay?"

"Whatever you need. You can even bring your bodyguards. Which way?" She gave the two men a grin as she passed them. "Where on earth did you find them, anyway? I've been looking in the wrong place."

"Would you believe they just turned up?" They walked on ahead, heads bowed in conversation.

Micah frowned, unexpectedly uneasy.

"A dangerous combination, those two women," Sam said as they fell into step behind them.

"Very," Micah said. "Sam, keep your eyes open. This place doesn't feel right."

"Nothing to do with the incinerated body back there?"

"No. I was here with Lily the day you turned up. There were shadows in the trees then, watching the children play. Watching her. I thought I saw them off but, well, here we are, back again."

Sam pushed out his lower lip as he thought, or sensed the area. "It's not one of our places."

"And yet I know what I saw. Keep your eyes open."

Up ahead, the path curved through the trees and they picked up their pace to catch up with Lily and Reid. As they rounded the bend, Lily stood near the edge of the path, her eyes closed. Micah hurried towards her but Reid stepped back to stop him.

"She's trying to get a feel for which way the killer went."

"I'm sure she is, but I need to be with her. I can help her," he protested. He had to help her. He knew that. No matter how much experience Lily thought she had, he had always been there with her, to guide her and keep her safe.

Reid, however, was unimpressed. "Really. Your arrival here is pretty convenient, isn't it, Mike? What's your surname by the way? Lily didn't say."

Micah knew that look. It was half threat, half enquiry, all cop. He didn't have an answer and she knew that. Somehow, she knew it.

Sam's hand slapped hard onto his shoulder, driving the air from his lungs. "Mike Angel, D.I. Reid. Lily's oldest friend and a holy pain in my ass. Doesn't approve of me, you see? Deeply suspicious sort of person. He's living in Rome these days but that doesn't stop him hopping on a plane the moment she had me ring. He just came this morning. Or was it last night, Mike?"

The blood drained away from Micah's face all over again at the barb, but there was nothing he could do about it here and now.

He was about to say something, to fall in with Sam's artful lie, when he was struck by a space in his world. An absence. A vital thing missing.

Lily was gone.

Chapter Twelve

The leaves all around her whispered words Lily couldn't quite catch. He had been here, no doubt about that. She would have known even had the charred corpse not indicated as much. She could feel him, taste him on the air. A taint that clung to the shadows between the dense trees—evil, actual physical evil. It reminded her of washing powder, something which should have smelled clean, but instead reeked of chemicals. She stood very still on the cracked concrete path, staring into the depths of the little piece of woodland, where the leaves shifted in the breeze and the voices went on and on.

Behind her, she heard them arguing. Reid, instantly suspicious of poor Micah, had wanted to ask all sorts of questions—would ask them all before she would let him return home with Lily and Sam—but right now she needed whatever Lily could tell her.

The murder scene had been much worse than Lily expected. Knowing Todd was burnt alive, knowing it in a way none of the others present could, because she had felt it last night as if it had happened to her, didn't help when faced with the sight of the blackened body, the gaping mouth. It would have been over in seconds, Reid assured her, thanks to the accelerant. And yet, it had lasted an eternity for Todd.

Even now the screams echoed around her mind. She'd thought it was Sam. She'd been so relieved when it wasn't. And now she felt empty, broken, ashamed. Todd was still screaming, and the other voices murmured on, disembodied souls, lost in this dark, dark place. Lily watched the trees and wondered if she should block them out or embrace them. Micah would know, but he couldn't just pop into her mind now and tell her what to do. Things had changed since he became corporeal, and to be honest she wasn't sure how she felt about that. It put him in a much more fragile position when it came to Sam, that much was clear.

No. If she was honest, she had put him in that position. She had agreed to Sam's deal.

She drew in a deep breath and exhaled, trying to shut out the unspoken accusations in Reid's voice when she spoke to Micah. And Sam's mellow tones trying to smooth over the cracks the angel's presence caused. No, she couldn't ignore it. She turned back, about to tell them to stop, to affirm their hastily concocted tale and hope Reid believed them.

That smell came to her again, clean, but not clean— washing powder, chemicals, detergent.

The bushes rustled behind her and something clamped over her mouth and nose, a huge hand smothering half her face. Panic speared her. She tried to scream but no sound came out. She fell, kicking, struggling, helpless, dragged down into the undergrowth. Twigs and brambles tore at her as he pulled her with him, moving too quickly for her scrabbling hands and feet to gain purchase or fight back.

Lily's heart hammered at the base of her throat as the figure of her attacker loomed over her, silhouetted against the distant light of safety, his gleaming eyes the only thing she could clearly make out.

A punch to her midsection drove all air from her lungs. He lifted his hand for a second and slapped a length of duct tape across her lips. She tried to scream again, but all that came out was a muffled cry. She kicked out at him but he merely raised an arm and cuffed the side of her head, sending her tumbling down a shallow incline through dead leaves and mulch, to lie at the foot, breathing hard, dazed and terrified.

"I know what you are," he snarled. "Satan's whore, handmaiden of the damned." He lurched over her and grabbed her by the hair, hauling her to her knees. "*M'khashephah lo tichayyah,* saith the Good Book, *Thou shalt not suffer a witch to live.*" Something flashed in his gloved hand—a knife—and Lily twisted in his grasp, trying to tear herself free. "We'll start with the simplest test, bitch, searching for his mark on your body. Undress yourself."

She tried to scream an obscenity at him. He grabbed her jacket and tore it from her back, tangling it around her arms, effectively binding her. His fingers dug into her skin through the thin fabric of her shirt and ripped it open. Releasing her hair, he pushed her headfirst down into the dirt again so her full back was exposed. The knife blade, cold and precise, bit into her skin at the base of her neck.

She cried out again but he didn't cut, just pierced her skin a fraction. It lifted and then descended again, not to stab her but to prick her skin, each jab eliciting a desperate cry of pain and helplessness.

"Tell me," he raged in his frantic low-pitched voice. "Tell me where the unholy one marked you. Tell me what he did. Confess it. Confess your wickedness to me."

"Lily!" Sam's voice echoed off the canopy, near, so near to her.

Bodies crashed through the trees behind them, Micah and Sam, tearing a path into the undergrowth for her.

"Lily, where are you?"

"Here!" she tried to yell, but the word was just a single strained vowel. "*Here! Here! Oh Jesus, please! Find me here!*"

Her attacker's foot slammed down on her back, pushing her beneath him. He seized her hair again, yanking it so her

155

head jerked back, her neck exposed.

Her inarticulate cry tore its way past the duct tape.

"He's going to kill me! Do something!"

She jerked down as the knife slashed through the air, severing her hair. Released from his hold, she crashed face first into the leaves which scraped her face and smelled of decay. He planted one last kick in her side to drive the air out of her, to leave her helpless and gasping. Then he was gone.

Sam burst through the trees above her and tore to her side, sliding down the incline in a fountain of leaves.

"Lily! She's here, Micah. Over here!"

He seized her, pulling her to him, holding her close in arms that seemed to tremble as wildly as her battered body.

"It's all right, sweetheart," he gasped, as if trying to convince himself as much as her. "We're here. It's all right. We're here."

It was Sam, her Sam. Sam's scent, Sam's warmth, Sam's fingers trying to brush away her tears and soothe her when he shared her terror. Sam engulfed her and she sank into him.

Micah and Reid thundered into the hollow, Reid already barking commands into a small radio. "Seal the exits. No, all of them. He's in here. Get that perimeter secure."

Micah stood over the two of them, his expression unreadable. Lily sobbed, reaching for him even as she clung to Sam's shirt. Micah took her hand in his, the warmth of his touch wrapping around her freezing fingers, and he dropped to his knees, holding her, reaching out to touch her face, stopping when he encountered the tape.

With a swallowed curse, he ripped it off. Lily screamed again, which made Reid spin towards them, even as her reinforcements flooded through the trees.

"Fingerprints!" It sounded like a curse.

Micah held up the offending article like something unclean

and it was snatched away into an evidence bag.

"Are you hurt?" he asked, in the gentle voice that was always there for her.

She shook her head, trying to swallow down the sobs of terror and relief that combined to steal her voice.

Sam's hand trailed through her ravaged hair, but he said nothing, just pulled her against his chest and rested his head against hers. Micah massaged her hands, trying to warm her, studying her face with his bluer-than-blue eyes, searching for something, anything, he could do.

"I thought..." he said at last, then stopped, helpless. His gaze rose to Sam's and then dropped to hers again. "I thought I'd lost you."

Lily didn't say a word, but pulled him to her so the three of them huddled together in the shadows.

Sam paced the lawn of the park while Reid took Lily's statement. She sat in the passenger seat of the car, shivering in a large grey blanket, nodding at something Reid said. A cop stood beside her, holding an oversized umbrella even though the misty drizzle had stopped now. The D.I. hunkered down in front of her, making notes and studying Lily with her penetrating gaze. Micah stood on the other side of the car, arms folded, scanning the tree line, in pure guardian mode again.

There had been no trace of Lily's attacker. By the time the alarm was raised, Sam reckoned, he'd already fled the park and vaulted over a wall somewhere. Lily's description was horribly vague. Big shadowy figure, a glimpse of fever-bright eyes. That was about it. Strong, fast, stealthy, religious nut—all the things they already knew.

Sam ground his teeth together and went back to pacing, trying to spread out his senses wide enough to trace the route the bastard had taken. It was no good. The aftershocks of the murder already committed here were too gruesome. They

157

swamped out the attack.

He'd come close to losing her. Just like Micah had said. For those dreadful moments tearing his way through trees and bushes, he'd been sure he would only find her body. It shouldn't bother him. But it did. Now he just wanted to throw up or tear someone limb from limb. He wasn't sure which urge would win out as yet, and he didn't want to stand still long enough to test any theories.

Reid looked up, catching his eye, and nodded. She was finished. Lily stayed where she was, huddled in on herself, her shorn hair and dirt-splattered face wringing out his heart. One of the medics arrived, replacing the detective. As Sam hastened to Lily's side, Reid intercepted him. He stared down at her, angry at her interference. She'd brought them out here. It was her fault that Lily had been put at risk. Micah moved around the car like a ghost, standing just behind the suddenly nervous doctor.

"I can't apologise enough," said Reid.

Sam glowered at her again. "You can start trying. He might have killed her."

She shook her head. "That isn't his MO, Sam. He kidnaps them first and tortures them before he kills them. I won't lie though, Lily was lucky. I want to tighten the security on her."

"Reid, your people were all over this park. That didn't stop him. Micah and I will be there for her from now on, every second if needs be."

Reid peered over her shoulder again, looking to where Lily and Micah stood, holding each other close. "And you're sure he's legit?"

"As legit as I am." Sam gave a brief laugh at the joke she wouldn't get. Well, that at least was true. He couldn't help himself. "Micah's loved her for years. He'd do anything for her. No way is he a threat. To me perhaps. But not Lily."

"I'm still going to run his details."

Sam frowned. "Why tell me?"

Reid pushed her auburn hair back from her face. "My brother was forever turning up with people like you, Sam Mayell. I learned to recognise those who aren't...well, let's just say entirely of this world, shall we? I'm not sure what side you're on, but I do believe you won't let this psycho get Lily."

"*Psycho*? An emotive word from so cool a professional."

"Technical term," she joked, though her grin was tight with tension. "I will catch him. And I won't let him get near another psychic." There was unexpected vehemence in her voice. He liked that.

"What happened to your brother, Reid?"

Her shoulders stiffened, a defensive posture he knew too well. "He's in a coma. Ever since someone like this attacked him. It doesn't look like he's ever coming out."

"And what about you? Are you psychic?"

She snorted a laugh. "Not unless it's contagious. I'm psychic as a brick, Sam. But I know them." She nodded back towards Lily again. "I know the good they can do. Seen it first hand. And I've also seen their fragility, their needs. She needs to be loved, especially after the shit life she's led."

Shit life? Had to be, he supposed, to leave her so closed off and alone. Reid watched his ruminations with altogether too keen an eye for his discomfort.

"You should ask her about her childhood, Sam. About her family. And about why she's here, living in a rented apartment when she has a mansion in the country to call her own."

He shifted from foot to foot, trying to drive out the wave of tenderness welling inside him for Lily. It wouldn't do any good. He had a mission, a job. He only had a couple of days left.

The thought made his blood chill. Instinct told him she was going to die. That was why he had such a truncated time limit. And Micah said the same thing. If both Heaven and Hell believe it, how could things turn out any other way?

"Your psycho isn't going to leave her be, is he?"

Reid shook her head. "He's marked her. He tested her as a witch and has convinced himself that she is. The hair thing, I don't know. Not yet. But it's the type of humiliation he revels in. He does nothing without reason, however insane his methods might seem to us. Rachel drowned when he subjected her to the trial by water, but Todd survived. He'd done some survival training several years ago. Problem is, a witch hunter expects a witch to escape drowning, so when Todd swam to shore, our killer was waiting for him. Survival meant guilt. So he burned him at the stake."

Sam shuddered. What would that maniac have done with Lily, had Sam not found them? He remembered the witch trials, the things done to those women and men who fell afoul of the Witchfinder General or similar psychotics over the centuries. He wouldn't allow that to befall Lily. Simply couldn't.

But, an insidious little voice in his mind whispered, you'll take her to Hell where they'll do much worse things to her, for all eternity.

"She's safe with Micah and me," he assured Reid. "I want to get her home now. Please, if you get any more information, let us know. But don't involve her like this again. It's too dangerous. He's watching her. And he's just waiting to make his move."

"Sam," Micah called. "They're finished." Lily stood now, snuggling into his side, her arms around him, her eyes huge.

"Time to go. Let me know what you can, Reid? Please?"

She nodded and bid him farewell, turning back to her work. Not as small as Lily, and certainly well able to take care of herself, she looked for a moment quite frail and lost in the twilight. Until she flicked a finger over the radio and began to bark into it again. Sam watched her with growing admiration as she stalked off.

But she wasn't Lily.

Sam sat in the front of the car on the way back, giving Lily the space she needed, the comfort which Micah could offer her effortlessly. Back at the apartment, he watched them, uncomfortable in the face of their understated intimacy, the way Micah calmed her simply by being there.

Sam couldn't even begin to think of a thing to say that might give her ease of mind. The killer had snatched her from right in front of them and they hadn't known. Micah had been the first to realise, not him. The angel had led the way. Only a fluke had brought Sam to her first.

He poured three glasses of twelve-year-old scotch, and neither of them asked where he had found the bottle. Lily wheezed as she tried to drink it. Micah, on the other hand, knocked it back in one go.

Sipping it more carefully, Lily paused only to yawn. She and Micah had settled themselves on the sofa. Sam pulled one of the chairs from the kitchen table and turned its back to them so he could sit astride it. Once she had finished her drink, Lily rested her head on Micah's shoulder and yawned again.

"You should sleep," Sam said, his own glass heavy in his hand, the alcohol untouched. "We'll be here."

"I know," she said in a very small voice which told him at once she didn't quite believe that would make any difference. "But I want to stay here."

"Lily, you've had a hell of a day," Micah said. "He's right, my bright one. You should sleep."

She poked her chin out stubbornly and shook her head. "You'll leave me in there. Alone."

Micah's bright blue eyes lifted to lock on Sam's. Devastated eyes, that looked right inside the soul.

"No," Sam said. "We won't."

"You want both of us with you, Lily?" Micah asked, a slight

161

tremble in his mellow voice betraying him. She nodded, already almost asleep in his arms. "Then...then we'll both be there for you."

Sam inhaled slowly, watching the angel's dilemma, feeling equally conflicted.

Lily pulled herself free and took Micah's hand, reaching out at the same moment for Sam's. He stared at her fingers, tiny little things, but so unbelievably strong. Sam lifted the glass to his lips, never taking his eyes from her hand, her invitation.

It wasn't what had been in his mind when he had suggested the three of them sleep together. But she knew that. Problem was, right now, this was what she needed and there was no way he could refuse.

He drained the glass, sighing heavily as he put it down. His hand met hers and Lily smiled, a shaky, relieved smile.

She led them to her room and almost collapsed on the bed. Both Sam and Micah caught her at the same moment.

"It's okay," Sam said. "You're safe now, Lily."

She swivelled her head, trying to take in both their faces at once. Failing, she pulled free of Sam and turned so she could sit down heavily on the bed, which bounced beneath her. She didn't look big enough to disturb a raindrop.

Lily winced and then brought her free hand up to her shorn hair, raking through it as if trying to work out what had happened. Shock, Sam realised, she was in shock.

"He—he—" Tears spilled from her eyes, cascading down her pale cheeks. "He cut off my hair."

Micah didn't seem capable of movement. He held on to her other hand as if afraid to let her go.

Sam knelt before her, carefully pulling her hand away from the mess the killer had left of her hair. He ran his fingers through the remains, stuck to her scalp with mud and water. "It's just shorter. With the right stylist, you'll love it. It'll be elfin.

A pixie cut. You'll see."

She gave a wary, disbelieving smile.

"Sleep now, Lily," said Micah.

She tugged at her ruined clothes and, belatedly, Sam realised she was still wearing the rags that remained after the killer had attacked her. As she pulled them off, the bandages across her back stood out against the pallor of her skin. She balled her shirt in front of her breasts.

"Here." Micah handed her another T-shirt, taking the shredded clothes she offered him and throwing them away.

They sat on either side of her as she lay down, closing her eyes, her breathing gradually dropping to the level of sleep. But when Micah tried to rise, her hand closed convulsively on his arm, stopping him.

"Lie down," said Sam, softly. "We'll talk tomorrow."

Micah sighed but obeyed him reluctantly, stretching out alongside Lily, on top of the bedclothes, still dressed, too tired to argue. Sam waited and then followed suit.

Lily's breathing levelled out again and finally, finally, he felt her body relax against his.

"Can you really find a hairdresser for her who can do that?" Micah asked, his voice unexpectedly warm and intimate in Sam's mind.

Sam stared at the ceiling, gently stroking the skin of Lily's arm, wondering what Micah's skin would feel like in comparison.

"Believe me, Mike, first thing in the morning, I'm going to track down a fucking award winner and threaten him until he makes her look like a fucking supermodel."

As sleep took him, Sam heard laughter ring around his mind, Micah's laughter.

Chapter Thirteen

Lily stirred, feeling two warm bodies stretched out alongside her. Cocooned between them, she had never felt so comfortable, so content or so safe.

Sam lay on his back, his strong chest rising and falling, a panther at rest. On the other side Micah lay on one arm, his face turned towards her, still sleeping, leonine in comparison. She had never imagined they would sleep, nor that they would need to do so. But there was something beautiful about them at peace she had never expected.

As if he sensed her gaze on his face, Micah's eyes flickered open. Bright blue, alert in that instant, and yet gentle, filled with love.

"Hello, my bright one."

"Micah," she breathed.

A hand ran from her hip, dipping down to her waist and up to the side of her breast. "Don't forget me, sweetheart." Sam. She could never forget Sam.

She smiled. Safe, she was safe. Lying here between an angel and a demon, she was safe. She would have found it ridiculous if she hadn't endured a nightmare the previous night.

"Did they find him?" she asked.

Sam's hand stopped suddenly and withdrew. He pushed himself up on one arm.

"No," said Micah. "I'm afraid not. But they will. Rest assured, Lily. They will."

"Or I will," Sam said in a far more threatening voice. He sat up, swinging his legs off the side of the bed. His whole tone changed as he stood. "Coffee? Then we'll sort out that hairdresser's trip, okay?"

Lily rolled over, staring at him in bewilderment. "Hairdresser's?"

Sam smiled. He was almost convincing. "We aren't staying holed up in here forever, Lily. You can't let him take your freedom away, not without a fight."

He strode out, probably in search of that coffee, she thought grumpily.

Micah kissed her cheek, his lips as soft as feathers, his scent as beguiling as ever. "He's right, though I hate to admit it. Get up, my bright one."

With both of them nagging her, what choice did she have? She struggled out of bed, feeling slightly dazed, as if last night had been a nightmare. But as she moved, the dozens of tiny wounds on her back ached in protest, and it all came flooding back.

"Oh God," she gasped, and her legs gave out beneath her. She hit the ground hard and lay there, trying to breathe until Micah's hands found hers and drew her up.

"Lily," he said, "you're okay." He helped her to stand. "You've got to believe that. He can't touch you with us here and we aren't going to leave your side. I swear it."

Sam dashed into the room, his eyes a little too wild for comfort. "What happened?"

Sudden outrage burst inside her. "I'm not an invalid, or a child," she exclaimed, shaking Micah off. "I'm not an idiot or crazy. I'm not—"

The sob came from nowhere, tearing out of her body, half

in terror, half in rage. She hugged herself and doubled over, trying to stop it before she broke down completely.

Neither of them moved and for that she was grateful. Slowly, determinedly, she gathered her strength and put her self-control back together. Shaking like a leaf in a storm, she straightened and then made herself face them. They stood side by side, angel and demon, light and dark, both completely silent, watching her.

"Don't treat me like one," she said. "Please. Don't."

Micah's breath escaped his lips in a sigh. It wasn't pity, but a strange combination of regret and self-recrimination.

"Given what happened last night, Lily," he said after a moment, "I thought you might be frightened, or defensive. I didn't mean to imply that."

Sam just looked confused but held his tongue. He didn't know, she realised. She thought he knew everything about her, even though she had only known him a short time. He seemed to know her intimately. But he didn't know the whole story of her past.

"They tried to lock me up," she said in a flat tone. "My family, my neighbours, everyone. My gran got me out, brought me home. And when she died they tried again. So I left the house and came here. They used to talk to me like that. *'You're okay Lily, it's going to be okay,'* until I thought I'd go insane anyway, just because of them."

Sam took a wary step towards her and when she didn't react, he wrapped his arms around her. "I'm sorry," he said. "I didn't know."

"I did," Micah admitted, his head bowed. "And I should have realised. Forgive me?"

Tears stung her eyes again. "Of course I do." She stretched out her arms to him and he took her from Sam, holding her close. "I hate this tension. It's like he's already here, with us all the time, breathing down our necks and making us turn on each other." She turned back to face Sam and reached out a hand, which he took, holding it gingerly. "I know this isn't ideal. But I can't lose either of you right now."

"You won't," Sam assured her.

Micah's chest expanded against her back as he breathed. "No," he said finally. "You won't. But it cannot last, my bright one. You know that?"

She didn't know what to say to that, so she ignored it, accepting only the first half of the statement. *No, you won't.* That would have to be enough for now.

Sam shifted uncomfortably, reading the same tension she did. He stroked her hand with his fingers and then fingered the shorn locks of her hair beside her cheek.

"At least let me try to do something with this. If you really won't come out."

She nodded and to her surprise realised Sam had turned his attention to Micah, as if asking his permission as well. Part of her knew she should be outraged, but she wasn't.

Before she knew what was happening, she was sitting on a chair in the kitchen, swathed in a towel, while Sam stood over her with a wickedly sharp-looking pair of scissors and Micah made an early lunch.

"Hold still," Sam told her calmly, holding the scissors up high. "Trust me now."

She did, she knew that. Even though all reason told her that it was foolish to trust a demon. But she couldn't help but do so when Sam smiled, when Sam asked. Micah cleared his throat, although he might have been suppressing a laugh, and she couldn't have that.

"All right then." She sighed. "Let's get started."

It took only a matter of minutes. The scissors blurred, the snips like the chorus of crickets in the evening on some sun-drenched foreign shore. Her hair brushed her cheeks and shoulders as it fell.

When Sam stood back, he wore a speculative expression. "Well?" he said at last. "Go take a look."

Lily went to the mirror over the mantelpiece and stared at the woman whose reflection stared back. A neat style framed her face. She looked younger, brighter, and far more chic than she could remember ever looking in her life. Her grey eyes were huge in a slender face and her copper hair flared out around her cheekbones in—just as he had promised—a pixie-like style.

"It's perfect," she managed. And the tears started to flow again.

Micah had never experienced cabin fever before. He might have hated going out but at least he had the option. In the confines of the apartment, he was aware of every movement of the other two. It was liable to drive him mad. Lily's scent was ever present, but so was Sam's. He passed so close on occasion that Micah could feel his body heat in the air. Lily slept for part of the afternoon, and the two of them circled each other as warily as possible.

When Lily rose again, she showered and dressed, taking her new hairstyle as a cue to pick herself up. In a plain white blouse and jeans, she had never looked so beautiful. As she entered the room, he froze, just watching her cross the living room, stop by the window and pull back the blind so she could look out.

"There's a police car across the road," she said. "I suppose it would be nice to go out, but I don't think Reid would approve. I'd like some fresh air though."

"What about the roof?" he asked, the words out of his mouth before he realised what he was saying. The roof garden, as they jokingly called it, was his place, his sanctuary. True, it was just a few clusters of potted plants and a ragged-looking deckchair now, but in summer, looking out over the city at night, it was so quiet, so peaceful. He'd never brought Lily there, though she knew of it. And since Mrs. Chandler moved into her retirement home, no one used it at all. Her plants would have withered and died without his presence. It was his place, his sanctuary. And if he had brought Lily there, she might have realised he could take human form. But now? What did it matter now?

Sam opened one dark eye but otherwise didn't move from the couch, where he was stretched out, pretending to read an old newspaper. How he thought he could fool them with his eyes closed, Micah didn't know, but Sam didn't seem to care.

"Mind if I give it a miss?" he asked.

It wasn't a question aimed at Lily, Micah knew. It was as important to Sam as to Micah that she should not be left alone for even a second again.

"No, we'll be fine," Micah said, trying to keep the relief from his voice. As they slipped out of the main door, Lily wrapped her hand around his arm and his skin tingled with her touch. His step faltered.

"You okay?" she asked. Micah just nodded and led her up the stairs to the roof.

The breeze was warm and all around them the city was humming with the wind-down to evening. Lights were flickering downtown, where the clubs and bars were just getting started, and the lines of cars heading home gleamed in the setting sun.

Lily stopped, inhaling the scent of jasmine and geraniums. They flowered profusely all around the doorway and doused the area with their fragrance, drowning out the mug of city air.

"It's beautiful," she whispered, her hand tightening on his arm. "I had no idea."

Micah found himself trembling. He had almost lost her last night. She had almost been taken from him forever. He wouldn't let that happen again, no matter what.

169

"What is it?" she asked.

He started. "What?"

"The way you were looking at me. The way your expression was almost—"

"What?"

"Dangerous."

He tried to smile, but couldn't make his mouth obey. "Do you know what angels were, Lily? In the beginning, I mean? The reason we were created?" She shook her head, waiting. "Vessels. Vessels to hold the Divine Will, the Word and the Light, the One. And then, as mankind strayed, He made us something more, enforcers of that Will. Soldiers, if you like, guardians, yes, but more than that. There was a war in Heaven. We fought, we killed, we did dreadful things. I sometimes think that caused the Fall, not the Morningstar, or the God Knife. What we did to each other. How could we ever recover the harmony we'd known? And yet, I'd do the same thing again. I'd take up a flaming sword and fight my brother."

"I see."

"Do you?" With a passion that surprised even him, he pulled her against his body. He was hard already, aching for her from head to foot. "I will not allow that madman to harm you. No matter what it takes. Do you understand?"

She nodded, her eyes darker now in the fading light, their colour melting to shadows with desire. He felt her pulse leap, saw it in her throat, just beneath her skin, erratic and ready for him.

"Lily." His voice rumbled from within and he seized a handful of her newly cropped hair, holding her back so his mouth could plunder hers. She squirmed closer, her nails clawing at his shoulders, pricking his skin through the light cotton of his shirt. "Lily, I could have lost you."

She gasped for a breath as he released her mouth, but her

lips continued to brush against his. "Never, Micah. Never in a million years. You know that, don't you? I love you."

They tumbled to the ground, heedless of comfort or luxury, pulling at their clothes until they could finally sink into each other and be one. As he moved within her, Micah cried out an exaltation that might have seen him cast out of the Holy Court forever if they heard. And they heard everything. He knew that, but he didn't care. He felt her body close and clench around him, heard his name on her musical voice, and he came, no longer caring about his fate, no longer able to care about anything but her.

Chapter Fourteen

It was the work of a minute to secure the door to the apartment, draw the curtains and plunge the place into darkness. Sam didn't want to be disturbed, not by anyone, especially not by Lily and Micah. That said, if their intimacy as they left was anything to go by, that wouldn't be a problem for a little while. No, Sam needed to be alone for this. He didn't want to expose a window into hell to either of them, or anyone else.

He stood in the centre of the living room and with one finger outstretched, concentrated on the fabric of reality. A brief spark greeted him, the warm glow of fire running beneath his skin like minute flames, worming their way down to coalesce beneath his nail. There was a hiss as magic met air and, slowly, he used it to draw a sigil, his finger leaving a glowing trail behind it. The symbol—once a forbidden word in a language now thousands of years dead and forgotten—fluttered, even though there was no breeze, and then twisted on itself, unfolding like the petals of some monstrous flower.

Darkness filled the void in its centre and a face with hazel eyes looked out, placid, calm, terrifying.

"Sammael? What is the meaning of this?" asked the Nameless.

Sam bowed his head but kept himself firmly on his feet. If he had to get out of there quickly, he wanted to be in a position to flee as fast as possible. "I have a question."

"Why do you not come here? Why is your location shielded from me?" Suspicion glistened in the gaze that beat upon him, but Sam held himself firm.

"After my last encounter with Asmodeus, I felt it politic to use a safer environment."

There was a long silence. Sam counted under his breath, wondering if he would actually be able to reach the door in time if the Nameless broke through Micah's wards on Lily's apartment. Evil couldn't enter uninvited. And Lily had only invited Sam, not the rest of the hordes of Hell. In theory anyway. But the Nameless was no ordinary demon.

"Did you indeed?" the Nameless chuckled at last. Something amused him about the statement. Sam just hoped the mood continued to be so genial. "Very well. Ask your question."

"I was given only a week." He paused, waited for a reply.

"That's not a question."

"Why only a week?"

"Why do you think?"

Oh good, thought Sam, questions answered with questions. The Nameless was good at that. He thought it amusing.

"I think that you plan to have her killed, to take her before her time."

The flawless face showed nothing for a moment, a beautiful mask, but then one eyebrow slowly rose. "I *plan* to have her killed? I think you credit me with too much, Sammael. I do not govern when a mortal life shall end. I merely read the book of destiny and wait."

Sam drew in a cold breath. "It's her destiny to die? Is that what you mean?" Both Courts had given a week. Both of them. What else could he mean? Sam's heart thudded dully and his head swam at the thought. No. Please no.

"Destiny is such a controversial word." The Nameless

looked past Sam's spell, at something in his throne room Sam could not see. "Is that it?"

"Wait. Is there a way to stop it?"

The drifting attention of the Nameless snapped back to Sam so quickly it was like a physical blow.

"And why, pray tell, would you want to do that? Mortals die. We collect their souls. Or else they travel to the light. That is the way of things." Sam felt himself studied, dissected, by that gaze and then dropped, like a plaything that no longer held a child's interest. Relief thundered through him, sharp and palpable. "Everyone knows that if a life is forfeit we will have a life, if a soul is forfeit we will have a soul. It matters not which soul. But we will collect one at the appointed time. Come back to me when you have more interesting questions. Or the next time I really will lose my temper with you, Sammael. You've been warned already. Don't make me send Asmodeus to do it again."

The Nameless waved a dismissive hand and the sigil sparked and died, the connection cut off. The bond of magic holding it to Sam snapped back, flinging him to the ground. He sat very still, nursing his head where an ache of colossal proportions was steadily growing.

"Shit," he muttered. "Shit, shit, shit." He had almost lost her once. That had been bad enough. But the witch-crazed maniac was going to come back. Sam knew that. And when that happened, if it was Heaven and Hell's appointed time, Lily was going to die.

A knock on the door brought him out of his daze. Moving quickly, despite the protests of both body and mind, he opened the curtains and headed for the door, rubbing the back of his neck in a vain effort to quell the pain there. He flicked back the chain and opened the door to reveal their other neighbour on the floor, Mr. Hopkins.

"Mr. Mayell?" The middle-aged man blinked at him in

surprise. "What are you doing in here?"

A grey man, Sam had decided on first bumping into him in the hall, some kind of civil servant or accountant who wore nondescript suits all week and nondescript casuals at the weekend. Looking at him now, Sam saw nothing to make him reassess the opinion.

"Oh, just waiting for Lily to get back. We were going to eat. Can I help you?"

"No. Not at all. I just wanted to see how she was. I heard about the commotion the other night."

Was it his imagination or was Hopkins peering past him, trying to see inside the apartment? Sam shifted, blocking the view more completely.

"Well, I'll pass on your best wishes then." *Leave*, he willed the other man. *Just leave.*

"And her...her guest?"

"Her..." *Her guest?* "Oh, Mike. Yeah. They've gone out. Are you sure I can't help you?"

Hopkins looked up into Sam's face for the first time, and his skin paled at whatever he saw there. If it was a shadow of the strength with which Sam was wishing him gone, it should have had him scurrying back to his own apartment in seconds.

"Things have changed since you arrived, Mr. Mayell," said Hopkins, clearly choosing his words with care. "I'm sure you haven't noticed. But this is an...unusual building. We look after our own, and our own problems. Always have done."

With that he left, walking quickly and quietly down the hall. Sam stared after him.

Had he just been threatened, however ineffectively, by an accountant?

Hopkins vanished behind his own door, and Sam stared after him for a few minutes more. To his surprise, he found his hands shaking. An after-effect of his contact with the Nameless, no doubt, one which would be easily solved by a large scotch. He poured it, the splash of the liquid unexpectedly loud in his ears, but he pushed it aside and drained first one glass, then another.

Their voices came from the hall outside, Lily's soft laugh, Micah's rumbling tones. Sam listened, envy rippling through his body. Sometimes he cursed his stronger-than-human senses. Sometimes they offered nothing but pain. Though he couldn't feel what had passed between them in the same way as he had while under Asmodeus's lust spell, he knew what they had done. The scent of their lovemaking travelled through the air ahead of them. It beckoned him, taunted him, and he reacted to it immediately, his body hardening.

What could he do? He was meant to be seducing them, but he constantly felt as if he was the one being seduced. Did they know? Were they doing it intentionally? And to what purpose?

No, it had to stop. He would have to stop it. If he left now...

But then Lily would die. He had to stop that too. He was so wound up in the threads of her life that he was losing himself, but no matter what, he would not let the killer take her, not in the way he had killed Rachel or Todd.

The footsteps stopped short of the door. The scent of desire wavered, and then changed. Like a weathervane in the wind, it swung around from love to fear, and Lily gasped.

He didn't think. In spite of his need to resist her, his body moved without hesitation, his quick strides taking him back to the door, which he flung open.

Micah stood in the hallway, cradling Lily against him. Her face was buried in his chest, and the angel's expression was caught between outrage and horror.

"What is it?" Sam snarled. "What happened?"

"Take it down," Lily sobbed. "Please Sam. Take it down."

Sam swivelled around to see her once-pristine white door

smeared with something red and sticky, and dangling from a nail hammered in it was a felt doll, hand-sewn with red thread. The noose around its neck was fashioned from bright, silken hair. Lily's hair.

Shadows dripped from the doll, tendrils of ill-intent and malice. Combined with the blood—he knew at once it was blood—he had no doubt who had left it there, nor what it was for.

Sam swiped at it, sending it flying across the hall. "What the hell is that thing?"

Surprisingly it was Lily who replied, her voice shaking wildly. "A poppet. It's a charm, a thing to bind or ward off evil. God, my gran used to make them, but—" She shivered. "Not like that. Oh God, Sam, Micah."

"Come inside," Sam said brusquely. "I'll call the police. Where's Reid's number?"

Lily sank onto the sofa while he punched the numbers into the phone. He spoke to her briefly and then slammed down the receiver.

"Who makes poppets in this day and age?" he asked. Micah shot him a glare, a warning and Sam forced his voice to be gentle. "It's more than a harmless charm, Lily. That thing had malevolence dripping from it. That's blood on the door."

"And any charm can be turned to evil intent in the right hands," Micah answered, sitting down beside her and slipping his arm around her shoulders. "That doesn't make the act of making a poppet evil. They've been used for centuries to ward off evil in all sorts of cultures."

Anger still simmered beneath his skin, but Sam walked it off, pacing back and forth.

"Your neighbour came over," he told her. "Hopkins? Real worried about you. He warned me off. Who is he?"

Lily gave him a bemused look. "Mr. Hopkins? He's been

177

here longer than me, longer than Mr. Cassini. I think he works for the city or something. Administration. He told me once he moves departments as they need him—medical, police, public affairs, all sorts of things. He's always been nice. Just a good neighbour." She paused, leaning back into Micah's arms again.

Sam bit on his lower lip and tried not to glare. He had no reason to be jealous, he told himself. If he clicked his fingers, she'd be his. All he had to do was say the word.

"You've never been the target of a serial killer before," Micah put in.

Sam shook his head. "There's more to it than this. Your grandmother made these things?"

"You really hate them, don't you?" Lily asked.

Rolling his eyes, Sam tried to plough on. Even the thought of it made his skin crawl, as if it was trying to get away from the poppet without the rest of him. "Did she or didn't she?"

"Yes. I have a journal of hers. She was a white witch, a psychic like me. She was the one who looked after me."

And got her out of whatever place her parents had locked her away, but Sam didn't really want to bring that one up again. "You have it? Where?"

"Downstairs. In my storage area in the basement."

Sam crossed to her. "Let's get it. I want to look at it."

"Now? Sam, the police will be on their way, won't they?"

"Then Micah will be here when Reid arrives. It'll take a few minutes, Lily, and it could be important. Reid's going to want to know about it. A poppet is an old charm. Seriously. No one makes them anymore."

"What are you saying?"

He didn't want to say it. He didn't even want to think it. "What if they used your grandmother's book to do it?"

The basement of the building was accessed by a narrow

staircase and looked like a rabbit warren of locked doors. They'd been designed for individual storage but most of the tenants didn't bother. Lily moved with accustomed ease through the thin passage to a door third from the end and fished the key out of her pocket.

"That's yours," she told him, nodding at the door to her left, which stood ajar. Sam rolled his eyes as if that was the last thing of importance. She gave him a nervous grin and opened her own door. She tried to flick on the light inside, but nothing happened. "Ugh, the electrics in this place are shot. My fault, I guess."

"Your fault?"

"Yes. Sometimes, when a spirit comes it seems to—I don't know—overload the circuits. Only sometimes."

Not since he'd been with her. She didn't say that but he could see it in her expression. He had stopped consciously trying to block her, but he suspected he was still having an effect. What spirit lost between Heaven and Hell wanted to come anywhere near a demon?

"Anyway," Lily sighed, stepping into the dark cupboard-like room beyond, "I know where it is. Just give me a second."

Sam stood back, admiring the way her rear swayed as she bent to rummage through a box on a low shelf. It was half in shadow and beautifully curved.

"Got it," she said, triumphant.

But as she stood and turned, an ancient-looking tome clasped to her chest, the door slammed shut between them. Sam cursed, and Lily's muffled cry pitched him at the door. The handle jammed as he tried to open it.

"Where's the key?" he yelled, though he knew the answer. She had it with her. "Lily? Lily, can you hear me?"

There was no answer, but another muffled cry of fear, words he couldn't make out. He hung off the handle, trying to force the door open with brute strength alone. Nothing happened. He couldn't get her out. He didn't have Micah's skill with locks and—

"*Micah!*" He made his sending loud and desperate. He didn't care if every supernatural being in the vicinity heard him. "*Get down here! Lily's in trouble!*"

The sound of a scuffle came from the far side of the door, then a thud, followed by Lily's voice, thin and stretched with terror. "Sam? Oh God, Sam, is that you? Stop it. Please, please, stop it."

Sam pounded on the door, his physical strength meaningless, futile. "Lily!"

But she didn't respond. She couldn't hear him, not through the heavy door. But his hearing was supernatural. He could hear her, hear her voice choking, her breath fading, her words. "I'm not... You'll...kill me. Sam, please don't."

Then silence, a terrible lingering silence like a shroud. Sam stepped back, staring at the door. He touched it with an outstretched finger, ready to summon all the fires of Hell to blast it out of his way. He'd pay for it but what did that matter? What did anything matter now? His skin warmed, glowed, readying itself for the passage of power.

Something came down hard and heavy on the back of his head, felling him effortlessly and sending him tumbling to the ground.

For a moment everything was wonderful. Burrowing through the box, Lily turned up items from her childhood that reminded her of good times instead of bad. Things she associated with Gran, from a china figurine to tattered photos, from old diaries to the small stack of her notebooks. She felt the soft leather binding brush against her fingertips and knew she had found it, knew by touch alone, though she hadn't laid hands on the book in years. She pulled it out, dust billowing around her, catching the light from outside.

A shadow moved, flickered across the corner of her eye, so fast she though she might have imagined it. She turned, catching Sam's gaze and smiling in her victory, hugging the book to her.

Then the door slammed shut and she was plunged into darkness. She screamed before she knew what she was doing, unable to move for fear of taking a tumble in the pitch blackness of the storage room. The noise of the lock slamming home broke the spell and she lurched forward, feeling for the door.

"Sam? Sam! Let me out!" She fumbled until she found the handle, but it was stuck, just as if someone was holding it from the other side, or had jammed it somehow. "Sam! Let me out!"

There was no answer. Breathing hard, she tried to push at the door, ramming her shoulder against it, the book digging into her ribs.

A hand touched her cheek, feather-light, and was gone. A low chuckle ran around the tiny room, bouncing off the boxes and forgotten oddments of a life she didn't really want to remember. Lily froze, trying not to breathe. Someone else was in there with her. Even her pounding heart seemed too loud.

"You know, for a witch," said a too-familiar voice, "you're mightily predictable."

The scream burst from her lips. She couldn't help herself. Sam's name was tangled in there amid the incoherency, and Micah's, but she knew they couldn't hear her. A leather-gloved hand slammed over her mouth, silencing her, the hand belonging to the killer.

Lily recognised his voice, his touch, the smell of him, all starch and detergent. She struggled against him, but he was so strong. Impossibly strong.

"Hush now, you little whore." His breath trailed over her ear. "It's holy work we're about here."

181

There was no way out of here. She knew that. Not for him or for her. Sooner or later Sam would get the door open but... But Sam had been the only person with her. Her breath hitched in her throat as the thought coalesced. It couldn't be. It didn't sound like him. It couldn't be Sam!

But who else could it be? The door had been locked, so no one could have been waiting inside. There was only Sam! And a demon could disguise his voice.

The hand lifted and she found herself spun around, her face shoved back against the door. The words that fell from her mouth came out in a babble. "Sam? Oh God, Sam, is that you? Stop it. Please, please, stop it."

Something pulled tight around her throat and suddenly she was fighting for breath. "Confess your congress with a demon, your practice of witchcraft and your evil arts. Confess what you are, witch, and save your soul."

"I'm not," she tried to say through sobs and the terrible constriction cutting off her breath.

He pressed in against her. "They won't get to you in time. No one is coming to help you. I am your only help. Confess what you are and save your soul."

"You'll kill me..." ...*anyway*, she tried to say, but the darkness around her was seeping into her mind, through her sluggish blood and breath.

"I don't even have to test you," her captor snarled, spit flecking against the back of her neck. "I know already that the water would reject you. I know what you are. I've watched you! Satan's whore, queen of harlots, a Jezebel and a Lilith. You fell so long ago, and as soon as I laid eyes on you I knew you for what you were. Confess it, and save your soul."

"Sam, please...don't," she gasped, and it was her last breath. The noose cut off her air and the world around her spun with shadows and spirals of light. She struggled, fought, tried to claw her way free, but nothing worked. Nothing. She felt her eyes close and something inside her gave way to despair. *"Help me, Micah, Sam, make it stop."*

Even with that final thought, everything slid away from her like molasses on glass.

Chapter Fifteen

Micah raced down the stairs, heedless of anyone in his way. He pushed past two of Lily's neighbours without so much as a word, their startled voices trailing after him. The basement door was swinging as he reached it and flung it open. In the narrow passage below, Sam sprawled on the floor, nursing his head as he struggled to get up. When he pulled his hand away from his hair, it was glossy with blood.

"What happened?" Micah yelled. "Where is she?"

Sam jerked up. "Someone hit me from behind." He reeled as he tried to stand, lurching towards the door. Micah pushed him back and bent his will to the locked door. A moment passed, two.

The lock clicked open and he pushed the door. Something was blocking it. He shoved harder and the same something, a dead weight, scraped across the floor to allow him access.

It was Lily.

For a moment it felt like the ground had fallen away from beneath his feet, like his whole body had frozen, hanging there between moments. Then her chest stirred, so weakly, her heartbeat giving a flurry like a dying bird.

Micah dropped to his knees and pulled her into his arms. A red line stood out on her neck, but there was no sign of whatever her assailant had used.

"Lily? Wake up. Talk to me. Lily!"

"Here, let me," Sam said, trying to push past him. Micah held firm. "Let me help!"

Sam's hands were aglow with demon-fire. He needed to vent it somewhere. Better he used it for good than for ill. All these thoughts ran through Micah's head but it still took a moment before he could persuade himself to stand, turn around and let Sam touch Lily.

The air sizzled, crackling with electricity, and in his arms Lily gave a huge gasp, gathered in lungfuls of air and jerked convulsively. Staggering back, Micah almost fell himself, but he kept his ground, standing with Lily in his arms in the deep darkness of the storage room, illuminated by the spark and crackle of demon fire.

Lily opened her eyes and looked up at Micah, only at Micah. "He was in here. I think it—I think it was Sam."

Strange, thought Micah, how easy it was to see someone else's heart break. Sam's face turned to stone, to carved ice. His eyes glittered with disbelief and the blood drained away from his skin, leaving him a pale comparison of himself, a hollowed-out shell.

Micah let loose the light within himself, let it flow over her and soothe her to sleep. It took an instant and then Lily wilted in his arms again, into a dreamless slumber that would help her recover and heal. He lifted his eyes to look at the demon again.

Sam took a step back, his back coming up against the far wall.

"No," he whispered. There was no rage. Not as Micah would have predicted. He'd expected the wrath of a thwarted demon but Sam's expression just held heartbreak. Just emptiness. Pure pain. "Micah, please, tell her no."

To an angel, the pain of another was like his own pain. Even the pain of an enemy, of a demon. And Sam's pain shattered him.

"She can't hear you," he managed eventually. "Let's get her back to her apartment. We'll talk there."

"Talk?" The word burst out of his mouth and the fury Micah had expected arrived in a deluge. "She was on the other side of the door. Dying! I could hear her, Micah. I could hear her being killed."

Ignoring him, Micah started up the stairs. Lily was no weight in his arms, no weight at all.

Reid was waiting at the open door of the apartment, already calling in a report on her radio. When she saw them her face brightened with relief then chilled with alarm.

"What happened?"

"He was in here," Micah barked, pushing past her. "In the basement. He nearly killed her."

"I-I'll call it in, get some EMTs in."

"She's okay," Sam said, though he lingered in the doorway, leaning on the frame. "Isn't she? She's okay."

Micah laid her down on the sofa, brushed his hand over her smooth skin and sighed. That fear again, that terror of losing her. It stole his strength, snatched away his self-control.

"She's okay," he said, more for Sam's benefit than anyone else's. "Aren't you, Lily?"

He glanced up over his shoulder. Reid was gabbling into that damned radio again, and in seconds her cohorts were scouring the door and the hallway, gathering evidence. But Sam hardly moved. He stepped inside, but not by much.

"Lily?" Micah called her back reluctantly, drew her from the sleep that would help and heal her. Her dove grey eyes opened and she stared into his face as if she hardly recognised him. Still dazed from his spell, still in shock from the attack. "Lily, D.I. Reid is here to talk to you about the poppet. Remember the poppet?"

She uncurled her hands around the book and sat up. As

her eyes snagged on Sam, she hastily dropped her gaze. "Tell him I'm sorry," she said in a low voice only he could hear. "Tell him." Micah nodded discreetly and drew back, letting Reid in to talk to her.

Sam waited by the door, trying to stay out of the way and out of sight, trying—in a way a man such as Sam could never do—to fade into the background. Micah took his place by the demon's side and watched the women talk, Reid leaning in close, radiating comfort and safety, Lily responding with the few details she could recall.

"She knows it wasn't you," he said softly, and Sam's dark brows drew together in a confused frown.

"That wasn't what she said. Anyway, I thought it would suit you if she believed it was. Neat way to get rid of me, isn't it?"

Micah grinned humourlessly. "Maybe. But I doubt even you could knock yourself out from behind." Sam was right of course. If Lily really did believe he had attacked her down in the basement, it would make Micah's defence of her soul far easier. But it would be based on a misunderstanding, if not a lie. Micah knew that. And he couldn't do it.

Reid's sergeant bustled in, getting a glare for interrupting her which he promptly ignored. So Reid listened to what he had to say and, as he finished, her eyes flicked up to meet Sam's. Her stare held suspicion and a shade of angry betrayal.

"Okay, Lily," she said in her calmest, most professional voice. "I'm going to have Dr. Graham check you out, and then I'll be back. Okay?"

Her voice was too bright, too brittle. Something inside Micah recoiled. Something was wrong.

She crossed to them and when she spoke it wasn't with the carefree tone. Her voice was heavy with suspicion. "So the storage area next to Lily's has a hole in the panelling, easily large enough for someone to get through at speed. And who owns that storage space, Mr. Mayell?"

"The building?"

Micah winced at Sam's insolent demeanour, but said nothing to interrupt. What could he say? He could guess what was coming.

"It's your name on the lease. Your storage area."

"One for which I never received a key. Ask Cassini."

"Oh, I will," she said. "Rest assured. Given Lily's initial belief that you attacked her, and your statement that you were locked outside, it seems strange, knowing that there was an easy way in and out the whole time. Doesn't it?"

Sam's upper lip curled in distaste, but this time at least, he held his tongue.

"And what about my statement, D.I. Reid?" Micah asked. "I found Sam almost unconscious with a head wound."

Reid cast a scathing gaze over him. It felt like sandpaper on his skin. "Well, that cleared up nicely. How convenient." She turned to go, but Sam caught her arm.

Reid snapped around to face him and at least three of her officers did the same, ready for an assault. But Sam just turned his hand around and spread his palm out before her. It was caked with his blood, most of it dried. Some still fresh.

"Is that convenient enough for you?" he asked. "Head wounds bleed a lot, D.I. Even a small one. Ask your pet quack. And I heal quickly."

Reid just stared at him. "I trusted you," she said at last.

"And you still can. I would never do anything to harm Lily. I can't."

And that at least, Micah thought grimly, was true.

It seemed to take hours. Lily sat on the far side of the room, surrounded by EMTs and cops. People scoured the hall outside and more of them swarmed over the basement. Micah and Sam sat at the kitchen table, watching it from a distance, lost in their own thoughts about humankind. Sam looked shattered.

Every few minutes his hands would start shaking again. He curled them into fists and then stretched out the fingers, as if trying to make it go away. Micah just watched him in silence.

For all his charm and the bonds upon him, Sam was still a demon, and if he did lose control here— He might not be able to hurt Lily, but there were a lot of other people in the vicinity.

"What's wrong?" Micah asked.

Sam looked at him as if he had lost his mind. "*What's wrong?*" He let out a long hiss of breath. "If you tell me to calm down and offer me a coffee, Micah..."

Micah smiled. "She's okay."

"Thanks to you. I couldn't save her. And some—some mortal overpowered me, left me helpless."

Sammael, the Angel of Death, the Seducer of Souls, an entity who had never been made subject to a being less than himself. Yes, it would hurt.

"She's okay," Micah repeated. "And she knows it wasn't you. In her heart."

Sam looked away, shook his head. "How could she ever forgive me?"

"You underestimate her."

"Or perhaps—" Sam sighed, "—I overestimated myself. He knocked me out cold, Micah. I couldn't open the door and then he came up behind me without me hearing a thing and knocked me out cold."

"And it's never happened before?"

"With a mortal? Are you kidding?" He caught the rise in his voice, Reid's glare, Lily's widening eyes. It took him a moment to swallow down his outrage. "No. It has never happened before. There are demons who can take me. Angels, sure. But no mortal."

Micah hummed as a new suspicion rolled through his mind. "So what if it wasn't a mortal?"

Sam groaned and buried his head in his hands.

The cops took their time about leaving, but eventually, with a great sense of relief, Micah closed the door on them. Which left him with the other two, each of them suffering, each of them in pain.

Words were going to avail them nothing, he knew that. Lily claimed she didn't trust Sam anymore and that was destroying him. The problem was, for the first time since all this began, Micah did trust him. How could he fail to? Whether Sam realised it or not, his burst of demonic energy had saved her life, given her the energy she needed to recover from the attack. But Sam didn't see it that way. All Sam saw was a failure to get through a locked door in corporeal form, a failure, in fact, to do the impossible. All Sam could hear was Lily dying.

There was nothing for it but to do the one thing he dreaded having to do.

"*Come here,*" Micah sent, and the demon looked up, his whole demeanour sharp and suspicious. Nestled in the sofa, Lily seemed to catch some hint of the contact as she too became still and alert, watchful. Micah hardened himself, closed off his feelings. What he was about to do was an act worthy of a bastard like Sam. He knew he had changed. It was inevitable when you strayed down forbidden pathways. His eyes lingered on Lily as the thought came to him. Even when those pathways were so beguiling.

Sam rose from his chair and crossed the room, his head held high, like a prisoner walking to the executioner's block.

"Sammael," said Micah. "You aren't welcome here anymore. The wards placed on this home constrain you, the bonds placed on your behaviour compel you. By the power of the Lord I name you a demon, Sammael, and I cast you out by the Word of the Creator." Sam took a step back and his face paled. Shock and betrayal etched lines on his face as the power of the angel entangled him, so much stronger than he'd ever given Sam to imagine. Now he understood though, what he had been playing with. Now he realised who he had truly underestimated.

"Micah, no." Sam dropped to his knees, gasping for air, trying to cling to the world while Micah's power forced him back into the shadows. "Please, no!"

The pain of it hit him and Sam screamed. There had to be pain for a banished demon. It was not the nature of banishment to be without suffering. Micah knew that. Although never formally banished from the Holy Court, all down the long years of exile on this earth, he himself had suffered, until they had assigned him to Lily. Besides, a demon was a demon, and destined to suffer for the crime of forsaking their holy birthright. The angel in him accepted this, rejoiced in it. Something else wept.

Sam's back arched as the gateway to Hell which he carried within him flexed and began to open. His head rolled back, his mouth opening wide, gaping with agony.

Micah stood before him, a rock without pity or mercy. He could show no mercy now. Not to a demon. Everything in his soul yearned to despatch Sam quickly and bind him in the inferno. "I send you back to the pit from which you—"

"Stop it!" Lily screamed. She ran to Sam's side and grabbed his arm, hot wind tearing at her hair and clothes. "Micah, no! You can't do that."

And there was the answer. In her face, in the love welling from her eyes. Micah lowered his gaze, releasing Sam with the merest thought. The tumult all around them fell still.

"You love him, Lily. As much as you love me." *Perhaps more.* Yes, that was his greatest fear, though he couldn't voice it.

She sobbed at the words, but didn't release Sam. Slowly, as if unable to believe what he was hearing, or that he was actually free, Sam turned towards her and wrapped his arms around her. Kneeling, he came up to her waist, and he pressed his face to her stomach. Tears streamed down her cheeks, silvering them.

"Don't make me choose between you, Micah." Her voice came out trembling like a reed. "I can't. I'm not strong enough." Her hands reached for him and he went, no longer caring about Heaven or Hell. She was all that mattered. Lily. And by extension, Sam. Because she loved him, and to lose him would hurt her. As he hugged her to his body, Micah reached down and tangled his fingers in the dark curls of Sam's hair.

Because she wasn't the only one.

He breathed the two of them in, their scents, their emotions, their love. "I think—" It almost didn't bear saying. But how could he leave it unsaid? "I think we've doomed ourselves to be together. What other way is there?"

"Love isn't a sentence, Micah," said Lily. "But how can this be? Isn't it wrong?"

"It isn't," Sam said. "You've changed us, Lily. I don't know how, or why. And I don't know what the outcome will be, what judgement they will hand down on us for it." He looked up, his chocolate brown eyes reflecting back their own images to them. "And part of me doesn't care."

Yes, Micah thought. How could anyone care about the future standing here, wrapped in the two of them, feeling emotions riot inside. Because in all of Heaven or Hell, or the earth between, there was nothing that felt like this.

"Come," he said, and dipped his head to Lily's mouth, capturing her sweet lips so he could kiss her and drive all concerns from her mind. Pleasure had its purpose and sometimes that purpose was comfort.

She groaned into his mouth, her body heating against his. Sam's hold on her tightened, his fingers stroking her skin where her shirt had pulled out of her jeans.

Sometimes that purpose was to assuage the growing hunger to join, to be one. Sometimes that was the only thing

192

one could do.

Lily's hands pressed against his chest, exploring the planes of his flesh through his shirt. His tongue danced around hers, penetrating deep into her mouth, while his hands slid up her back beneath the blouse. His fingers brushed her skin and then encountered Sam's doing some exploring of their own. Micah's heart thudded, very loud, a crazy rhythm as he struggled to maintain some last vestige of control.

"I want you." Lily's lips fumbled against his, her hips arching towards Sam. She looked at Micah with eyes that had gone beyond desire into some ancient and limitless place of pleasure, of need. "I want you both." Her face flushed with shame, but she didn't look away.

"It isn't wrong, Lily," Micah said. "Love is all. That's what He always says. So this can't be wrong."

Micah moaned as his mouth took hers again and that control he thought he could cling to slipped out of reach.

Lily wasn't sure how she moved. It felt like floating, buoyed up between the two of them, set aglow from within by need and desire. Micah guided her backwards, through the bedroom door, but Sam eased her down onto the edge of the bed. Micah was still kissing her, his mouth moving in perfect time with hers, his hands resting now on her shoulders.

Sam knelt in front of her and slid his hands between her knees, pushing them inexorably apart. His fingers moved up her thighs, stopping as he reached the crease where her legs and body met. Micah released her, moving behind to massage her shoulders before bending to kiss her neck. Sam bowed his head towards her mons and inhaled deeply. His nostrils flared as he did so and he shuddered from head to foot.

Micah's teeth grazed the line of her jugular and she lost herself in the gasp of sensation the touch induced, her head falling back to the angel's shoulder. Sam teased her through the thick material, rubbing against her until she arched up again. He moved quickly, unbuttoning her fly and pulling off her jeans. She sat naked from the waist down, one man behind her, his fingers trailing down towards her breasts, his mouth making her skin shiver, and the other kneeling between her feet, like a supplicant before a queen.

Sam bent again, his tongue trailing a line from her hip to the very edge of her downy hair. She cried out, trying to wriggle free as he teased her, tickling her sensitive skin. But Micah's hands pinned her arms to her side and then slipped down their length. He caught her thighs, pulling them apart for Sam, holding her open for him, her arms still trapped beneath his.

Her demon grinned, his eyes sparkling. Very slowly, his hands brushed back her pubic hair, parting it so that her vagina was revealed to him. Gently questing fingers eased her body open for him, and tenderly Sam bent to her, his breath dancing across her skin. Lily inhaled, waiting for his touch, his maddening, magnificent touch.

But before Sam's mouth could claim her, Micah released her thighs to the demon's grip and began some exploration of his own. His fingertips trailed down the neckline of her shirt, peeling back the material to give his lips access. He slipped the buttons free and his hands cupped her breasts through the lace of her bra, brushing his thumbs against her nipples until they hardened, the texture of the lace making them even more sensitive. They ached for him.

Sam's tongue darted forward, swirling around the edge of her vagina, the tip tasting each fold of skin, as if drawing back the petals of an exotic flower. Her clitoris throbbed, and inside her the now familiar melting of desire seized her. His lips brushed the hood of her clit, easing it back and he sucked, hard.

Lily groaned out her need and Micah turned her face to the side so he could kiss her again, his mouth hot and demanding as he pulled her shirt down her arms, the material teasing her flesh. She leaned back against his chest as he unhooked her bra and filled his hands with the full weight of her breasts. He shifted behind her, the bed's movement nearly throwing her off balance.

Part of her was shocked at where she found herself, afraid of the spiralling emotions, the whirl of desire and of the prospect of two men. As a fantasy it was wild and uninhibited, but as reality— She trembled at the prospect.

Sam's tongue pressed into her depths, deep inside her, curling and unfurling. Lily's blood surged through her body and she called out his name. His fingers bit into her skin, holding her still so he could continue his intimate caresses. The breath hitched in her throat.

Micah moved and she fell back, her upper body bouncing onto the bed, thrusting her hips at Sam's face. Micah's mouth closed on her right breast, the pressure of his mouth wringing another cry from her.

She stared at the ceiling, her body rippling with sensation as they licked, sucked and drew groans of pleasure from deep inside her. She couldn't help herself. The idea of the two of them together was bad enough. Her stomach clenched with just the thought. But the reality. Oh, the reality.

Micah switched breasts, his hands still smoothing her skin, electrifying it with every touch. And Sam—oh God, Sam—Sam licked her from clitoris to perineum and back. He slipped his hands under her ass cheeks as he drove her passion higher, squeezing them, pulling them gently apart. His teasing fingers probed the edges of her anus, spreading her own juices all around the tight hole, easing gently inside, stirring her body higher and higher. A stuttering cry broke from her lips, fear and desire and blind need combined. She wanted more. So much more.

Her clitoris burned for him, for them. Lily pressed herself

against Sam's mouth, arched her chest for Micah's. She had no idea what this was leading to, and yet it was inevitable. Micah lifted his head, and she opened her eyes, watching his assiduous expression as he watched her, waiting for her to come.

At the thought, she lost control in a blissful surge that exploded from Sam's mouth and coursed through her body. Her back and hips started to lift but her lovers pushed her down with gently determined hands, holding her there so that the only way to express the joy, the rapture was to cry out and shudder beneath them.

Micah brushed his fingers through her hair, his touch so light, so tender that she wanted to cry. As Sam rose from his knees, she gazed up at them both, dark and light, her lovers.

"Lie still," Sam told her. "Let us."

And what could she do but obey? She closed her eyes and surrendered herself to the sensations as the bed shifted again, rolling her body from one side to the other as Sam climbed up the length of her and stretched himself out alongside her. Two mouths closed on her, one on each breast, two sets of fingers caressed her body, stimulating her all over again until they entwined together at the delta between her legs. Madness, she told herself, but such bliss.

"This isn't over yet, my bright one." Micah smiled against her skin. His breath set every nerve ending sparking. He slipped one finger deep inside her, then two. Or was it just him?

Her inner muscles clenched and both of them sighed.

No, she reminded herself. This wasn't over yet. And part of her prayed it never would be.

"Roll over," Sam told her, "on top of him. Take him into you, Lily. Show me how you love him."

Half dazed, she tried to lift herself. Four hands helped her, cradling her, positioning her where they wanted until she found herself astride Micah's glorious body, the length of his cock

196

pressing to the most intimate parts of her body. She rocked against him, unable to hide her smile.

Desire flickered across Micah's face, his blue eyes glowing from within. He entered her, and she slid down his whole length until he filled her, stretched her. Her body pulsed around him and she tried to press closer. His hands closed on her hips, holding her still, refusing to let her take him as every instinct told her.

Sam's fingers parted her ass cheeks, a silky smooth liquid coating them. What it was or where he got it she neither knew nor cared, but she welcomed it, relished it. He worked it around the rose of her anus, carefully probing until she opened to him. First one finger, then two, easing their way inside, stretching her. She cried out at this forbidden pleasure and all it implied, and Micah lifted her, his broad length stimulating every fibre of her being.

Sam's body pressed against her back, his cock resting between her ass cheeks while the warmth of his skin flowed over her. His breath played against the nape of her neck, stirring the delicate hairs there. His hands closed over Micah's, the two of them holding her, holding each other. All it took was a simple flex of her hips, forward onto Micah and back, so that Sam's slick cock slid into her ready anus.

Lily flung back her head and cried out his name. They stilled, letting her adjust, letting her burning body absorb all they had to give until she wanted more again. So much more. Then Micah thrust and it was his name on her lips. She pulled herself up the length of Sam's cock in a luscious slide and then thrust back to impale herself right to the root. Not pain, not as she might have thought, just raw pleasure, as close to agony and ecstasy as anyone could endure.

Sam growled, the noise cascading through her. She bent forward, taking Micah's mouth with her own demanding lips, teeth and tongue. Sam and Micah thrust in tandem, one, then the other, filling her, branding her, making her theirs and theirs alone. Micah kissed her, his teeth grazing her lower lip, and white hot lust speared through her. She couldn't stand it.

"Lily," Sam gasped, his body straining. She clenched hard around him as Micah surged up between her legs again. Her angel's eyes darkened, filled with her reflection, the hunger in her own face, and behind her shoulder, Sam's face, Sam's desire.

The demon pushed himself deep inside her and the bright spark of her orgasm ignited. Two men filled her, played with her, brought her body to the throes of the most exquisite bliss she had ever dreamed of. Sam moaned, burying his face into her shoulder and Micah gasped as her body seized him, riding him despite his best efforts to contain her. Sam's teeth grazed her skin, his breath, his tongue washing over her and then he bit.

The world coalesced to just the three of them, and in a brilliant rush of energy and pure joy, Lily came. Her body claimed them both. Sam cried out her name, emptying himself inside her, and Micah's orgasm brought his back up off the bed, arching like a drawn bow. Her inner walls contracted with need, with want, and he came, pumping up into her until she shuddered into stillness once again.

Lying there in a sprawl of limbs, sweat-sheened bodies entangled on the expanse of her bed, Lily breathed easily once more.

"I need you." A body pressed against her mouth, and she was not even aware which of them it was anymore. Hands soothed her ravaged body, caressed her tortured muscles, and eased her into something resembling sated sleep. "I need you both. I always will."

Chapter Sixteen

Sam woke to fingers trailing delicate lines across his chest, teasing the dark hair that sprinkled around his hardened nipples. Lily laughed as he stirred beneath her touch, the low chuckle she gave rumbling through his body like his own. She rocked towards him and gave a little sigh, her mouth parting as she did so.

"Yes?" Micah asked, his deep voice so gentle that it seemed to caress Sam's ears. He was fucking her, pressed along the length of her back, making love from behind in a gently rolling rhythm. The movement set Sam's cock stirring and Lily smiled, her eyes opening to find his.

"You're awake," she said. "I thought you might sleep all morning."

Sam cupped her breasts, lifting them, pinching her nipples between thumb and forefingers. "So did you think to start without me?"

"Can't wait forever." Micah thrust a little harder. Lily cried out, and her features softened as her desire took hold of her. God, he could watch her for eternity, Sam thought, caught in a moment like this.

Sam edged closer so he could kiss her. As their lips met, her mouth turned demanding, drawing him into her, devouring him. He brought his hand down to her clit, finding it unerringly, brushing against the surge of Micah's cock as he did so. They both stiffened, then gasped, and Sam smiled against Lily's ravening mouth.

"You're incorrigible," she told him and wrapped her arms around him.

"My turn," he told her.

Micah laughed as he withdrew, relinquishing her. He rolled onto his back, spent and languorous now. Sam pulled Lily astride him. She complained for a second, only as long as it took for him to slide inside her and pull her firmly down on him.

"Tell me what you want," he asked.

She tossed back her head, lifting herself and dropping down his length again, impaling herself in an act of pure pleasure.

"I want you."

"And what do you want to do to me?"

"I—" She glanced to one side, to Micah. Sam glanced too, couldn't help himself. The angel was watching them with an indulgent smile on his face.

"Are you going to allow her to tell me?"

"It's nothing to do with me, unless she needs me involved. Do you, Lily?"

She smiled and closed her inner muscles around him so hard it was Sam's turn to gasp. "I want you like this, spread out, but, like the other night, tied to my bed. Mine. I want you to be mine."

He flexed his hips, driving deeply inside her. Lily's body rippled around him and he knew he'd lose it. No matter how much he wanted to make it last, no matter how much he wanted to bring her again and again, he knew he would come. She would make him.

"I am yours. I want the same."

"You'll let me tie you up?" She seemed surprised. Her eyes

flicked to Micah again.

"Both of you," he assured her. "And will you return the favour?"

Her hips swirled as she came, her body taking him with her. He arched up from the bed, just as he had watched Micah do last night. He couldn't help himself. But she fell forward first, sated, exhausted.

As Lily slumped down on top of him, Micah's mouth found hers. Sam watched them kiss, lying beneath them, unfulfilled but floating in a world of perfect peace. The angel broke away from her and reached out, his fingertips tracing the lines around Sam's mouth, his eyes. Light blossomed between them, holy light, the contact of divine creatures. Nothing could compare to the sensation, Lily astride him, Micah's touch. He stiffened, the pulse beginning anew, lines of pleasure arcing through him like lightening. He came with a cry of iridescent pleasure and Lily gave that same low laugh, the one which coiled around his heart and loins, binding him to her.

"I fear you'll be the death of me, Lily," he moaned, closing his eyes and feeling all strength ebb from his body.

"Are you planning on going back to sleep, Sammael?" Micah asked. "I'd heard so many stories, I'd expected more stamina."

Lily slid down between them, wriggling into the narrow space. "What sort of stories?" she asked with a giggle.

"Well, let's see," Micah went on, "there was the Duke of Aquitaine's second wife, and his daughter, there were a couple of queens, and at least one Empress, wasn't there?"

"I'm not listening to you," Sam groaned, wishing only for silence and peace, and for this closeness never to end. Though he could never admit the last part.

"Ah, but you are," Micah teased. "How many nuns, Sammael? I never really got a definitive number."

Growling in feigned bad humour, but inwardly smiling at them both, he rolled out of the bed, flicking the sheets carefully back over Lily's body. "I'm making coffee," he said. "Best damn thing humankind ever invented, coffee."

"Just be careful you don't meet another woman on the way to the kitchen," Lily called after him. The two of them collapsed into gales of laughter. Sam didn't bother to hide the grin on his face when they couldn't see it. Stupid, to feel this much pleasure out of the bedroom, but there it was. A warm glow—friendship, amusement.

Love?

He huffed out his breath through his nostrils. "You'd have to deserve love in the first place," he muttered to himself.

The shower started up in the en suite. Sam ran his fingers through his hair. He needed a shower too. But later. Right now, he just wanted to spend some time with Lily and Micah, enjoy this while he could, while it lasted. It was only a matter of time, he realised that, but while it lasted—

Lily's arms slipped around his chest and she pressed her face against his back.

"Thanks," she said.

"My pleasure." No denying that. His body still hummed with the aftermath of the pleasure, trembled with the promise of more whenever she touched him. Like now.

A knock sounded against the front door. Lily sighed and bent her head forward against his back as she sighed.

"I'll get it."

"No. Let me." The last thing he wanted was her opening the door to the killer.

"You've got no clothes on and I doubt that Mr. Hopkins or Cassini's hearts would be up to the shock." She laughed. "I had some forethought." She stretched her arms wide and did a twirl to show off her silken robe. It covered her at least, but given the nature of the material it didn't do much to disguise the curves beneath.

"Still," he told her, catching her arms to hold her back as she tried to walk away. "It only takes a second to throw something on. Don't answer. Promise me."

"All right," she sighed. The knock came again, a little more urgently. "But be quick."

He was already tugging on his jeans when Micah appeared from the bathroom doorway.

"What is it?" the angel asked. He had only a towel wrapped around his waist and water glistened in his golden curls.

"Someone at the door."

A muffled voice came from outside the apartment and Lily laughed. "It's okay," she called into them. "It's only Mr. Hopkins."

A spike of ice drove itself down Sam's back. Why couldn't she do what she was told for once in her life? Even if it was only— He stiffened. "Hopkins was here yesterday. Before the poppet. Before the attack."

"And Hopkins has been here longer than Cassini." Micah's expression darkened. "He used to take care of the keys."

"Like the key to my storage? To Lily's? To mine?" He didn't wait for an answer, but burst into action, speeding out into the living room, Micah close on his heels.

Lily stood at the door, totally relaxed, talking to her neighbour, apologising for all the fuss of last night. But Hopkins, old and grey, a harmless man, glowered past her. Right at them. Sam skidded to a halt. He couldn't move, couldn't lift his feet off the ground. Micah slammed hard into his back, almost bowling him over. Malice flooded Hopkins eyes and suddenly they glowed, like twin stars.

"Lily!" Sam yelled, a moment too late.

Hopkins' hand lashed out, seizing her, pulling her through

the door with a strength impossible for his appearance. Lily screamed, her legs kicking, hands tearing at his arm. But the old man, the grey man, wasn't frail anymore. He moved like smoke and liquid, flowing between moments like a demon, and yet not like one at all. He glistened as he moved, his body so strong, so impossibly strong. He lifted Lily off her feet and they were gone. The door slammed behind them.

The barrier holding Sam back disintegrated and both angel and demon fell, a tangle of bodies, disentangling themselves.

Sam tore the door open and sprinted outside. There was nothing outside, no one, not even a sign. He wasn't human. Hopkins, whatever he was, wasn't human, demon or angel. The way he moved—

"Sam! Micah!" Lily yelled. Her voice echoed down the stairs leading to the roof, accompanied with bangs and crashes as she tried to fight back. Sam's heart lurched. This was pain. Pain and terror such as human beings felt almost every day of their pitiful existences. Helplessness.

"Move!" Micah roared, racing past him. It was like a binding spell snapped, recoiling on him like a broken elastic band.

Angel and demon thundered up the stairs, bursting out onto the roof, into the chill embrace of the morning. Sam followed Micah, but just beyond the doorway the angel stopped, as if he had run into the same invisible wall that had held Sam back earlier. The wind howled around them, tearing at skin, clothes and hair. But Micah didn't move. He stood like a pillar of stone, his body tensed but still.

Sam's head swam in horror. At the edge of the roof, Hopkins stood over Lily's kneeling form. A length of black leather around her neck acted as a noose, cable ties secured her hands, and his foot pressed against the small of her back.

"Stay away or she dies," Hopkins yelled at them.

"You're planning to kill her anyway," Sam growled, edging closer. "What are you? Why do this?"

"I do it for the Lord," Hopkins shouted, lifting his face and his voice to the stars. "I do it for the path of righteousness."

Light sparked in his eyes, like sparks of static electricity, and his body shifted subtly, a dark shadow straining to be free of the puny body housing it.

"He's a Nephilim," Micah said, his voice shockingly calm on the tumultuous air.

Sam hesitated. How could he not? The children of angels and humans were the stuff of legends, even in Hell. Mankind had thought them giants, or monsters, and Sam found it hard to disagree. Demons operated under certain restrictions. Not so for the Nephilim. They couldn't die. They were stronger than all but the Nameless himself. Short of the intervention of an angel of the highest order, they couldn't be stopped. And angels were forbidden from interfering.

The Nephilim ran amok in the world, pleasing themselves. It had taken the Great Flood to wipe out the first generation, an act of the Creator himself. Yet Nephilim were still born. And sometimes, with that sort of power, without the proper guidance and care, they went bad.

Hopkins grinned at them, jerking his arm up so the noose tightened around Lily's neck. She whimpered, her chest heaving with a sob. She tried to keep still, but how could she with her whole body trembling?

"Stay where you are, Sammael," Hopkins warned. "I haven't decided how she should die yet. Hanging would be more traditional but a fall from this height will leave her smeared over the pavement and be just as effective. Quite a mess though. Bound to cause a snarl up in the rush hour traffic."

Sam clenched his hands into fists, his nails gouging into his palms. He had to do something, anything. He had to distract him, to get close enough.

But close enough to do what? Rush him? Even if he could overpower Hopkins, Lily would fall.

"Micah," he hissed, "we can take him, can't we? If we go together?"

But Micah stood still as a statue, his teeth chewing on his lower lip.

Humming to himself, Hopkins began to tie the other end of the noose to one of the spars securing the aerial.

"They're your lovers, aren't they?" he asked Lily. "A pathetic demon and a corrupted angel? You did that, didn't you, witch, corrupted him? A slut with appetites so depraved that one wasn't enough. You weren't the first and you won't be the last. And yet they betray you now. For all your wiles, they stand back to watch you die."

Hopkins faced them, grinning from ear to ear, his mouth stretching far wider than a human's. Behind the taut lips, his teeth were too sharp, too bright.

"Come on then, both of you. Try it. I know you want to."

Sam threw himself forward, building up the momentum for his attack in his rush across the rooftop. Lily struggled, trying to free herself, but she couldn't, not in her precarious position. Ready to tear Hopkins limb from limb, Sam barrelled into him. Alone.

It was like hitting a rock. The air burst from his lungs and he crashed back to the rooftop. Hopkins stood over him, laughing, but as Sam tried to rise, the Nephilim slammed a foot down on his chest, crushing the air from him. He bent down and lifted Sam by the throat, holding his struggling form high in the air over his head.

"You're a fool, Sammael. An egotistical, sex-crazed fool. You could have been so much greater but you let your loins lead you for eternity."

"Micah," Sam tried to say, but the word escaped his lips as a feeble bark. *"Micah, please. Help us."*

With a disgusted snarl, Hopkins hurled him down onto the

roof again. "He won't help. He isn't allowed. So many rules, dictating what you two may and may not do. Some you can ignore, but not this. The Creator himself laid this down as an incontrovertible decree. The Nephilim are the children of angels. You have no power over us and he is forbidden to intervene."

"Why are you here?" Micah asked, his voice wavering. "Why are you doing this? Witch hunts are below you, surely?"

"Not for one such as her. And the other two. Interfering in destinies, in the destiny of the righteous and the damned, in the pre-ordained paths of their souls. And when they're strong, when they're really strong, like she is, they call me, time and again—Ashkelon, Wiesensteig, Essex, Salem, Whitechapel. I know what a witch is. I can smell out their sin. They have concourse with the Nameless himself, make themselves his whores and entertain his creatures." He slammed his foot into Sam's side and blood filled his mouth. Sam coughed, trying to drag himself up again, but Hopkins was too strong, too quick. "My task is to cleanse the world of them, but I offer them the chance of repentance. I'm not without a heart, Sammael. I will be welcomed back to the Holy Court and into the arms of my father. Which is more than will ever happen to you. To either of you."

Sam spat out his own blood and strained to free himself. Lily was so close, almost within reach, but Hopkins held him pinned to the roof. And Micah—Micah was just standing there. Just standing there.

Micah's first instinct was to give in to the rising wave of righteous fury that swept through him like a purifying fire at the sight of Lily in such peril. As Sam hurled himself forward, the angel surged forward to help him, to join the fray and attack.

A cool touch of light on his shoulder stopped him.

"I told you that you should have come home, Micah," said

Enoch's voice. It rippled through the air, like dawn itself. *"There's nothing you can do. Not against one of our Lost Children. She must die."*

"No," he breathed. "No, Enoch. It's wrong. Our Creator wouldn't want this."

"He's Nephilim," said Enoch. *"If you harm him, you'll be damned."*

Sam fell, his body crushed and broken. Blood drenched his chin and his eyes, his black and endless eyes, filled with agony, with despair. Lily shivered on the edge of the building, the noose and her precarious balance the only thing holding her back. He would lose them. If he listened to Enoch, he would lose them both.

"I wanted to spare you this," Enoch sighed. *"Why wouldn't you listen to me?"*

The cold gripped him then, the wind of the morning, the chaos that swirled around them.

Sam was pleading for help, for rescue, for both of them. Lily sobbed, her shoulders shaking. Micah could hear her saying his name under her breath, over and over again.

Hopkins sneered at him.

"He won't help. He isn't allowed..." Hopkins ranted on, giving his convoluted reasons. But Micah could no longer hear him. Enoch swirled around him, trying to draw him away.

"Come home, Micah. You crossed the line with her. It's over. There's nothing else you can do."

"I can't leave them. You said I had a week!"

"And you interfered. You pushed him and he acted earlier than expected. You can't save them. Sammael might survive. His masters will realise he didn't fail, but they want her soul. They want her dead as much as anyone so they can collect."

The callous way he said it exploded like shards of betrayal through Micah's body. "She isn't evil! They can't take her."

"She had sexual congress with a demon, Micah. And with you, both of you. By her own standards, she has transgressed. She doesn't have a hope. She's damned."

"We're all damned," Micah snarled and tore himself free of Enoch's restraints.

He sprinted across the open roof, bearing down on the startled Hopkins, who instead of readying himself to face the furious angel, stood there, staring in shock. His mouth gaped open like that of a fish.

Micah took him about the waist, bearing him forward towards the edge, diving headlong into the space beyond.

"Save her, Sam," he sent, not even sure if the message would reach him, but trusting in his need to punch it through to the wounded demon. *"Save her."*

Hopkins screamed, a high and desperate sound of denial, of rage. He clawed at Micah's hands and face, but the angel held on, pushing him off the edge of the building.

"NO!" Sam screamed, trying to reach him, trying to stop him.

But Micah couldn't let go. He had to be sure.

The wind snatched him from the roof's edge and he fell, still clinging to the Nephilim. Lily's face was a snapshot of horror as he flashed by, her eyes wide, tears lining her face, and her mouth stretched in terror. She pitched forward, trying to throw herself after him.

"No, my bright one!"

Sam's hand seized her, pulled her back, and Micah smiled as he fell, holding on to the screaming Nephilim. The shadows came from nowhere, swirling through the morning light like ink in water to coil around them, to snatch them both from the world and into the anguish of the new eternity he had chosen.

Chapter Seventeen

Sam's arms closed around her, his body warm, his touch gentle and desperate to ensure her safety, but Lily could feel nothing. Though he had quickly undone the noose and freed her hands, she still felt them there. She couldn't breathe, couldn't feel her fingers. She couldn't feel anything. Micah was gone. Her world was over.

"What was he?" she asked, surprised to find she had a voice at all. Even more surprised to discover it sounded so calm and in control.

"A Nephilim, the child of a human and an angel. Stronger, faster, demented. Micah was forbidden to confront him. All angels are."

"But he did."

"Yes," Sam said, holding her as if afraid to let her go. "He must have stood high in the ranks of Heaven to be able to take a Nephilim, forbidden or not. Why did he never say anything?"

What did his status matter? Her mind whirled with outrage. Micah was gone. The shadows had snatched him out of the air, right in front of her face.

"I don't care," Lily snapped. "Where is he, Sam? What happened to him?"

"He fell."

She stared at his pale, stricken face. "No he didn't. I saw the shadows take him. He didn't fall. He never made it to the ground."

"No, Lily." That vicious edge of patience freaked her out. He sounded like a wire about to snap. He sounded like she felt. "He *fell*, as angels fall. He fell from grace. He gave himself up for you. The shadows took him to Hell."

She shuddered, her body jerking around a cold ball of shame in her core. "It's my fault. It's all my fault."

Letting her go, he turned around slowly until he faced the spot where Micah had taken Hopkins over the edge. He stared at it for a moment as if it might hold an explanation, a reason, and then, flinging his arms wide, he howled.

The noise tore through her, primal and agonised, tortured with rage.

Lily wrapped her arms around the steel in him, tried to quell the tears in her eyes, the sobs in her throat, the reflected anguish within her body and mind.

"The Nameless said they'd take a soul today." Sam gasped out the painful words, words that grated across his ravaged throat. "Said they didn't care which one. So when Micah offered, they took him. Instead of you. Fuck it, Lily, maybe this is what they wanted all along. They played us both to get him. To get Micah."

Lily dragged herself up to her trembling feet, swaying as she tried to stand. "We've got to do something, Sam." She grabbed his shoulders, shaking him hard. "We've got to get him back. He isn't dead. He can't die. We've got to go and bring him home!"

"Go where?" he yelled into her face. "To Hell? Like a fucking inverted Orpheus? You'd go to Hell to get him back, would you?"

Lily slapped his face. The crack of skin on skin sounded sharp and loud in the morning's brightness. Things like this shouldn't happen on a spring morning, she thought absently. They belonged in the night, in the darkness or the storm. Not

211

like this. Things like this shouldn't happen at all.

"You know I would, Sam," she told him, her vehemence stunning him even more than her slap. He flinched back from her, his dark eyes full of the hard lines of her face. "I'd do it for either of you. And you're going to take me there. Understand?"

Sam didn't move for a second, just stared at her. Slowly, his arms came around her again. His touch was tentative, careful. "You don't know what you're asking."

"I'm asking you to help me get Micah back. Whatever it takes."

"Lily, I'm a demon. Being here with you has changed me, but if we go there—if I take you there—I'll be as I was. Worse than I was. I'll be one of them again. And by the time we reach him, there's every chance Micah will as well."

"He'll still be Micah. You'll still be Sam. I believe that."

He shook his head, little jerks of denial. "But you're wrong, love. So wrong. You have no idea."

"I trust you. Help me to get him back."

"I won't leave you. I'll stay here with you. I will keep you safe. Don't ask this, Lily. I'll be everything for you, and more. Don't, Lily, please."

She pressed her fingertips to his bloodstained lips to silence him. She knew what he was saying, what he was offering. But how did you tell a man willing to sacrifice everything he was for you that it wasn't enough? She needed Micah too. And if it had gone another way, she would have asked Micah the same thing, for help to rescue Sam. So even though she feared it might shatter his newly reacquired heart, she asked.

"Help me get him back, Sam. Take me there and help me rescue him."

Sam slumped against her, bowing his head so his forehead rested on hers. How could he resist her? Nothing would sway her. He knew that now. Slowly, he nodded.

It wasn't until Lily got back to her own apartment that she started to shiver. Sam left her in her bedroom, muttering something about getting ready which she didn't catch. She didn't care. Her skin crawled, as if insects swarmed beneath it, burrowing through the epidermis, and she stood in the middle of the bedroom, staring at the rumpled bedclothes where the three of them had lain. It seemed like an eternity ago. But the imprint of his body was still warm. She picked up the pillow, pressing it to her face, and inhaled the scent of warm cinnamon and musk.

Micah.

Dropping the pillow back down, Lily turned away. She rubbed her arms, trying to rid herself of the feeling of Hopkins' touch. Condensation still blurred the mirrors in the bathroom, where Micah had showered, and water dewed down the length of the glass door.

Where he had been.

"*Micah, please talk to me. Please be here.*"

There was no answer. She knew there wouldn't be, but she had to try anyway.

She stepped into the cubicle and turned on the shower. Hot water drenched her—hair, robe, skin—pounding onto her and sluicing down her body. She ripped off the robe, leaving it like a wet rag swirling 'round her feet. She picked up the soap and scrubbed at her skin, trying to rid herself of a taint, a curse, something vile. She didn't know what. But for this to have happened to her, for Micah to be snatched away from her, there had to be something wrong with her, something evil. The type of thing that deals with a demon to seduce an angel, that couldn't be satisfied by just one. A Lilith, as Hopkins had called her. A Jezebel. A witch.

Sam's voice came from the bedroom. "I'm ready." He

sounded different. Lily switched off the water and stood there, suddenly cold. Sam's voice came again, hollow, dangerous. "Lily, come here."

The lilt of humour was gone. She'd forced him into this, she knew that. He was hurting too and she had disregarded that, pushing past his feelings in her need to get Micah back. She had created this new, bereft Sam, this hollow man.

Another sin to face. Something else to atone for.

Wrapping herself in a towel, she rubbed the water from her hair. It stuck out in tufts, dishevelled, and she ran her fingers through it, scraping it back from her face. It would do. What did vanity matter now?

When she stepped out of the bathroom, however, she froze. Sam waited for her, blocking the doorway, her only means of escape. But he didn't look like her Sam anymore. Sammael. That was the being standing opposite her.

Clad only in tight leather trousers, his skin seemed to glisten, as if the olive complexion carried a permanent sheen of sweat, a glow from within. His eyes, dark and endless, had melted from their dark brown to an endless black, the black of his hair, of a demon's soul. His lip curled into a sneer and Lily took an involuntary step back.

"If you're ready, if you still want to come, we should get going."

She glanced down at the towel. "Like this?"

His eyes raked over her body so intimately that she felt naked, even if she wasn't. But there was no affection there, no tenderness. Her Sam was gone. The demon had taken his place. "Hardly. As inventive as you are with sex, I doubt you'd survive five seconds naked in Hell. They'd have you every way before you took six steps." He nodded towards the bed. "I brought your clothes."

Clothes was an overstatement. Lily cast an appalled look at the small pile of leather and metal on her bed.

"You can't be serious," she said with a laugh. "I'm not wearing that!"

He moved faster than the eye, slipping between moments. His hands seized her upper arms, and he shook her, not gently. His face bore down on hers and she didn't know him anymore.

"You'll do whatever I tell you."

"What? So Hell is a big old S&M party?"

Sam lifted her, his hands digging into his upper arms. She struggled to balance on the very tips of her toes, her heart beating faster than she thought possible.

"Without the safe words," he snarled. "This is no joke, Lily. As far as anyone else is going to be concerned, you are mine, body and soul. If they think for a moment that you're a free mortal walking their highways, they'll take you from me. And I won't be able to stop them. Understand? It's bad enough that by doing this we'll risk unbalancing all creation. If they take you, they'll keep you and break all realities apart, but that's nothing to what they'll make you endure. If you're so set on doing this, Lily, you'll do everything I say. Now tell me you understand."

Somewhere, she found her voice. It sounded very small. "I understand, Sam."

"Call me Master."

Something inside her shrank back at the malice in his tone. Something else, something she remembered from that night in his apartment, unfurled, dark and sensuous. Lily lifted her chin and gazed deeply into his endless eyes. So this was what he wanted, was it? Or what he needed perhaps? Well, so be it. For Micah—and for Sam—she could do it.

"Yes, Master."

"Lower your gaze," he growled.

She dropped her eyes, hooding them with her long eyelashes. It brought his broad chest into full view and another surge of that warmth she recognised as lust swept through her.

"You need to learn your place. Here, now. Before any other demon lays eyes on you and knows you for what you are. There will be no second chances, Lily." He lowered her from her tiptoes, his hands running roughly down her arms, making her body quake with unexpected need. His breath rippled across the skin of her chest and neck. "They won't listen to pleas, or reason, or to anything you can say. And there isn't much you can say with half a foot of dick down your throat. They like to hear you scream. So from this moment on, you're mine."

"Your slave," she said. His eyes flashed, a hint of red danger in their depths. "Master," she added quickly.

"Better," he admitted, grudgingly. "Drop your towel." She shook it free. If areas of her skin were scrubbed raw, he passed no comment, merely looked her over like he was inspecting merchandise. "Up against the wall," he said and turned away.

Lily backed up until she felt the cool touch of her magnolia-painted bedroom walls against her shoulder blades and buttocks. She clasped her hands in front of her, knotting her fingers together as she watched him bend over the clothing on the bed. She couldn't tell what he picked up, something small which he held in one fist as he approached her, looking so out of place that it would have been laughable. If it wasn't for his glare. If it wasn't for the way her treacherous body was reacting.

Micah, this is for Micah, she tried to tell herself. But she knew she was lying. This was for Sam. This was for herself. Her stomach muscles tightened and her cunt grew wet and ready.

The world slowed, focused on each moment, each sensation.

"Lower your eyes," Sam said again, his mouth a hard line, and she obeyed, gazing at the floor, at his bare feet. They were perfectly formed, treading across the cream carpet, leaving slight indentations behind them which took a moment to spring up.

216

A thin line tightened around her throat and the warmth of his fingertips guiding it did nothing to assuage the sudden chills that shot through her. He fastened a collar around her neck, pulling it tight enough to be felt, but not so tight as to be uncomfortable. But she was aware of it, she couldn't fail to be.

Breathing a little faster, she kept her eyes trained on the handsome lines of his chest, on the way his pecs curved as he moved. He was holding something else in his hands, a length of leather, like a leash. Catching her wrists, he pulled them up above her head and tied them there, the dado rail providing the anchor, her arms stretched as far as they would go.

Her heart raced as the sensations of the morning returned with a vengeance. Was he doing it on purpose? Making her relive what Hopkins had done? And by extension what happened to Micah? Oh God, he wouldn't, would he?

And yet, her demon stepped back from her, his gaze travelling over her skin, and with a surreptitious flick of her eyes, she saw the smile on his face as he drank in her body, the way she trembled.

His nostrils flared and before she knew what was happening, he slid his hand between her legs, a finger tracing a line between the slick folds of her labia. He brought it up to his mouth and tasted her.

"All ready and waiting, I see," he said.

She said nothing, praying he would laugh and make some sort of smart comment so she would know he was still her Sam, that nothing had really changed and this was just a pretence. But he didn't.

Sam cupped her breasts, weighing them in his hands, the pads of his thumbs teasing the nipples to erectness. Lily bit her lower lip and closed her eyes.

"No," he said. "Look. I want you to watch."

So she did. It was as simple as that, she realised. What Sam wanted, she wanted, and it was not just because it had to

217

be that way. She felt it, pulsing away inside her, the need to please him, to submit to his dominion.

She watched him run his hands over her body, observed the way he stimulated her, teased her most sensitive places. Nothing was safe from him. He would and could take anything he wanted and there was nothing she could do about it. And she didn't want him to stop.

Sam bent to take the tight bud of her left nipple in his mouth, his teeth grazing it, slowly increasing the pressure to the point of pain. Or rather pain and pleasure combined. It formed a direct connection between her breasts and her vagina, a line of fierce desire slicing through her body. She groaned as he rolled the other nipple between thumb and forefinger, squeezing so tightly that it struck again, pulsing in her groin.

He released her suddenly and without warning. The breath rushed out of her, but he was already gone, his back turned to her and he bent over the bed again. This time he brought back two pieces of metal. At first she wondered if they were some kind of weird tribal weapon, but when he placed the cold curve of metal against her breast, she knew she was wrong. The intricate design cupped the outer curve and clipped against the nipple, cold teeth that bit into her tender skin, enflaming it, and making the blood pump even harder in an effort to reach the abused centre. He fixed the other to her and stood back to admire his work. Like metal tattoos, they embraced her, teased her and dragged against her skin in the most delicious cruelty.

The corset came next, a sheath of black leather which he stretched around her, lifting her decorated breasts so they sat cupped in the bodice. He hooked up the back, pressing close to her, his musk overwhelming her now. But he didn't caress her again. His movements were all clinical, cold. He tugged the laces until the corset squeezed all remaining air from her chest, cinched in her waist. The nipple clamps brushed against the bodice and Lily groaned despite herself, rocking her hips in a vain effort to alleviate the building tension.

Sam caught her hips in his strong hands and pushed them back, stilling them, his touch a warning.

But he didn't pull away this time. His fingers dimpled the cheeks of her ass, pressing into the soft skin, massaging her body so that she undulated according to his lead rather than her own will.

"Tell me how good it feels," he commanded.

"It feels good," she breathed. "Oh God, it feels good." His fingers bit a little harder and she remembered. "Master," she finished hurriedly. "My Master."

The word sent shards of pure lust running through her veins. Her clit throbbed with need, but he ignored it, driving one finger, then two deep inside her, working against her G-spot until she was shivering and crying out. The metal clamped around her nipples rolled and tormented them, twin points of fiery pleasure that mirrored the violence of her need below. Her vaginal muscles spasmed, locking around his hand as if to hold him tight, or devour him. She felt the white heat of orgasm cresting over her, ready to break and she reached for it, the cry of joy hanging ready in the air.

Then he stopped.

Sam pulled out of her before she came and the pleasure cut off as if a wire had been severed. Bewildered, betrayed, she stared at him, her chest heaving, sweat sliding down the line of her cleavage, her legs shaking.

Sam slowly undid his trousers and drew out the magnificent length of his cock. Already erect, the head purpling with its hunger, he ran his hand up and down the shaft, watching her face as he pleasured himself. He took his time, the bastard, his fingers teasing his own skin, drawing the moment out.

"Please." He wouldn't come like that in front of her, would he? He wouldn't just wank off when they could fuck and— Oh

God. "Master, please."

Light sparked in his eyes, a demonic light of triumph, of conquest.

"Say it again."

Like she needed prompting. "Please, my Master. Fill me, Sam. Fuck me. Take me away. Please."

Sam pressed close to her, his body moulding to the length of her, and his mouth silenced her, his tongue plundering her mouth, reaching deep inside her. She returned his kiss with a ferocity which startled even her. With agonising slowness he slid his hands down to lift her, hooking her legs around his waist. It only took a flex of his hips and he slid deep inside her, filling her, his girth stretching her.

Lily gasped, her whole body arching to meet him, taking him so deep inside her that she was sure he must now be a part of her. That they were one being and could never be parted.

Sam thrust, his body taking what he wanted without thought for her, without a care. He fucked her without tenderness, without compassion, his mouth ravenous on hers, teeth and tongue grappling with her. Lily stretched out her hands, wriggled her fingers in a vain attempt to gain the freedom she no longer wanted.

Sam rammed himself against her, bracing his hands on the wall to either side of her, slamming himself into her willing depths. His tongue penetrated her, delving deep and churning the rising current she could no longer fight.

It might never end, she realised. She might be bound here forever at his mercy, subject to his every whim. Micah might be lost to her, never to be won back, but Sam—Sam was here for her, for himself. Sam was taking her, consuming her, taking everything she was and recreating it according to his image, his needs. And she would let him take whatever he needed, whatever he wanted. Without reservation.

Sam growled with his release, emptying himself into her

and triggering her own orgasm, a wild and abandoned scream of joy, of need fulfilled. They sank against each other, drenched in sweat and exhaustion, breathing hard as their foreheads pressed together and they stared obsessively into each others' eyes.

"Do you understand?" he asked, his chest heaving, his arms wrapped around her, holding her close. "Tell me you understand, Lily, or this can't go any further."

She shook against him, aftershocks still tremoring through her body. He could feel that, surely. He could feel how he affected her, how he made her feel.

But if this was how it had to be, this was how it had to be. There was no arguing, no dissent. What Sam wanted, Sam got, Sam took. And that was that.

"I understand," said Lily solemnly. "Whatever you say. Until we have him back. Help me, Sam."

"I will," he promised, in tones just as serious as her own. "You know I will. And now don't speak of it again. Promise." He untangled her legs, lowering her away from his body.

She bowed her head, lowered her eyes to the ground, even as her legs trembled and went from beneath her. There were only two words that conveyed all she felt, all she needed to say, every promise she owed him and he deserved.

"Yes, Master."

Chapter Eighteen

Sam paced the living room, waiting for her, wishing she'd see reason. He had hoped that showing her what was in store for her would frighten her enough that she would leave well enough alone. But not Lily. Oh no. She responded to him. More than responded. She turned it back on him, dominating him with her willing submission.

He should have known. He should have learned by now. But he kept on doing it. Underestimating her. Just like Micah had said.

Thoughts of Micah twisted his stomach. His enemy, yes, but one so close at this stage that he was something else. A friend? A lover? He didn't expect to feel this way about anyone. Let alone both a mortal and an angel.

The sound of Lily clearing her throat brought his eyes up to the bedroom door. He swallowed hard on his tightening throat, unable to do anything about the similar tightening in his groin.

The corset was the least of his worries. True, it presented her body, moulding it for him alone. The tight leather skirt she wore barely covered her ass. Beneath it she wore nothing. His fingers twitched at the thought that he could slide them in there, with unrestricted access. Leather cuffs hugged her wrists and ankles, all the better to hold her in whatever position he desired, given a frame to which he could bind her. The studded leather choker around her throat forced her to lift her head proudly, but she kept her eyes demurely cast towards the floor, a perfect contrast.

Lily had applied a little makeup to her eyes, a little blush to accentuate the flush of arousal beneath her skin, and she had painted her lips scarlet.

Sam couldn't deny it. She was perfect.

So damned perfect it sent chills through his body, followed by waves of hunger.

"You're ready?" he asked.

He wished she would say no. That she would shake her head and back away in fear. But she didn't.

"Yes, Master."

The words sent shudders through him and his insides knotted with need. Blood pounded and an echoing pulse answered from the sperm damned up in his cock. Damn it, damn it, damn it. All he wanted to do was to push her back onto the bed and...

The bed they had shared with Micah.

Damn.

"Come here," he told her, forcing his voice to be calm and in command. "Hold on to me."

She stood against his back, all the long, warm, curvy length of her pressed against his skin. Carefully, she wrapped her arms around his waist and before he could catch his breath, she turned her head and pressed her cheek against his back.

"Is this permitted?" she asked in her soft and sultry voice.

"It is. Now hold on."

Never before had he found it so difficult to draw the sigil to open the way to Hell. His hand shook. That shouldn't happen. But Lily changed him. She changed everything. Perhaps that's why Heaven and Hell were so interested in her. Or the reason the Nephilim had been drawn to her in the first place. Or perhaps it was all about Micah, as he had said. He didn't know anymore. How could he tell one end of this tangled web from the other?

Sam curled his hand into a fist and tried again, more controlled now, more confident on the outside at least. Inside was a different story. He traced the word of opening and the line of fire hung in the air for a moment before it twisted and began to unfurl. A warm blast of air rolled over them and Lily's grip tightened.

So she did feel fear. And she trusted him to protect her. Too late he realised why she was doing this.

She trusted him.

Sammael clenched his teeth together, leaning back against her as the gateway opened. Beyond he saw an empty chamber, just what he had wanted. Taking a deep breath, he reminded himself what he was, what he was doing. He closed his hands over Lily's, holding her against him. Her fingers wriggled for just a moment beneath his firm grip, then fell still. Trusting him.

Damn it, why did she have to trust him?

Sammael stepped through the gateway, dragging her with him, and closed it behind them.

The heat made drops of sweat stand out on his skin, and behind him Lily exhaled, a breath of surprise which played on his flesh, maddening his rising lust. This place was part of it. Hell always aroused him. Down through all the endless years his best and worst moments had taken place here, until now. Until Lily and Micah.

The demon in him growled and began to uncoil, grabbing back control from the conscious rational being he hoped to be. Forcing it back down took all his willpower, willpower which faltered when he caught Lily's scent in his flaring nostrils. Sweet, rich, musky, like spiced honey, like a drug, her body pressed to his, the faint hint of fear clinging to her just making the concoction all the more addictive.

"Lily, come here," he growled.

Obediently, she stepped in front of him, her eyes dutifully downcast. Oh, she played the part all right, she played it wonderfully. Not the slightest hint of rebellion.

And why would there be? Here and now, in his domain, his world, she was his. All his.

Sammael pushed her back against the wall, running his hands down her sides, pulling her hips towards him so she could feel his arousal, sense his needs. Her pulse quickened and she breathed a little faster, spreading out her fingers against the rock face on each side of her slender form.

Bending his head, he captured her mouth, his kiss designed to brand her, to remind her that here she had nothing but him, and was nothing, to make her realise his dominance was no charade.

A moan sounded deep in her throat, that music of submission that he had come to expect of her. She would fight him, at some point, he knew that. When she realised they weren't going back, that they weren't going after Micah. Then she would fight.

And then he'd punish her.

His cock twitched at the thought.

"I was wondering where you'd got to, Sammael," said Asmodeus. Sam jerked around, rage blazing within him. The demon king of lust stood a little way down the corridor, hands on his hips. "We're gathering in the audience chamber. You won't want to miss this."

Then his eyes snagged on Lily and he grinned. "Or maybe you will. Is this her, then?"

He sauntered forward. Every element in Sam's body rose aggressively, but Asmodeus didn't seem to notice. He slid by him, pressing into the space around Lily. She shrank back against the wall and looked to Sam with desperate eyes, her

225

heaving chest inadvertently thrusting her decorated breasts up at Asmodeus.

"Pretty," he drawled, and ran a fingernail along the bare flesh of her shoulder, leaving behind a vivid scarlet line.

"I haven't finished breaking her in as yet." Sam didn't bother to keep the warning from his voice. "I want her to be perfect when I present her to the Nameless." If he was seen as the one who delivered both Micah and Lily to the Nameless, his position would have risen greatly since he was last here. By the way Asmodeus withdrew, he knew he was right. Besides, no one, not even Asmodeus, would be fool enough to tamper with someone destined for the Nameless.

Sam smiled. Now this, while definitely useful, could also be fun.

Asmodeus shrugged as he withdrew, as if it was nothing of any consequence. "Later then, pretty one," he promised Lily.

She shrank back, her face very pale in the shadows. Something unexpected lurched in Sam's chest, and the thoughts of a moment ago were like ashes in his mind. To see such fear on her face, such terror.

And what would the Nameless put there? He swallowed on a dry throat. Come to that, what would *he* have put there?

"What's happening in the audience chamber?" he called after the demon king. Asmodeus looked back, laughed and his old confidence returned with a vengeance, making Sam grind his teeth.

"Come and see, Sammy boy. You really don't want to miss this." Then he was gone, down the winding tunnels.

When Sam turned back to Lily, she slumped back against the wall, her eyes huge and afraid.

"Did he hurt you?" Sam asked rapidly. "Bespell you?"

Lily shook her head. She only whispered his name, terrified someone else would hear and know her for a fraud. "Sam?"

Sam sighed, the demon within him quashed at the thought of her carried off by Asmodeus, turned into something like Lara. Hadn't the Nameless said Lara had been just like Lily once, bright and innocent, a perfect vessel? His stomach twisted in on itself. And there were worse fates. She could really end up in the hands of the Nameless. Or he could lose himself, as had so nearly happened minutes earlier.

And what would he have done to her? He didn't want to think of the answer.

Sam took her hands, enfolding them in his own in what he hoped was a comforting gesture. He couldn't say anything that might betray them, and here anything could be overheard, to be used against them. Knowledge was a currency, so was flesh. He drew Lily against him again, gently this time.

"We must go," he told her in even tones, while his eyes bore into hers, begging her to trust him a little longer. "We need to find out what's happening in the audience chamber. Remember, Lily, you have to remember."

Her fingers tightened on his briefly and she lowered her gaze once more.

"Master."

The first thing Micah could feel was the cold. It surrounded him, sank teeth into his skin and seeped its poison right down to his bones. Deep in the marrow, he felt it freezing him, and part of him no longer cared.

Micah came to lying on stone, shivering, naked. He'd always been told that Hell was hot, all fire and brimstone, but this cell was draped in ice from the ceiling to the floor. Ancient ice, black and shining, smooth as glass. Curled in a foetal position, a newborn in a frozen womb, Micah tried to will himself to move. And failed.

No sound greeted him but his own ragged breath, the breath which misted and plumed in the air before him. Tears slid from his eyes, but they froze as they reached his jaw, hanging from him like tiny stalactites, crisp and sharp in the frigid air.

Lily was safe. He had to remind himself of that. It was all that mattered. Lily was safe.

In tackling the Nephilim, Micah had expected oblivion. But maybe his judgement was still to come. It would have been easier, though, to have been wiped out of existence in the moment he bowled Hopkins off the rooftop. To have ceased to be once she was safe. No such luck. The shadows had snatched him from the air, swathed him in darkness and void.

And now he was here.

No sign of Hopkins either. Micah was alone. Was this it then? His punishment? To be here for the rest of eternity, frozen and alone, gradually eaten away by the ice, or smothered in it as his own tears sealed shut his eyes?

But Lily was safe. That sparked a small warmth deep inside his heart. Sam would protect her, keep her from harm. Lily was safe and Hopkins was gone.

Gone where?

Micah struggled to move, his body protesting, his skin almost adhering to the ice beneath him, but he ignored that pain. What did pain matter? He stood, holding himself still despite the powerful urge to shiver and let his teeth chatter. A dim light came from a door before him, like something from a dungeon, ancient oak set with a small metal grill. Ice rimed the metal, sheened the door as if it had been frozen shut centuries before.

He was alone, but outside the door a torch was burning. He stared at the wavering point of light, of heat, wishing it was nearer. As an angel he had never known cold like this. He'd never known the way it ate into the heart and clung there, fist-like, while tentacles of discomfort weaved their way through his limbs, under his skin.

Outside someone coughed and muttered a curse. Micah stifled his first urge to call out for help. If he was where he thought he was, no help would be forthcoming. Better to keep silent and wait for the inevitable. Because he knew it would come.

A face appeared in the grill, bright eyes above the flash of a grin like a knife blade. Then it was gone. Micah waited, listening to the sound of booted feet fade away and then return, accompanied by another, more intimidating figure. The keys grated against the lock. Not that they needed an actual lock. This was for show, for intimidation, for in Hell everything was about perception. Fear in the mind was a much more effective tool than anything else, but it needed certain props. And for each mind those props were different.

So this was his fear?

He gazed around himself with unexpected interest. It would never have occurred to him that cold and imprisonment could terrify him, and yet it did. He felt the rush of it up his spine, a rush made even worse when the door opened and Asmodeus entered.

Suddenly Micah understood that this was only the beginning of their exploration of his personal torments. The uncontrolled lust that the demon could instil was another facet he dreaded. So what was he afraid of? He began to fear that he himself was only starting to find out.

Asmodeus smiled and Micah closed his eyes, waiting. A quick snort of breath and Asmodeus spoke, his voice echoing strangely in the icy chamber.

"Sammael was right about you. Come. You have an audience."

No need to ask with whom. Only one thing in this desolate place could demand an audience in that manner. Asmodeus turned away, not even waiting to see if Micah obeyed. When he didn't move, he heard the sound of other feet, the ring of metal against metal, but he kept his eyes closed, willing this to be a dream, unable to admit his own place in it. Asmodeus laughed, a low, dangerous chuckle that crawled over Micah's flesh.

"It's going to be like that, is it? Passive resistance? I don't think so."

Metal snapped shut around Micah's wrists, weighing down his arms. It only took seconds. He didn't even feel the hands securing him, but at the tug of the chain attached to the manacles, his eyes flew open. His feet slipped on the ice and he fell heavily, his hands dragged out before him. When he looked up, Asmodeus held the other end of the chain, a thick length of shining metal. The bands around his wrists gleamed like silver.

"Get up, Micah. Or I will drag you there on your pretty face."

The chain slackened for just a moment, enough for him to get some purchase and struggle to his feet. Asmodeus rolled his shoulders, watching his discomfort with undisguised pleasure.

"Better," he growled. "Now, follow."

Without another glance back, he strode off out of the cell, and Micah had to follow or fall again. He had no doubt that if he tripped, he would indeed be dragged the rest of the way. Asmodeus was a King of Hell. He'd have no qualms about proving that in every way possible.

Eyes followed him as he was tugged down the corridors, demons and damned alike watching him with the same hunger. He could feel their thoughts slide over him like a molester's hands. He was beautiful to them, and here, beauty was a thing to be corrupted, defiled. Not for the first time, his fear edged a little deeper into his heart. This time it lodged there like a cancer.

The corridors wound around like a labyrinth, twisting and turning, leading him past more doors, more chambers, through areas with air like molten gold, and areas even colder than his cell. Micah kept his eyes trained on Asmodeus's back, not wanting to look at the beings which leered at him from all directions, not wanting to acknowledge the ever-growing group that followed behind him, like a pack of wild dogs scenting fresh meat.

The walls opened up and they entered a vast chamber, high-domed and lit with columns of burning fire. It was full of beings—great and small, terrifying and pathetic—but all of them paled into insignificance before the one seated at the far end. Enthroned on a dais, the Nameless lounged, his eyes as beautiful as they had always been, his face the image of the angel brought before him. But his mouth formed a cruel and mocking curve and when those hazel eyes latched onto Micah's, his grip on the arms of his throne tightened, his nails gouging into the ancient stone.

The Nameless leaned forward, dismissing Asmodeus with a negligent flick of his hand. The chains crashed to the floor at Micah's feet, where they weaved back and forth like snakes, waiting for their Master's command. The Nameless said nothing, but rose slowly to his feet, stepping down from the dais to approach his prisoner.

Disgust crawled through Micah's stomach, but he kept his peace, clinging to calm like a drowning man to driftwood. The Nameless walked around him, inspecting him, and then came to a stop before him. With a grip like a vise, he caught Micah's chin and wrenched his head up so that their eyes met.

"Greetings, my brother. It has been far too long."

Micah's eyes stung. Yes, brothers. They had been brothers, and much more. Twin souls, duplicate spirits, created together and forged directly from the Divine Will.

"Lucifer." A gasp of fear and excitement flew around the assembly of the damned. He dared to name the Nameless. And why shouldn't he? He shocked them, surprised them. But what did it matter what they thought? They would have him eventually. All of them. Micah understood that. Might as well face it.

"Beloved," said the Nameless, in a twisted version of the voice that once Micah had known as well as his own. The music in it was gone, and yet lingered on the edges like a ghost. Was he surprised to be named, to be acknowledged for the being he had been? "He's betrayed you too."

"No," Micah said, filling his gaze with the riot of colours in the eyes that beheld him. "No. I chose this. I knew what I was doing."

"For a mortal? For that woman?"

"Yes." There was no fear in saying it, no regret. Lily still lived. Hopkins had not taken her and that was all that mattered. And knowing she yet lived, that Sam was with her and would protect her, was enough. A seedling of renewed strength stirred in his soul. "It was worth it," he assured them all.

Lucifer smiled, not the derisive curl of before, but one tinged with pity. Endless pity, such as he possessed in the first days. This was the soul that wept for grief even as he had taken up the knife forged to kill the Creator, the knife he still wore at his side. This was his brother, and his brother wanted to weep for him.

"Poor Micah. Sammael will just bring her to us anyway. You'll see." When Micah tried to shake his head, Lucifer held it still, his grip tightening.

"And Hopkins?"

"Hopkins?" Lucifer gazed at him uncomprehending for a moment, then understanding flashed in his eyes. "Oh, the Nephilim. Already ransomed."

The cold reopened a hole in the pit of Micah's stomach, and fear came pouring back in, along with betrayal and bile. "Ransomed?"

"Yes. Someone wanted him back. They left us you."

"But I—" But what could he say? The Nephilim had but been true to his nature, however twisted that had been. Micah had known what was forbidden and had ploughed on anyway, with Lily, with Sam, with Hopkins.

"You were betrayed. Just as I said. Poor Micah." The stone grip softened, became a caress. Hands flowed down his neck, across his chest, while Micah stared at the floor, at the weaving chains, and tried to shut out the growing darkness all around him, creeping through the cracks in his pitiful defences. "Come. Be one of us now. Revel in the power to which we were born, brother."

And why not? a dark insidious voice within him asked. Lily was gone, Hopkins was free, and he was trapped here, at the mercy of the Nameless and his hordes. Creatures like Asmodeus, like Sammael. Micah's eyes burned with tears he could not shed.

"I cannot." His throat felt scorched and barren.

The aura of friendship bled out of Lucifer's voice, his brother and friend no longer, the Nameless again. "But you will. Eventually."

He stepped back and the chains shot upwards, wrenching Micah's arms out to the side, holding him above the ground, helpless. Micah hung from them, his whole body exposed. All Hell roared its approval.

The Nameless circled him, eyes no longer sympathetic. "Where to begin though?"

Several voices called out vile suggestions, and Micah's skin shrank back around his frame with the images they conjured in his mind. Images no doubt aided and made more vivid by the powers of the Nameless and his minions.

The Nameless stopped behind him. He smoothed one perfect hand up Micah's back and down again, nails scraping in his wake. "No. First a reminder. Of what he was. Something that will stay with him for eternity."

The hand came to a rest between his shoulder blades and then lifted until only one nail remained. Long and sharp, it picked the spot right in the centre of his back, where his spine stood out stark and prominent, shoulder blades flaring on each side.

"A gift to mark you, Micah. A gift to turn you. A gift you will never erase." The Nameless sank his nail into Micah's back, deep through skin and bone, burrowing between his vertebrae. Shards of darkness, of demonic energy seeped from it like poison, worming their way through his skin, changing everything they touched.

Light began to slip away from him, but Micah clung to his consciousness as the shards did their work. They trailed lines across him, back, up and down beneath his skin, coils and whorls of shadows that stretched and burned, chilling and killing as they went. The pain grew, like acid inside him, and the dark point in his heart began to unfurl. Micah cried out, in spite of his resolve, his head thrown back to give voice to the agony.

Abruptly it subsided, still there, but muted.

"Get him mirrors," said the Nameless in a bored voice. "I want him to see."

They were brought at once, two huge mirrors in ornate baroque frames that should have flattened the frail figures porting them. The slaves worked in silence, aligning the mirrors on either side of him. The chains lowered him enough so that he could stand, though he was still held in place, his ordeal far from over. Micah's chin dropped forward to his chest, but the Nameless was there again, lifting him, stroking his cheek and wiping away the involuntary tears of pain.

"Look," he urged.

And without wanting to, Micah obeyed. His sight swam in and out of focus for a minute and then fixed on his image, a

234

reflection of his reflection. His arms outstretched, his back knotted with straining muscles, his buttocks clenched, and now reaching across his shoulders and down his spine, a tattoo drawn in something that simmered like oil, black with a rainbow hue. It was stylised yet detailed and there was no denying what it depicted.

Angel wings.

Micah stared at the ink beneath his golden skin, the way it writhed and coiled, still moving, still consuming him. The pain had dulled now to a constant ache, designed to be eternally there, beneath the surface of his suffering body. Lifting his eyes, he found the Nameless watching him.

"Want to see what it can do?"

"No." The word was a breath, a plea and—he knew it as soon as he said it—a mistake. The sweeping curve of the smile returned, slicing through the handsome face before him.

"Ah, Beloved, how I adore it when you deny me," he said and planted his hand on Micah's chest.

The ink on his back flared to incandescent agony, searing through his flesh, white hot and relentless. Micah screamed because there was nothing else he could do. His voice bounced off the ceiling and the walls, broke against the watching assembly, who laughed and jeered and lusted for him.

When the pain subsided and he slumped in his chains, he opened his eyes to find himself looking at the crowd gathered around, at the way they reached for each other, hungry and aroused.

"Asmodeus," said the Nameless. "Time for your gift too. Perhaps both together. And then we'll see the mighty of Heaven crawl for us."

Asmodeus stepped before him, but Micah couldn't tear his eyes off the crowd, off two faces in particular who gazed on impassively as Asmodeus took his face in his massive hands and bent to kiss him. The spell of lust ignited within him, pumping through his body, seizing it and shaking it like a terrier with a rat. Micah gasped as the demon released him, and his flesh responded as if a thousand lovers kissed and caressed him. He writhed in his chains, his body aching to be touched, to be taken.

A figure fell against his legs, thrown there by unseen hands, a woman, small and fine-boned, with large dark eyes. At a glare from Asmodeus, she reached up her shaking hands, taking his cock tentatively. Her golden hair fell down her back and she smiled up at him. A small, frightened smile.

"I had an angel once." She stroked his balls, tracing a fingernail up the pulsing vein to the head. "He loved me so much he told me what he was. I bore him a child. I adored him but he wouldn't come when I needed him and so I fell. He even looked a bit like you. I loved him so."

She took him in her mouth, swallowing him while one hand cupped his balls.

"Good, Lara," said Asmodeus, stroking her hair as if she was a dog. "Make him come for us."

Micah strained against his chains, his eyes searching frantically for the pair he had seen, lost now in a sea of faces, in the red mist of arousal. Lara worked her throat along the length of his cock while her hands probed between his ass cheeks, forcing their way into the tight hole. He groaned. Sperm damned up in his balls and her tongue tickled the vein on the underside, teasing him to higher levels of arousal and blind need.

"Not yet," the Nameless commanded.

Lara released him at once, but only long enough to force something down the length of his engorged shaft, a cold metal ring, as icy as the chamber in which he had first found himself. Then her mouth descended again, her fingers returned to their teasing penetration. The ring tightened around him, shrinking in contact with his body heat, blocking any hoped for release, trapping him as effectively as the chains that held him in place.

"No," he moaned, trying to force his lust-drugged eyes open, trying to fight the darkness swelling up inside him. The chains dragged his arms out further, and Asmodeus kissed him again, pouring more of the agony of arousal into him.

Beyond them, beyond Asmodeus's kisses and Lara's devouring mouth, beyond the Nameless and his tender caresses of damnation, the crowd had turned on each other. Cries of ecstasy and torture, of lust and pain combined, echoed his own. And one other sound. One voice. A small sigh of dismay. Micah's eyes snapped open and he found her.

Lily stood in the midst of the damned, Sam's hands travelling over her corseted stomach, dipping beneath the short leather skirt she wore, his mouth biting into her bare shoulder. She leaned back against her demon, her eyes almost blind with lust, their last sight only of him, of her fallen angel and the things they did to him. She cried out and began to shake, tears springing from her eyes like diamonds in the infernal light.

"No," Micah gasped. "Please no."

The Nameless slapped his hand hard into the small of Micah's back, and the tattoo ignited like sodium in water, white hot and violent. Lara swallowed his endlessly pulsing cock, her throat working him, her wicked fingers teasing and probing. Asmodeus's mouth devoured him.

Micah tried to tear himself free, struggled against the tsunami of despair, desire and rage. Instead it surged up inside him and swept everything else that remained of his former self away to darkness at the roar of his release.

Chapter Nineteen

Sam's firm touch encircling Lily's body was comforting rather than arousing. She was certain that with the sight before her, the anguish on Micah's face, nothing she saw would have aroused her. And yet her body had betrayed her, just as Micah believed she and Sam had betrayed him. She had seen the belief on his face, etched there amid the lust and the horror. And all the time her body had throbbed for Sam's touch.

With gentle hands hidden behind cruelty, Sam lifted her over his shoulder, carrying her out of the audience chamber, away from the surging mass of bodies which were even now leaving their first partners and searching for another. He strode as if he wanted to carry her away to fuck her in some darkened corner, but his fingers caressed the bare patches of her skin and she hid her face in his shoulder to hide her tears.

Once the noise fell away behind them, Sam lowered her to the ground, letting her lean back against the wall to get her bearings. They stood in silence, neither looking at the other, the image of Micah strung up and tortured, of Micah sinking into damnation, still vivid in their minds.

"Breathe," Sam told her at last.

She gulped in air, choked and doubled over, coughing and retching. She could still hear it, the noises of the chamber, running through the stone walls like distant thunder. Sam rubbed her back absently until the coughing subsided.

"Better?" She nodded and he took the leash attached to her collar again. "We should get moving."

"Where, Master?" She could ask, if she was careful. He wouldn't punish her for that, not if they were alone, so long as she kept the right tone, just in case.

"Back home."

Lily planted her feet firmly on the stone, staring at him. Shock made her forget herself. "Not without him."

Anger flashed in Sam's eyes but though his temper flared, he didn't lose it. "You saw him. There's nothing we can do now. We're getting out of here."

She dropped to her knees, pressing her forehead to the ground. "Please, don't. We can't leave him like that."

Sam growled a curse deep in his throat and somehow she knew she'd won, whether he liked it or not. He couldn't stand to see Micah trapped here any more than she could.

"Get up," he told her. "Stay close and do exactly what I say." She did as he told her, and as she stood before him, his hands closed on her upper arms, squeezing them so tightly that they bruised. "Exactly what I say, Lily. No arguments. Swear it."

"Yes, Master," she chimed.

But his grip tightened still further, his eyes blazing. She squirmed beneath his painful touch. "No. No games. Swear it."

He meant it. More than anything he had ever said to her, he meant this. She stilled, taking the pain, using to remind herself what they were doing and why. Using it to remind her that this was his love for her forging this determination. It had to be. The alternative was—

She nodded, her expression solemn again. He needed to believe her. To be able to trust her as she trusted him. "I swear it, Sam."

He released her and the blood surged back into her arms, where scarlet bands stood out in the dim light. He breathed a little more easily and that made her own breathing calm.

"Right then." He shifted uncomfortably, his hands curling and uncurling. "We'll go and see what we can do. But Lily..." She lifted her chin, ready to argue, ready to defy him. "Lily, really..." He exhaled, stretched out and threaded his fingers through hers, pulling her carefully against him, as if he feared to hurt her, or feared to let her go. "It might be far too late."

He led her down the narrow passages, trails which wound in and across each other. Several times she was sure they were doubling back on their path, but Sam didn't waver. She followed dutifully in his wake, her eyes lowered, the leash in his hand drawing her on. Those they encountered chilled her to the core, eyes that trailed over her body, followed her hungrily. Her skin itched as if unclean, but she didn't try to brush off the sensation. If she showed her discomfort, they would know. They would see it as a weakness and that would damn them both. And Micah.

Micah... In spite of her resolution to be strong she shuddered at the thought of what she had seen, of Micah, of what they had done to him. When Sam stopped, she fell still behind him, never lifting her eyes to see the being to whom he talked. A blaze of heat washed over her, sweat prickling on her skin. But she didn't care. All she could think of was Micah, the pain in his eyes, the anguish, and finally the insane lust. It hadn't looked like him when Sam carried her away. It hadn't looked like her angel at all.

"They're finished with him," said a rasping voice. It trailed over Lily's exposed skin like sandpaper and she knew his eyes were on her. "For now anyway. They plan to have some fun with him though, and for a long old time." He laughed, a dreadful hiccoughing sound that jerked at her insides. "Damnation, we all do, Sammael. I'd say you're high up in the line given you brought him here."

"Yeah, probably." Sam's voice had a smirk buried in it that

made her shift her stance with discomfort. "But I want to see him first, Xaphan. He put me through some rings up there. I want to see that he knows it was me who put him here. And there's her, of course. I want him to see her."

Xaphan snorted and that surge of arid heat flared around them again. "Aye, well, who wouldn't want to see her? It'll drive him over the edge, if Asmodeus and the Nameless haven't done so already. They took him back to the ice cells. Give him some cooling-off time. He was wild by the time they finished. Damn near tore his way through that bitch Lara's head."

A hand closed on Lily's thigh, not Sam's. This touch was cold and dry, like frozen suede. It squeezed and she flinched back, unwilling to cry out or make trouble for fear it would give them away.

Sam's fist moved in a blur, slamming down on Xaphan's arm. There was an audible crack and Xaphan howled, staggering back from them.

"You don't touch what's mine," Sam snarled. He shoved Xaphan back against the wall. "Never!" Driving his fist into the demon's stomach, Sam pounded the air from him. "Ever!" His knee crashed up and Xaphan doubled over with a curse and a rush of breath. "Touch what's mine!"

Xaphan slid down into a heap at their feet. Sam stepped over him and, with the leash drawing her forward, Lily had to follow, picking her way carefully so as not to brush against his slumped figure. Her heart was pounding, but she kept her head bowed and wished she had some way to reach out to Sam, to show him, what? That she appreciated his care? That she loved him?

They rounded another corner and she stumbled. Strong arms caught her, Sam turning so fast that he moved between moments. He said nothing, just stopped her fall, and raised her up onto her feet, pausing only to brush a strand of her hair back behind her ear.

But he said nothing. Just turned away and led her on, down into the depths of Hell, down into the cold.

The temperature dropped steadily as they descended, ice creeping up the surface of the stairs. With Sam ahead of her, Lily doubted she would fall far, but the heels were high enough that she was certain she might take out an ankle before he saved her. But there again, barefoot wasn't an option here.

At the foot of the stairs, the dungeon walls sparkled with frost. Snow piled up against the walls, and the only light came from flickering torches, pallid against the darkness and the cold.

"Stay quiet," Sam ordered and she nodded.

The corridor opened out to a round chamber, doors leading off in every direction. In the centre, hunched over a brazier, was the most repulsive-looking little man Lily had ever seen. His skin was the colour of corpses, mottled with liver spots and stretched so tightly over his frame that it looked thin as paper. His eyes loomed out of the face, far too large.

"Sammael, is it?" he wheezed, peering at them. "Been a long time since I had you down here, Sammael." He rubbed his hands together, the knuckles cracking as he did so. Then he turned his gaze on Lily, his eyes turning piercing. "Brought me another treasure, have you?"

Sam folded his arms and the leash tugged Lily closer to him. For that she was grateful. "No. I want to see the angel."

The old demon laughed. "Not much of an angel left about him now, boy."

Sam grinned, showing all his teeth. "Just the same. I need some time. Alone."

"Alone? Ah, Sam, that'd be more than my job's worth. Now maybe if your friend here would care to distract me for a time..."

Lily swallowed hard, trying to figure out how she could bring herself to let that thing touch her, but swearing that if it helped Micah, she would do it. Sam, however, had different ideas.

"I'll let her entertain you with a knife, perhaps? But certainly not by herself. I thought all of Hell knows I'm training her for the Nameless. Even Asmodeus has more sense than you do, Charus. Get out and give me room."

Grumbling, the old demon shuffled off, leaving them alone. Sam grabbed the key hanging by the cell door and fitted it to the lock.

"Remember, Lily, do what I tell you. If I say get out, you run, understand?"

"Yes, but—it's Micah..."

Sam levelled his gaze at her, his mouth a hard and unyielding line. "Did you see him back there? It'll be worse by now. Much worse."

"What do you mean?"

Sam swung the door open and stood there like an escort, waiting for her to enter ahead of him. Lily stepped into the ice-encrusted room, and her feet came to a halt as if frozen to the spot.

Something growled from out of the shadows. Something hungry. Cold speared through her and only the flat of Sam's hand coming to rest against the small of her back propelled her forward.

"I can't see," she whispered.

"I can see."

The voice clawed its way through her, Micah's voice. His voice and yet not his voice. Nothing like it.

He growled again and the sound of his chains accompanied the sound. She flinched back but Sam stopped her, his body firm against hers, determined.

"He can't hurt you. Not chained up." Sam took a step forward and Lily was forced to do the same.

"Micah?" she asked, her whole body trembling.

As her eyes adjusted to the darkness, she picked out his body, his arms stretched above him, chained to a stake in the centre of the room. His feet were similarly restrained at the base. For a moment, she pictured Saint Sebastian as seen in countless portraits, bound to a tree, shot with arrows. Of course that wasn't how he died. They beat him to death.

Micah's eyes gleamed in the dim light and then, as they fixed on her, blazed red. His nostrils flared. "I can smell you."

"Micah?" She couldn't make herself reach out to him. Never in a million years had she dreamed she would hesitate now.

"I can smell your fear." He jerked forward, the chains wrenching his muscles, straining to contain him.

Sam's body hardened and his stance changed, subtly shifting his hip around her so he stood in front, partially shielding her.

"And you, Sammael," said Micah. "Don't think I'll forget what you did. You brought us here. You damned us."

Sam opened his mouth as if to protest, but then closed it again. Lily glanced up just in time to see his Adam's apple lift and fall as his throat worked.

"She's mine," said Micah, and his voice dipped to ripple across her skin. "Always has been. Always will be. And now, Lily—" She shivered, as if he touched her, as if he trailed his fingers up the nape of her neck. "—now I don't have to behave anymore."

Closing her eyes didn't help. Neither did concentrating on Sam, his warmth, his body pressed against hers. Her pulse made her ache. She wanted him, wanted them both.

"Touch her for me, Sam. Let me hear her gasp in pleasure. Let me hear her moan."

"Micah," Sam said, his voice thick with arousal. "We're here to help you. To free you."

"And what would I do if I was free? To her, to you. What would I do?" He laughed, a low and dangerous sound that echoed off the ceiling and walls. "Touch her for me. Run your hand up those long legs and let me see her quiver."

Sam moved slowly, as if only reluctantly obeying. His hand closed on her thigh, sliding up to the edge of the skirt, to the curve of her ass. So intimate a touch made her damp for him, for them both.

Micah inhaled, nostrils flaring again, and the red light in his eyes grew intense. His lips drew back from his teeth in a rictus smile and his face, stark in the shadows, beautiful and yet skeletal, strained closer.

"Make her come for me, Sam. I want to see her come. I want to see you come."

The chains groaned under the pressure, the metal grinding together. And behind him, the wood creaked.

"Sam," Lily said. His eyes were closed, his face strained in ecstasy, like a man enchanted. She tried to pull back, but his hand closed on her skin, digging into her buttocks to hold her against him. "Sam!"

"Take her," Micah commanded, writhing towards them. "Throw her down and fuck her for me, Sam. Make her scream. Make her come. And then give her to me."

Sam turned with a snarl, pulling her towards him. Lily cried out in alarm and Micah groaned. Sam's grip hurt. His mouth when it closed on hers bruised, his teeth grazed her lips. This wasn't like him, wasn't like either of them. She knew them, knew their hearts, their souls. She'd felt their love, their minds touching hers, entwining about hers to carry her through the darkness. And here they were, consumed, defiled.

Tears stung her eyes like acid and she tried to fight her way free. But Sam was too strong, too powerful. And Micah's laughter goaded him on, each command he gave more violent. Pain lanced up her arms as Sam twisted them behind her back and forced her to bend forward, so her sex was bared to him. She sobbed his name.

And abruptly everything went still.

Sam let out a ragged breath and released her. Staggering forward, Lily landed on her knees by the door, the ice biting into her skin.

"You bound me." Sam's voice grated on harsh breaths. His hands spread wide on either side of his hips, the fingers flexing as if he wanted to curl them into fists, but restrained himself. "You bound me to her so I wouldn't hurt her." His chest heaved as he regained his self-control. Lily struggled to her feet, watching them, her whole body shaking. "How could you ask me to do so now, Micah? How could you, of all people, ask—"

The wood crashed as Micah pulled the chains free.

"Lily! Get out!" Sam yelled. "Shut the door. Get out now!"

Micah took him in a single leap and the pair of them crashed to the floor, grappling together. Lily backed out, gripping the door, her knuckles white. She'd promised Sam to obey. But Sam was in danger. Micah forced him down, his body stronger, wilder, his hands tearing at her demon. Sam twisted beneath him, and their mouths met. Violent, needy, animal, they kissed.

Mesmerised by what she saw, Lily didn't realise anyone was behind her until a hand fell on her shoulder, another closed on her mouth, and the door slammed shut.

Sam's body betrayed him. Micah was strong, always had been, but the newborn demonic Micah was more than that. He was ravenous. His mouth consumed, his hands raked Sam's skin, their legs entangled.

"I know you want me, Sam," Micah snarled. "You did from the start. Now say it. Tell me."

"Yes, I want you."

Micah flinched as if struck. Hadn't expected that, had he? Looking to dominate, to force himself on another, but when the other was willing, however unexpected...

"You know I want you," Sam insisted, and brought his own hands up to frame the former angel's face. Micah's nostrils flared. Something of the features Sam knew bled back into the animal expression there.

"Sam." His voice was still a growl, but a low rumble now, a warning buried deep inside it. So dangerous, his lust barely contained.

Sam leaned in to him, capturing his mouth. He'd kissed Micah before, but not like this. He poured himself into Micah's mouth, kissing him as he kissed Lily. As lovers, not rivals teasing one another.

Micah's hands grabbed his upper arms, the fingers digging into his muscles but, finding no restraint or fight in the body beneath his, the touch gentled.

"You know I want you," Sam repeated, pulling at his leather pants. "And she's watching, isn't she? Looking through the gap in the door? Come on, Micah, she wants to see it as much as you want to do it."

He pulled himself out of Micah's stunned grip and turned around, ready for him, eager to tell the truth. He'd waited a long time to have Micah to himself, and if it was going to be this way, so be it. He'd take everything the angel had, and then give some back as well. And it would be good. Damn good.

But Micah didn't pounce.

"She isn't there." The strength in the voice faded. "Sam. She isn't there." It sounded like Micah again, the Micah he knew.

Struggling up from the cell floor, Sam found Micah standing over him, his naked body still glorious, still marked with wings right down his back, but the eyes, narrowed in concern, were blue. Bright, lapis lazuli blue.

"Micah?"

The angel stretched out his hand to help Sam up. "I'm—" He inhaled slowly and let the air out in a long rush. "Yes, it's me. I think—" He frowned and shook his head, like a punch-drunk boxer. "You brought Lily *here*?"

"She wouldn't take no for an answer. Where is she? Lily?" He reached the door and tugged it open. The room outside was empty. Not even a sign of Charus. "Lily? Come back. It's okay."

Micah pushed past him. "She's gone. There's no trace of her, only—her scent." He lurched down the corridor following whatever invisible after-trace of Lily only he could smell.

Sam's instincts for danger were screaming inside his gut. "Lily?"

No answer. Great. He'd brought her here, told her to trust him and now she was lost. Lost or taken. *Shit!*

He hurried after Micah, hunting each corner and shadowed nook in a vain hope he'd find her hiding. Nothing. Not a sign. The angel strode on ahead, almost out of sight in the icy shadows.

"Micah?"

Micah stopped abruptly.

"*Go back.*" The warning swirled through his mind, desperate and stained with fear. "*Hide. They're coming.*"

"*Too late.*" He knew it. There was a scuffle. Not even a scuffle. Micah didn't fight. He knew it was useless.

And so did Sam.

"Sammael?" Asmodeus's voice boomed down the hall. "Sammael? Are you intent on spoiling all our fun? I've got the angel. Now where's the girl?"

Where's the girl? They didn't know. His heart surged inside him, hope springing up like a geyser. They didn't have Lily.

So who did?

His newborn hope fell as if turned to stone. So who did?

Walking up to where Asmodeus and his lackeys held Micah wasn't quite the hardest thing he'd ever done, but it felt like it. They moved like hyenas, seizing his arms and forcing them into manacles, but it was not the first time that had happened. Nor, he feared, the last.

"Where's the girl?" Asmodeus asked again.

Sam tried to keep his face impassive. "I thought you had her."

The blow came as expected, swift and brutal, snapping his face from one side to the other. "Don't be impudent. The Nameless wants her now. Where is she?"

Sam spat out blood, bright and red on the icy steps. It gleamed there, for just a moment before a desperate figure threw itself on the spot, licking it up, sucking at the spot. Sam felt his stomach twist. This was a demon? Was this his own instilled nature as well? It disgusted him. They all did.

He turned to face Asmodeus again. Something glinted in the king's dark eyes, dangerous and out of control. And something else. Fear?

"I don't know. She was here. Right outside. Someone took her."

Asmodeus snarled at him, anger winning out, rage draining the blood from his face. "Took her? Whoever took her will spend eternity wishing he'd kept his dick to himself. Bring them," he told the other demons. "They can explain it to the Nameless themselves."

Hauled down the tunnels by hands that tore and scratched, that bruised and bit, Sam tried to reach for Micah's mind. Perhaps together they could sense her, feel her presence. Perhaps together, even now, they could find her. The angel was carried ahead of him, unconscious or just completely passive, Sam couldn't tell. But he didn't fight. Not like Sam. He couldn't help himself, even when every struggle of his was punished tenfold by his captors.

Finally, beaten and bloodied, he was dumped unceremoniously at the foot of the dais that held the throne. The Nameless sat forward, watching him bleed and cough, watching him try to drag himself off the ground.

"Well, Sammael, it looks like in trying to steal one of my presents, you lost the other. So they tell me, anyway."

"Tell you...?"

"My Lord—" Asmodeus began angrily but the Nameless stopped him with a wave of his hand.

"Silence," he said, his voice unnaturally calm and controlled. One might say even blissful. "We have guests."

Sam twisted around so sharply it hurt. From the far side of the hall a group of beings clad all in white were approaching. Not just clad in white, they glowed with light, the luminescence making the blackness of the walls of Hell even darker. They looked ludicrously handsome in their neatly tailored jackets, pressed trousers, the crispest shirts. All white. All perfect spotless white.

Shit, thought Sam, they look like a fucking boy band. It was a short leap from dressing in that sort of getup to singing in close harmony.

But they weren't. He knew that. They were angels. A host of angels.

One stepped forward, his golden eyes coming to rest on Micah, and the placid mouth sank into a hard line. Another stepped forward then, also golden-haired, but in a style which fell over his eyes in an oddly human way.

"Lucifer," said the first angel and bowed his head in greeting.

"Raphael." The Nameless nodded, a gesture unparalleled in all of Sam's infernal experience. They were acting like equals. "And Enoch too. I am honoured." He didn't sound it.

"We've come for our brother," said Raphael.

The Nameless stilled, and his eyes bored into them. "You took the Nephilim in his place."

"We have no Nephilim. We have come for Micah."

Pushing himself out of the chair, the Nameless stalked forward. "Micah is mine. I have marked him."

"And yet here he is," Raphael concluded in his musical voice, "uncorrupted by his sojourn here. Our brother, if you please. And the mortal."

"The woman you were going to allow to die," Micah interrupted. "What right do you have to come here now and claim us, to swoop in and save the day?"

Raphael's jaw fell open, his mouth slack for a moment before his grace reasserted itself. "Micah, you forget yourself."

Micah rose, his muscles rippling beneath his torn and blooded skin. "I think I only begin to remember myself. You've forgotten me. You and all my so-called brethren. This isn't a place of healing, Raphael. You have no business here."

But the angel stood firm, glaring at his supposed subordinate. "I am one of the seven who stand before the Lord, Micah. He has sent me to untangle this and I will do so. Where is the girl? Where is the Nephilim?"

Sam gagged, as in his mind elements slotted into place. *Click, click, click,* so easy, so simple, so bloody obvious. "Who traded Micah for the Nephilim?" he blurted out into the taut silence.

"The Creator himself," snarled the Nameless, clenching his hand into a fist around the hilt of his knife.

Raphael shook his head. "Not so. He loves all, but He would never make an exchange like that."

Micah stared at them, angry, betrayed, but silent. No, not at them all, at one in particular, one who would not meet his gaze. "Enoch," Micah said at last. "Enoch, did you lie?"

Enoch, the Metatron, let out a sigh which deflated his

chest. "What choice did I have, Micah? I tried to make you leave. I tried to stop you. But you wouldn't. I had no choice but to leave you here and take Hopkins."

To Sam's amazement, Micah nodded. "What parent would do less for their child?"

Tears started in Enoch's eyes. They glistened as they slid down his cheeks. "I never dreamed he would escape. I meant to keep him with me, out of harm at last. But he...the first chance he got, he fled. I trusted him and he fled."

"Then where is he?" Sam interrupted. "And where has he taken Lily?"

Freezing water burst over Lily's face, dousing her in a terrifying reality. She flinched back, a scream on her lips, and found her hands tied behind her back. She spluttered her way to consciousness and opened her eyes to find Hopkins standing over her with a wide, shallow bowl.

"Good. You're awake, witch. We can begin."

"You're dead," she gasped, trying to wriggle her hands free. "I saw you fall."

"Yet you're the one I found here in Hell." He laughed, dropping the bowl. It clanged against the stones and rolled around with a deep ringing sound. Beyond him a lake stretched out, wide, dark and deep.

"Welcome to the shores of the Acheron." Hopkins knelt beside her and stroked her hair.

Shivers ran down her spine, but she held herself still, unwilling to give him the satisfaction of seeing her fear. Still grey and colourless, he didn't look harmless now. He moved like quicksilver, so fast she couldn't follow. Though he wore a pale suit, his eyes sparkled like cold fire and his mouth was a thin, hard line of hate.

"They say that those who try to swim across are dragged

down by the souls of the damned, who also attempted to escape this place, or who never managed to cross. Trapped between worlds, they wait in watery graves, pulling the unwary down with them. Suicides, murder victims, the massacred, the unavenged, the forsaken, those who never embraced their lives and souls, those who never accepted their deaths, they all wait in those depths."

"Let me go." She tried to keep her voice calm and controlled. "Please. Let me go."

His hand slid down the side of her face, his touch clammy and disturbing, intimate but at the same time repulsive. He stroked her neck but stopped at her shoulder, his eyes fixed on the mark left there by Sam's teeth.

"I can't do that. You're a witch, the concubine of a demon who would give you to the dark Lord himself." He gazed at her with wide, washed-out eyes and tried to smile helpfully. "I'm saving you. Why can't you understand that?"

He leaned in closer and Lily could smell his breath, rancid and ancient. This was a creature as old as time, one who had persecuted countless women and men, physically and mentally torturing them, isolating them from their families and homes, until finally he killed them. Just as he had killed Todd and Rachel. Just as he had tried to kill her.

"They called me Jack, when I liked to cut. And how I liked to cut. They called me the Witchfinder General before that, and Inquisitor. Titles have power, especially titles like that. They instil fear, get the blood pumping. Do you know that in the first days, humankind spilt human blood for the Lord? They sliced open their sacrifices, or drowned them, or garrotted them, all to the glory of His name. And those who were special, marked, or tainted like you, they were the most powerful sacrifices of all. It's an age-old tradition."

Lily's stomach twisted and he leered in closer, his hand closing on her shoulder, pulling her towards him. She did the only thing she could and slammed her forehead right into the bridge of his nose.

Pain blinded her. Hopkins howled as he staggered back from her, but it served her nothing. His fist cudgelled into the side of her face, knocking her to the ground. Without her hands to save her, she hit the rocks hard, and stars danced before her eyes.

He seized her by the back of her neck, dragging her up. "You like it rough, do you? Fucking bitch!"

He hit her stomach hard, driving his fist up into her and knocking all the air from her. Gasping, blind, her body screaming in agony, she folded over his blow. Another crashed into her in precisely the same place, his knee this time. She heard a crack and knew it was something inside her. Blood filled her mouth and she couldn't breathe.

"We'll see how you like it wet."

He plunged her into the black and near-stagnant waters.

Lily's eyes flared open and she struggled, remembering the sensation of drowning too intimately from her vision of Rachel's death. Air bubbled up from her mouth, sheened with light, like particles of pure magic in the dark water. Beneath her, weeds swayed, stirred up by her struggles. Her feet scrabbled against the stone but she couldn't find purchase, and her body wasn't strong enough to tear itself free of Hopkins' grasp. He pushed her deeper and her lungs strained, needing to breathe, fighting to breathe. Her heart pounded and thundered in her head.

The weeds undulated like long hair in the water, parted and closed. Behind it two points of light sparkled and, to Lily's panicked horror, resolved into a face, a woman's face. She surged up, pale and wan, her sunken cheeks bruised. Lips brushed Lily's and suddenly Lily knew her. Rachel.

"*Breathe, Lily.*"

Rachel opened her mouth and air flowed over Lily's lips, little bubbles, trailing away, wasted by Lily's shock. Rachel shook her head, the strands of hair swirling around their faces, and tried again. Lily forced her lips to part and breathed. The blackness cleared, and from her left she saw another face, as pale and lost as Rachel.

"Breathe, Lily. You must breathe or die."

Todd kissed her and the air he imparted was blazing hot, a total contrast to Rachel's, and it warmed her rapidly freezing body.

Hopkins' hands bit into her scalp and shoulders. Pushing her deeper, holding her down. She kicked and struggled, feeling her hair tearing out by the roots, but she couldn't get free. And her body still strained to breathe.

Rachel surged up again and Lily met her greedily.

"Help me," she thought, pleading with all she believed that they would hear her. *"You have to help me."*

She needed to breathe. Her body was reaching the break-point, her own instinctive urges gaining control. Her sight was falling away to the darkness of the lake. She had to breathe. Had to.

Chapter Twenty

Micah willed himself to be still, to capture the inner calm and let it cradle him. Panic would gain nothing. Rage would tear him apart. He needed to think, to be calm, to feel. He needed to find her.

All around him the chamber exploded in wild accusations, shouts and threats. The Nameless and Raphael all but snarled at each other, Enoch was still trying to plead his case, and Sam was yelling the loudest of all.

Something long forgotten inside him unfurled. Something he had put aside so long ago that it remained no more than a ghost of a memory. Now it roared back into life from deep inside him.

"Be silent!" Micah roared, and it was as if that *other* rose up within him. Pure and powerful, it shook its way through him, transforming as it went with the heat of a refiner's fire.

His voice shook the earth as only the voice of an archangel could, coupled with something else, something greater powering it from behind. They fell still, even Raphael and Lucifer, stunned. Micah didn't care. All he could think of was Lily back in the hands of the Nephilim.

The Nameless stepped towards him, the knife in his hands now, the blade glinting ruddily in the light. "Brother, you will not bring that light here. If you do I will snuff it out. If you speak the Word, or His Name, I will—"

Micah glared at him and whatever Lucifer saw in his face, it stopped him. But the blade still remained in his clenched fist, the blade that could kill gods, let alone a demon or an angel. Any angel. Even one as powerful as the Morningstar himself.

Micah could feel the fire of the Creator within him now. It had been so long that the dizzying feeling of being swamped by such endless power stole his breath. It felt euphoric and at the same time terrifying. Once he had lived only for moments like these, consumed with this fiery zeal. Now he felt like nothing more than a vessel to be used.

"I can find her." He had to force the words out. "She lives, as yet, and I can find her. For with Him, nothing is hidden."

"Micah, you can't dream to use Elohim's power to seek out the mortal?" Raphael exclaimed.

A spark of rage ignited in the vortex of energy overwhelming him, and Micah recognised it as his own. "Well, why not? I fell, remember? I fell and you left me here to rot so Enoch could save his spawn. As he's been trying to save him throughout time. And failing. Just as he failed the child's mother. How many lives has the ruling to leave the Nephilim be cost? How many innocent souls? How many who turned to the Nameless for salvation under his torture?"

He burned inside, the energy coiling through him, making his anger blaze even brighter. He had to find her. He threw back his head and gave himself up to the power, losing himself in it, becoming it.

The Nameless gave a howl of rage and thrust the knife forward in a savage attack, but Micah was gone, a column of fire which swirled around them, licking up the length of the chamber. It snuffed out all other fires, drained the light from the angels. And then it took off, like a serpent of flames, roaring down tunnel after tunnel, razing the ground as it passed, scourging the labyrinths of Hell.

Light blasted across the surface of the water, roaring like a dragon released from its den. Lily gave one last, desperate kick and felt her foot connect with his legs. The next moment Hopkins was torn away from her, flung out over the water, and Lily burst from the lake, gasping for precious air. Strong arms pulled her clear, dragged her onto dry land, arms which flickered with fire, which glowed from within with the light of the sun. Micah's arms. She knew their touch as well as she knew her own. Micah cradled her, held her.

"No!" Hopkins shrieked, splashing through the water towards them. "No, she's unclean. She's tainted. She has to die to be saved. She has to die."

Lily forced her eyes open. Hopkins stood in the water, drenched and raving, screaming at her, and at her angel.

"*Rachel, Todd*," she called with her mind. And they heard her.

Hands surged up from the water, clawing at his legs. His cries turned inarticulate and he fought back, struggling to free himself.

"Father!" he cried, as they dragged him lower. "Father! Save me. Father!"

The black waters of the Acheron closed over his face, flowed into his gaping mouth and still he cried. The number of hands multiplied in response to his struggles, more and more pulling him down. And then everything fell still. The lake stretched out, an endless black sheet, reflecting only the lights on the shore.

Lily looked up into Micah's face. He was just visible inside the column of fiery magnificence that held her. And yet the flames didn't burn. Rather it felt like sitting in a pool of sunshine. She smiled and saw him smile in return. Behind her other figures moved, hurrying towards them or rushing to the shore.

A man in white threw himself towards the water but fell to his knees before he reached it, keening in grief and pain.

Another bent towards him, placing a hand that was not quite comfort enough on his shoulder.

"Enoch," he said. "It's over."

"He lives," Enoch sobbed. "He lives on in there. Draw him out, Raphael. Please, I beg you. Draw him out."

But Raphael shook his head. "I may not. His victims have him now, as is their right. Forever. It's their salvation, my friend, to punish him. There are so many of them."

"And only one of him."

"I know. But he threw away his chance of Heaven when he slew them. Time and again."

A woman stepped forward from the ranks of the damned, her golden hair tumbling around her frail, bruised body. She wrapped her arms around her chest and fought to make herself approach the angels, terrified but determined. "Enoch?"

Lily stared as the woman who had taken part in the abuse of Micah stumbled forward.

"Enoch? That—that thing was our son?"

Enoch and Raphael spun around as she fell to her knees, keening and weeping, her whole body shaking with grief and remorse. No one went to her aid. Not a single one of them, angelic or demonic.

Lily's heart twisted for her, but she couldn't move. It hurt too much to move.

Sam dropped to his knees before Lily, blocking them from her view. "You're all right. Are you? All right? Lily?"

She tried to draw in a breath and everything hurt, all at once. She took it in with a sob and a cough which developed into a racking agony that shook her. Blood filled her mouth again and her sight wavered, darkening.

"*Lily,*" said Micah, directly into her struggling mind. He glowed from head to foot, her angel, so much more powerful than she had ever imagined. "*Lily, stay with us.*"

She was trying. Couldn't they see she was trying? But it hurt. It hurt so much. And she felt so tired. Blackness welled up around her, from within and without, as if she too was falling into the dark water, pulled down by dead hands.

She curled against Micah, her head on his burning shoulder, and her hands reached for Sam. He wrapped his fingers around hers and called her name, over and over, trying to draw her back.

Her eyes fluttered one last time, exhausted, heavy, drained, and she saw another figure bearing down on them, beautiful and terrible, a dull and vicious blade raised in his fist. Her fingers tightened on Sam's hand and she tried to cry out.

"*Micah!*"

But it was Sam who moved, Sam who rose like a shadow, so quick, so supple, Sam who stepped between Micah's back and the Nameless's blade.

Sam who folded over, who fell.

And Lily found her voice, in a scream.

The knife slid through his skin, in between his ribs and deep inside him. Sam stared at it, detached, unable to believe that it was really happening. The knife was created to destroy the Creator, and instead, it was inside him.

The last few times he'd been stabbed like this it had hurt. Damn, it had hurt. But not this time. This time he felt nothing but bewilderment.

Of course, the last few times he'd been stabbed, his body had reacted instinctively, beginning the healing process immediately.

But not this time. No, this time even his body let him down.

Heal, he told his body. *Heal!*

The Nameless jerked his blade out and blood followed it, bright red, glossy, pumping through the hands Sam pressed against the wound. His legs jerked and he fell, all strength flowing out of him with his blood.

The Nameless cursed and backed away, retreating to the demons as the angels closed ranks in front of Sam.

Angels, he thought. *Protecting me. What a joke!*

Lily called his name, the sound high-pitched and desperate.

"*It's all right*," he wanted to tell her. "*It doesn't hurt.*"

And then it did.

Holy shit, it hurt. Fire and ice warred inside him, stretching barbed wire through his veins. His breath burst from his lungs and he arched his back up off the rock floor. Micah and Lily were with him, trying to hold him, comfort him. Even hurt as badly as she was, Lily struggled to pull him into her embrace, telling him she loved him over and over again.

"Raphael," yelled Micah, and the voice was not entirely his own. Sam felt it roaring through his mind, and through his tortured body. He remembered that Voice from long ago, knew it as intimately as he knew anything, and he wept to hear it again. The tears felt like acid on his face. "Raphael, you have a sacred duty."

The Angel of Healing bent over him. "But he's one of the fallen, Lord. One of them."

Micah's face didn't change, implacable, carved of stone. "No. He never fell. He was ever mine. He just did not remember until he saw the threat to my existence. Now, perform your sacred duty."

Raphael shuddered and looked into Sam's face with his endless golden eyes. With a touch that fell like morning raindrops, he laid his hands on Sam's stomach, his face stilling in concentration.

Everything fell still around him. The encroaching cold fled at the golden touch and Sam breathed again, a deep breath of relief. The pain faded with his exhalation and he slumped down in Micah's arms, Lily holding his hands, the sweet darkness of rest rising around him.

Micah smiled, and it was not just Micah's smile. "I am pleased," said the Voice. "I am well pleased."

The shadows weren't so frightening anymore. Sam closed his eyes and slept.

Chapter Twenty-One

Micah floated in the nexus of power and light, a distant observer of the events unfolding. His horror rippled out when Sam took within his own body the knife intended for the Creator, changing the world, changing reality, and the Spirit with him reacted with detached surprise.

"*You care.*"

Of course he cared. The thought was bitter and sharp with shock at the expectation that he would not.

"*For a demon?*"

For him. For her. Of course he cared. He loved them.

Micah closed his eyes, but that couldn't hide him from the Light, from the Word, or the Voice. The Creator surrounded him, cradled him, filled him. He was a vessel filled to overflowing.

"*I have need of you now, Micah. Enoch will be banished. I have need of a Metatron.*"

An image came to Micah's mind of Enoch walking a rain-drenched street while the lights cast yellowed puddles of light back up at his stricken face. Banished to earth, to walk amongst mortals. Banished as Micah had been.

"*You were never banished.*"

And yet, he was never called home until it suited the angels. He was left to guard and defend mankind, left to his own devices until he was barely an angel anymore, let alone the highest among them. Even the other angels forgot who he had been.

"*You served. You did your duty.*"

"I fell," Micah said. "I did what I did for love."

"*Of course. That is your primary nature. So did Enoch. And Lara. It's just a different kind of love. One which I better understand than yours.*"

"And because you don't understand it that makes it wrong?"

Micah felt the presence waver, searching for something. It couldn't be found in Micah's hostile mind, that much was certain, so it stretched out further. Searching and finding, drawing back what it needed. A way to communicate. A way to plea the case.

"I never said that," said the voice of a young woman. Her hair ran in silken lengths of gold down her back and her eyes were violet. Light spilled from them now, light and love instead of fear and hunger. Lara drifted closer, swathed in light, but he knew it wasn't Lara. Just her form. Lara as she should have been. She too was a vessel.

Micah knew that he should be glad it wasn't Lily. No mortal could have survived such a joining. But Lara? All he could remember were the things she had done to him, the things she had helped Asmodeus and the Nameless do. And all the others.

And something else. *I had an angel once.*

An angel who had failed her. She had been like Lily, but she had been damned. But first of all, she had been like Lily. A perfect vessel. Who loved an angel and was ruined because of her love.

Something sharp and painful wrenched within him and he recoiled.

"I never said it was wrong, Micah. Love is all. But you are

damaged too. I can help her heal. I want to help you heal."

"You can't," he snapped. "Nothing can. Look at them, at Lily and Sam. They almost died for me. And now you want me to leave them. To desert them for you."

"I am your Creator."

Tears stung his eyes. Micah tried to hold them in, defiant to the last. And they burned.

"I have saved Sam," the Creator continued. "I have wiped away every sin, every ill deed he ever did. I will send them back together, to comfort one another. But I have need of you. First of Angels, Eveningstar, come and stand on my left-hand side as is your rightful place."

The tears broke free. Ever since the war in Heaven, when he had been forced to side against his brother, Micah had been excluded from the Holy Court. The forgotten angel, the wanderer, the one they never mentioned. Even the other angels forgot about him. His place was on earth, his role guiding mankind, guarding those who could make a difference, until it reduced from guarding them all, to a nation, to a group, and finally a single individual. Lily.

The thought of her sent a pang through his shattered heart.

"You didn't trust me," he said, unable to keep a sob out of the words. "When Lucifer betrayed you, you lost your faith in me as well."

Lara's hand touched his cheek, gentle, tender, her skin soft and aglow with light. "No. I trusted you." An image of him cradling Lily came to mind, an image of him kissing Sam. "I trusted you with the most important task of all. Saving her, and giving him the opportunity to come back from the shadows. Who else could I have trusted, Micah?"

"And now you'd take me from them?"

Lara's face showed confusion and Micah felt the light

within him withdraw, the golden waves of sunset drifting to purple night.

"No. Perhaps not. Perhaps your task is not yet done. But I still have need of a Metatron, one to speak for me and be my Herald."

Micah frowned, staring at the face he had hated, listening to the voice he had never ceased to love. "If you will redeem a fallen soul, I think you might have one more deserving than me. She should never have fallen. It wasn't her fault that the imbalance was created. Yet she has had to pay for it. Because the angels punished Enoch for telling her the truth and made him leave."

"It was the law. Divine law."

"Which can't be wrong, can it?" Micah couldn't keep the sarcasm out of his voice.

The Creator didn't laugh. "No. It cannot. So what are we to do, Micah?"

"You've saved the damned before. Rescued them, raised them. The Magdalene, Saul, Lazarus. You harrowed Hell. There's an imbalance, isn't there? A mortal walks in Hell, so there must be an imbalance. Step in. Right it."

Laughter rang through the air, the type which lifted the soul, which made all who heard it smile as well.

"You would command me, Micah?"

Micah's lips drew up. He felt more joy than he had since the dawn of time.

"Do as you will, my Lord."

Darkness flowed over him, not the black cold of fear and terror. This was the warmth of sleep and comfort, the sense of being cradled and held safe in the night.

The light that was Micah, and yet was not Micah, glowed, arms enfolding Lily and Sam. It pulsed and then surged in sudden brightness. Micah pulled away, lifting from her embrace, rising into the air. Lily cried out and, on the far side of the cavern, so did Lara. The damned woman convulsed and threw back her head when the light engulfed her. For a moment the two of them hung above the earth, their feet not quite touching it, their bodies totally relaxed. Lily struggled to her feet, but Raphael's touch stilled her. Ancient beyond his appearance, the golden eyes told her to be still, to wait.

Damn it all, she didn't want to wait. "Micah!"

Sam stirred fitfully beneath Raphael's hands, and the Nameless began a string of curses, his demons shying back from Lara and her glowing form.

"He can't do this," Asmodeus shouted. "She's mine. I won her. She will always be mine."

But he didn't try to pull Lara down, nor did the Nameless attack. They stared, rooted to the spot by whatever was occurring. The light pulsed once more, bright as a supernova, and Lily hid her eyes.

When she looked again, when the glare had left her vision, both Micah and Lara were gone.

"No." The strength seemed to weep from her body and she sank back to her knees beside Sam. Raphael's solemn expression did nothing to comfort her. "Where is he?" she asked.

"That I do not know." He sighed. "Neither you nor Sammael can stay here, not once we leave. The balance has been restored now and you are no longer safe. The Nameless and his followers will want revenge, on both of you."

Lily glanced down. Sam looked so pale, but his face was still and free from pain.

"The knife has done its work, but I believe I have saved his life." Raphael reached out one elegant hand towards her. "Let me take you home."

Unthinking, she slid her hand into his. "But where is Micah?"

Raphael shook his head slowly. "That has not been shared with me. All I know is we have a new Metatron, one to replace Enoch."

"Micah?"

The world shifted around her, swirls of light and colour weaving together until, quite suddenly, it resolved into her bedroom. Sam lay on the bed, and Raphael, his white-gold hair looking slightly less perfect than it had when she first saw him, stood on the far side.

"He will need rest," said the angel, looking down on his patient with a curious expression. "And he will need love. He is not what he was and he will find that hard to deal with for a time. I trust you will undertake to care for him."

"Of course," she said, trying to shake off the dreadful feeling of numbness. Micah was gone. Gone forever. Taken from her, and from Sam.

Raphael shimmered, his form moving like morning mist evaporating in the sun, and then he was gone.

Lily stood there for a long moment watching Sam sleep. Satisfied all was well, she limped to the bathroom, shedding her clothes as she did. Raphael's touch had cured her ills as well, every bruise and scrape banished from her body. But he couldn't help what scars remained inside. She washed, drenching herself in hot water, and dried her hair. But she never felt a thing. Satisfied at last that every last trace was gone, she crawled under the duvet and curled up against Sam, holding him, watching him.

His eyelids fluttered the moment before he awoke, his thick lashes trembling against his cheekbones. Lily smiled as his eyes opened, the deep brown of dark chocolate or black coffee. They reflected her face, much as his exhausted smile reflected hers.

"You're alive." She pressed her hand against his chest to

268

feel the beating of his heart.

"Am I? Should it hurt this much?"

"I think it's generally a good sign."

He tried to smile. "Where's Micah?"

Her face froze, and answering panic filled his. Beneath her hand his heart rate increased.

"They said—that is, Raphael said there was no Metatron, not after Enoch was banished. So—"

"So Micah volunteered?"

She shook her head. "I don't know. But he's gone."

Sam rolled onto his back, staring at the ceiling. "I guess it makes sense. I never realised who he was. If I had..."

"Would you have been nicer to him?"

He grinned that same old wicked grin. "Christ, no. I'd have been even worse."

She gaped at him. "Sam, you said Christ. You've never said Christ before."

"'Course I have." But he hadn't. She was certain. She was about to say so, when Sam said, "The bloody Eveningstar. How did I miss that?"

"I've never heard of the Eveningstar."

"I'd say no mortal ever has." He rolled back towards her, stroking her hair as he spoke. "In the beginning—I mean, in the *very* beginning—God created only two angels. The Morningstar and the Eveningstar."

"Lucifer and Micah?"

"Yes, as it turns out, the strongest, the most beautiful, the closest to Him, designed to be his sons and his vessels. Even when He continued to create others, they were the closest, his Beloveds. But Lucifer wanted to be more. When the Creator brought mankind into being, he couldn't understand why. What need did the Almighty have for such paltry beings as these? And worse, they were given free will, something Lucifer believed

269

they did not deserve."

He kissed her, his lips brushing gently against hers.

"That doesn't hurt?" She smiled.

"No," he said. "No, that doesn't hurt at all." He kissed her again, pressing a little harder and his eyes blurred with desire. "Where was I?"

"Free will."

"Good thing, free will." He trailed his fingers through her hair, pulling the duvet up over them both, and Lily snuggled closer. "Lucifer rebelled and forged that knife." A shudder ran through him and his ardour cooled a fraction. "The knife that could kill the Creator, that would drink in divine power. Is that what it did to me, Lily? Wiped out all traces of the divine and the infernal?"

"Raphael only said you would be changed, but he saved your life."

Sam sighed, his eyes distant. "Changed, yes. I feel changed."

Lily slipped her arms around his waist, stroking the skin of his back. It felt like silk, and he groaned as she touched him. His body arched towards her and his erection pressed against her thigh.

"Sweetheart," he sighed. "You make me happy to be alive, no matter what."

"You're meant to rest."

"With you here? Not possible. Rest is the last thing on my mind." He cupped her breast, ran his thumb over her nipple until it stiffened and ached for him.

"Please, Sam, tell me what happened. Tell me about Micah."

He moaned, closing his eyes, but when he opened them she saw resolution there. "Okay, if I can make it fast. There was a war in Heaven when Lucifer revolted. But his brother stood against him. Or at least refused to stand with him. No one knows the full story except the two of them and the Creator himself. When Lucifer was defeated, bound and cast down to Hell, taking those who had joined him with him. The Eveningstar...he vanished, I suppose. Or talk of him stopped. Like most of the others, I assumed he too had been banished. But if it was Micah—which it was, of course—he was sent to earth, to guard human beings, an angel of spiritual guidance. Such an overlooked role. The angels all looked down on him for millennia, when all the time, he was watching over the Creator's most treasured creations."

A sudden surge of pride welled up inside her, love and devotion for the angel who had been her only friend. Even as it swept through her, the tears came as well. He was gone.

"Ah hush, love." Sam kissed her face where they fell and his mouth came to hers wet and salty. "All will be well. I don't know how, but all will be well."

He held her as she cried, kissed her and stroked her shivering skin. As her tears dried, and her body warmed beneath his touch, he rose above her.

"I'll take care of you, Lily. And keep you as safe as ever he did. Safer. I swear it."

She was about to answer, to tell him she knew that, when she realised they weren't alone. Another body breathed the same air, shared the same space, radiated warmth. The foot of the bed shifted as someone sat on it.

Sam froze, staring at her beneath the covers, alarm and anger warring in his eyes. He lifted his finger to his lips, warning her to be silent and still. Too afraid to move, images of Hopkins looming from the shadows still clinging in her mind, Lily shrank back beneath him.

Sam hurled himself at the foot of the bed in a flurry of bedclothes and desperation. Two figures thudded to the ground, rolling together. Lily scrambled to the end of the bed and saw them struggling together, two forms, like morning and night, dark and golden.

"Micah!" she exclaimed.

Micah flipped Sam onto his back, pinned him to the floor and grinned, a wild and reckless grin. All down his back, the elaborate sketch of wings still decorated his skin, from his shoulders down to the back of his thighs. But the other wounds were gone.

"You're going to have a hard time protecting her as a human if that's the best you can do."

"A human?" Sam gasped, fighting for breath as he tried to free himself.

Micah laughed and released him, then pulled Sam to his feet and dragging him into an embrace at once powerful and tender.

"Yes, a human. A mortal. And one without a taint of sin. You never fell, He said. So you have nothing to repay. He's wiped out everything you did, because the knife destroyed the demon. Not you."

"That—that's impossible."

Micah rolled his eyes. "Don't ask. It's ineffable. Part of His nature."

Lily gripped the bed sheet, staring at the two of them, unable to believe her eyes.

"Micah?" she said. "Micah, you're here?"

Micah smiled, brighter than she had ever seen him, the weight of the world he used to carry gone. He snatched her up in his strong arms and whirled her around, laughing when Sam had to dive out of the way.

"If you'll have me. Both of you."

Lily kissed him and they fell onto the bed, her hands pressed against his chest.

Sam joined them, sliding against her back, his hands

teasing the sensitive skin of her waist. He kissed the nape of her neck and then lifted his head to give Micah a long and intimate look. "I see you still haven't got the hang of appearing around her with clothes on then."

"I don't need him with clothes on." Her voice sounded husky with need. "But I don't understand. We thought you were the Metatron."

"I was," said Micah, "at least for a while. It came naturally because once that was my purpose. But now he has another."

"Who?" Sam asked, planting another series of kisses along Lily's shoulder blades.

"Lara," Micah said with a smile. That brought Sam up short, with eyes wide. "Once she was like Lily, and she had a guardian angel. Enoch loved her, as I love you, but he broke the cardinal rule, the one thing agreed upon by Heaven and Hell. He told her who and what he was. The Holy Court took him away, but she had already conceived his child, a child she bore and became the Nephilim. Without Enoch there to protect her, Asmodeus seduced her effortlessly and she was damned. But some part of her remained, at the core, her perfect nature, probably why Asmodeus and the Nameless took such delight in corrupting her. She didn't deserve that. Not to pay for Enoch's transgression, not to see the monster her child became without her, not to be so degraded by the ranks of Hell. So He took her back."

"That, um...that won't go down well with some of the heavenly host," said Sam.

Micah grinned, the edges of the expression manic with delight. "Yes. That thought appealed to both of us too."

"And you?" Lily asked, drawing him against her.

"I have a new mission." For a moment her heart lurched. If she lost him again, even with Sam to comfort her, how would she stand it? They were meant to be together, the three of them. She understood that now. She finally believed it. He must have seen it in her eyes, because his finger traced an invisible line along her jaw and he captured her eyes with the wondrous blue of his own. "I'll take care of you. Of both of you. And I intend to begin right away."

"Really, Mike?" Sam drawled.

But Micah wasn't joking, nor did he rise to the bait of Sam's nickname. "Really."

His kiss took Lily's breath away. Rolling onto her back, she gazed up at the two of them. "But if I have a child, won't it be like him?"

"Not if it's Sam's child," said Micah. "He's human. The conception of a Nephilim is a chance in a million and not all of them turn evil. How could they with a mother such as you." He kissed her, taking his time to enjoy the sensation, making her body pulse for him even harder. "But I can see that the creative spark is suppressed in me. I can keep that from happening. It's within my power now."

"Your power," Sam interrupted. "Yes, we never discussed your power, nor the secrets you kept."

"Secrets we can share later. Right now, I'm busy."

Lily groaned and arched towards him.

Sam grinned at her, while Micah's mouth worked its way down her body, too intent on her to look up.

"I think he missed you," Sam said, his hand sliding over Micah's shoulders in a caress.

Then he leaned in to join them. Both mouths closed on her breasts at the same time. She cried out, her hips lifting from the bed. Two hands pushed her back down, teasing fingers sliding inside her. They moved in unison, the perfect pressure on her nipples making her whole body melt beneath them.

Sam took command of her, lifting her astride his lap. She took him inside her, unable to wait, unable to draw it out. Not now. Later on they could make it slow. Now, she needed them.

Oh God, she needed them both so badly.

Micah's teeth grazed her shoulder and he filled his hands with her breasts, rubbing them against Sam's chest until he too gasped. He was so hard inside her, like iron wrapped in velvet. His penis shuddered as her body closed around him.

"What do you want, Lily?" Micah asked.

"Both of you." The reply was instantaneous. She didn't need to think. What was thought at a time like this? "Both of you inside me."

Micah's chuckle ran through her, as deeply sultry as Sam's, the sound of it making her body spasm with need.

Micah's fingers, damp with her excitement, teased the sensitive skin of her anus, sliding inside, stretching her in readiness for him. If she winced, or cried out, Sam gave a series of gentle thrusts which drove away the pain and brought her to the brink of orgasm. Maddening, patient, he rocked into her, but never let her go all the way.

"Please, please," she said over and over.

He kissed her to silence her and Micah's ministrations continued, his fingers curling up inside her ass, drawing all her consciousness together to a single point of pure pleasure.

Micah's hand withdrew, cupping and stroking Sam's balls. Suddenly it was Sam's turn to gasp, his eyes fluttering closed in ecstasy. Lily rolled her hips, circling them while still holding him inside her. To her delight, she heard the same words spill from his lips.

"Please, please, please."

She started to laugh, just for a moment, before Micah's cock found its way into her, working deep and deeper inside. She could feel them both pressing against each other, only a thin wall of her flesh keeping them apart. They filled her so completely that she could never imagine being apart again.

Nor did she have to, she realised with a wild surge of joy.

Whatever happened, whatever the future held, they would be with her always, angel and demon, her perfect lovers.

Lips on her neck, hands on her breasts, three bodies moving in unison, in perfect harmony, Micah's half-suppressed groan of need, Sam's deep and reckless laugh, everything coalesced into a single perfect moment. Lily's world shattered and re-formed as she came, bringing them both with her to a new reality where they would never be parted again.

About the Author

Rhiannon Leith didn't mean to write erotic sci-fi, fantasy and romance, it just worked out that way. And when you find something you're good at…

She's written stories about vampires, djinn, psychics, angels and demons. All of them are very naughty indeed.

To learn more, please visit her website www.rhiannonleith.com and get a taste of fantasy on fire.

Kidnapped by rebels...or rescued by love?

With a Touch
© 2010 Rhiannon Leith
The Guild Chronicles

As a prized psychic, Eva's lived her entire life inside the Guild Compound. While sex isn't exactly forbidden, she's rarely indulged—such intense contact could swamp her sensitive gift. A chance encounter with Aidan, a sexy Guild Security Officer, rocks her to the core when she sees herself entangled in his arms. She fights the unfamiliar surge of lust and tries to focus on the job at hand, the interrogation of the subversive Rafael.

Yet she discovers that he's no terrorist. In fact, his capture is a ploy, a way for him and Aidan to infiltrate the Guild with one goal in mind: Eva.

At first Eva fights her captors, but once outside the Guild's walls, she realizes she is free. Free to live and love as she pleases. And her two rebels please her indeed, introducing her to erotic pleasures she never imagined. They break down the barriers imposed on her mind and body, making her question everything she's ever known.

Even as Eva dares to dream of a future with her lovers, she fears for their lives. The Guild wants her back. And that's not all they want...

Warning: Contains two irresistible rebels working "undercover" to win the woman of their dreams, an evil corporation, rough sex, tender sex, sex with mild bondage, sex intensified by psychic connections and an oh-so-passionate ménage à trois.

Available now in ebook from Samhain Publishing.

When the craving takes hold, the only thing to do is ride it out...

Midnight Craving
© *2010 Lolita Lopez*
Midnight Vice, Book 1

Patrolling Houston's gritty supernatural underbelly has its perks. For Isla Alvarez, it's working alongside nephilim SWAT Officer Jace Lane. Ruggedly handsome and possessed of mad skills, Jace embodies everything she's ever wanted.

Unfortunately, the demonic blood pumping through her veins keeps them separated, since relationships between human descendants of archangels and demons aren't actively encouraged. Staying away from him, though, is impossible after she winds up on the receiving end of a nasty sexual-compulsion curse, courtesy of a sadistic vampiress. Suddenly Isla is overwhelmed with a life-threatening lust only Jace can sate.

Jace's principles were once strong enough to resist his longing for the alluring Isla, but in the face of her desperate craving, his desire breaks free—leaving him wondering if she's not the only one affected by the spell. He'd be more than happy to satisfy Isla's increasing need for sexual release, if they weren't in a race against time to reverse the curse before it turns deadly.

For Isla, it's not just her life she's worried about losing. It's her heart.

Warning: contains wicked-hot shower sex, raging-hormone-induced naughty language, driving under the influence (of overwhelming lust) and smiting of demons and vamps.

Available now in ebook from Samhain Publishing.

GREAT
CHEAP
FUN

Discover eBooks!

THE FASTEST WAY TO GET THE HOTTEST NAMES

Get your favorite authors on your favorite reader, long before they're out in print! Ebooks from Samhain go wherever you go, and work with whatever you carry—Palm, PDF, Mobi, Kindle, nook, and more.

SAMHAIN
PUBLISHING

WWW.SAMHAINPUBLISHING.COM

LaVergne, TN USA
21 March 2011
221062LV00001B/70/P